You and Me Dancing to Gershwin

PACIFICA ACADEMY DRAMA SERIES
BOOK FIVE

CHRISTINE MILES

YOU AND ME DANCING TO GERSHWIN

Pacifica Academy Drama Series, Book Five

Published by Sealed With a Swoon Books LLC

Copyright © 2020, 2022 by Christine Miles

2nd edition

Cover Design by The Killion Group, Inc.

*For the dancers, musicians,
and lovers of rock music and all things theater.*

Books by Christine Miles

Adult Contemporary Romance

Timing is Everything Series

Last Time We Loved (Book One)

First Time We Laughed (Book Two)

The Time We Met (Book Three)

This Time It's Forever (Book Four)

Smart is Seriously Sexy Series

Off-the-Charts Chemistry (Book One)

Passion Under the Microscope (Coming Winter 2024)

Young Adult

Pacifica Academy Drama Series

Me, Shakespeare and the Anti-Love Club (Book One)

The '68 Camaro Between Kenickie and Me (Book Two)

Teddy Brewster's Hold On Me (Book Three)

Silver Bells for Me and (Saint) Nicolas (Book Four)

You and Me Dancing to Gershwin (Book Five)

Summer in Winter Wonderland (A Cozy Mystery)

Chapter One

I sat back and stared into his eyes. Though they weren't exactly *his* eyes. But my artistic interpretation looked pretty close. Dark. Slightly narrow. Piercing me, as if he wanted to read my soul. He'd stared at me a few times like that back in November. The phrase "bedroom eyes" drifted through my mind.

Heat barreled through me and went right to my face. I shook my long blonde hair until the thick locks shielded my burning cheeks. Then my mom's voice filled my head.

Alexis Evelyn Pfeiffer, good girls *don't think things like that.*

I sighed and lifted my head.

Study hall had just started, and I loved this part of my school day.

Mrs. Ferguson left us alone unless we "forgot what the word whispering meant." So it was almost always quiet. And she, like right now, typically stayed seated at her desk while we sat wherever we wanted at the long tables in her classroom. Student after student in navy-blue cardigans covering white polo shirts with our bottom halves in khaki skorts or pants.

Because she rarely walked around the room, I treated study hall as my personal art class; my second favorite and much-needed emotional release. Plus, being a *good girl* in my house meant always being ahead in all of my honors classes.

My eyes drifted back to the intense pair I'd been working on here and there since we'd returned from winter break a couple weeks earlier. A long time to be working on one set of eyes, but they had to be absolutely perfect. Like everything else in my world.

I titled my head right and squinted at my work in progress.

No. His eyes still weren't dark enough. Weren't *mysterious* enough.

"Who is that? Because it's so not Henry."

Natalie Carlisle's quiet, yet razor-sharp voice, caused me to jolt.

I folded my sketch book with a *slap*! As Natalie sat beside me, I peeked at Mrs. Ferguson, glowering at me through her large, round glasses

"Sorry," I said to her, which earned me a curt nod before she went back to her computer.

I faced Natalie. The light in her deep brown eyes matched her wicked grin.

"Whoever you're drawing looks *hot*," she whispered.

Actually, the subject of my art project was ridiculously *hot*. But her comment caught me sideways and I straightened. "Henry's hot. In his own, unique way," I softly, and not very convincingly, added. Then guilt latched onto me and my shoulders slumped.

Natalie's mouth eased into an apologetic smile. "You're right." She lifted her shoulders. "But you're supposed to remind me when the old Natalie comes out."

I nodded. "But there are parts of the old Natalie I'm used to and don't mind. Like your honesty." *Even though it occasionally stung. But only because she spoke the truth.*

She leaned toward me, her black hair falling forward and down her left shoulder. "Lexi, I like Henry. He's smart, totally awesome to you and, yeah, cute in his own way."

Yes. What many girls at Pacifica Academy would consider the perfect boyfriend.

"But he's way more into you than you're into him." She pointed at my sketch book. "Obviously." She lowered her hand. "This is going to sound way harsh, but you need to break up with him and go after who you really want. Does he go to P.A.?" Her eyes widened. "Wait a sec. Those eyes..." She reached for my book. "Let me see—"

I swiped it off the table and hugged it to my chest.

Only one person in this school might know about this. *Him*. But Heather was so caught up in her new boyfriend and the beginning stages of the spring musical, I had a strong feeling she wouldn't say or do a thing.

Natalie smirked. "So he *does* go to this school. Which would explain why his eyes look familiar." Her smirk faded. "Why haven't you told me who it is?" Hurt flashed across her face. "Lexi, I consider you one of my best friends. Practically a sister."

Guilt crushed my insides and I reached for her hand. "Nat," I whispered, "you know I feel the same way about you." I squeezed her fingers, and decided right now I couldn't be a *good girl*. "I swear I'm into Henry. He's everything you described and more." I mentally cringed at the lies tumbling from my mouth. But I didn't want to get into the fact I'd stupidly let myself like a boy who I'd *thought* liked me, too.

Natalie lifted her eyes to mine, and I gave her my bright smile.

"I'm drawing a picture of my celebrity crush. That's why he looks familiar."

She narrowed her eyes. "I don't believe any of this."

Of course she didn't. I wouldn't believe me, either. I still shrugged and released her hand.

"I'm letting this go," she mumbled. "For now." She paused, then said, "You seem to also be forgetting Shane and I have spent *a lot* of time with you and Henry since Snowflake Formal." She shook her head. "Even Shane can tell there's something off with you two."

Shane being Natalie's super sweet, funny, Ken-Doll-of-a-looking boyfriend. He also happened to be a P.A. theater star and meant he knew what convincing acting looked like.

But I said, "Maybe Henry and I don't have obvious chemistry." *Like you and Shane, and every couple we're friends with.* "We're still getting to know each other."

She peered at me a few seconds before turning to open her backpack.

I guess all this meant my parents' *good girl* was "perfect" at everything but acting. And I would definitely have to start a new art project for study hall.

* * *

I dropped my Trigonometry book into my backpack and reached for a notebook. Then icy fingers covered my eyes, and I halted.

"Hey cutie," Henry murmured into my ear. "I've been thinking about you all afternoon."

I managed a smile as he removed his fingers. His hands were always cold. Like he'd just had them in a freezer.

I faced him. Guilt pressed me down at the sight of his huge grin for me. His girlfriend. Because Henry Callaghan had walked up to me after school one week before Snowflake Formal and nervously asked me to our second biggest dance of the year. There'd been no reason to say no, either. Though I'd been foolishly hoping *another* boy I'd spent a lot of time with in late November and early December would ask me.

Henry's grin deepened and it matched his illuminated, light-brown eyes. "I have a surprise for you."

His shaggy, red-headed, freckled looks reminded me of the actor who played Ron Weasley in the *Harry Potter* movies, but minus the deeper voice and British accent. Henry was more on the lanky side than solid and not super tall. But with me being barely over five-foot-three, most of my friends and classmates towered over me.

I forced myself to return his boyishly sweet and genuine smile. "I like surprises."

At that moment I spotted Heather walking down the noisy, chaotic hallway between her boyfriend, Nicolas, and *him*. Noah Sanchez. Also known as the subject of my art project and one of her best friends. The three were laughing together, and Noah's deep smile and shoulders shaking from whatever they thought was so funny slashed something deep inside me.

Everything, including Henry's voice, faded into a haze as thick as one that shrouded San Francisco on a dreary, January morning.

If Noah had possessed the courage to ask me to Snowflake Formal and...vice versa...I knew I'd be walking with them, right beside him, and holding his hand that had to be warm.

Heather and Nicolas looked my way and sent me huge smiles. Heather even waved. Their actions caused Noah's dark, piercing eyes to land on me. Which caused his smile to slip.

Another slash, but this one made the haze evaporate.

I focused on Henry, burst into laugher, and placed my left hand on his upper arm. "You are so *funny*," I said around my idiotic giggling. Perfect little *good girl*? No. Not right now. But I'd figure out some way to make amends with the universe for my awful behavior.

Heather, Nicolas, and Noah passed us, and I released a quick breath.

Henry's eyes widened and his grin transformed into confusion. "I didn't know Mr. Thatcher being gone today and canceling Mathletes was funny."

I blinked twice, then laughed-shrugged. "It's just the way you were saying it, I guess."

Oh, my *goodness*. I needed to get back to me. Super-sweet Lexi Pfeiffer. Henry didn't deserve this phoniness. And I'd promised myself when he'd asked me out on a second date after Snowflake Formal that I'd let go of Noah Sanchez and give Henry—us—a chance.

I'd also been tired of being the third person in the phrase "three's a crowd" while with my friends and their boyfriends. I wanted what all my friends had after being single for so long.

With that thought, I grasped the folds of Henry's cardigan and smiled up at him. "What's my surprise?"

His deep grin returned. "That Mathletes was canceled." He placed his hands on my waist. "I can walk you to the studio. Maybe give you a *really* long goodbye?" he quietly added.

I was being totally ridiculous. Henry was very cute in his own, unique way—not too bad of a kisser, either—and treated me better than I truly deserved.

"Sounds perfect!" I released his sweater. "I just need to finish loading my backpack."

I faced my locker, but he managed to keep his hands on my waist.

Yes. I liked him. And the closeness with a boy I'd avoided for a long time.

Henry and I would find our chemistry, and everything would be extraordinary.

Chapter Two

I walked into the dance studio and breathed in the familiar scent of pine, bleach, and glass cleaner. Most people would probably find the smells overpowering. To me, it smelled like the place where I hung my heart. My true home. I'd spent years dancing my heart and soul out on this polished hardwood floor, and in front of the shiny mirrors lining the studio's right side.

"*That* was some kiss, young lady."

I yelped and twirled left in the direction of my aunt's mock stern voice.

She strolled toward me with her arms folded while staring at me through her narrowed, hazel eyes. "I'd ask how Henry's doing, but *that* kiss answered my question." She fanned her face, which made the wisps of golden hair that had fallen from her French braid flutter. "Ahhh," she teased. "To be eighteen again and in love."

I shook my head and dropped my backpack on the nearest of the metal chairs set up along the studio's left side. "Aunt Daphne, Henry and I aren't in love." *But maybe we could be.*

She laughed. "Then what would you call *that* kiss. Just raging, teen hormones?"

I groaned. "Eww. I can't talk about this with my aunt. No way." In truth, she felt more like having a much older sister, even a best friend, but she was still my aunt.

And my long goodbye with Henry may have appeared on the hotter side of embraces, but his kisses, though pretty good, didn't make anything inside me tingle, shiver, or melt. Nothing like the way Natalie described her kisses with Shane. Or what my other girlfriends had to experience when they kissed their boyfriends.

I'd actually never experienced kisses like that with any boys I'd dated.

"Okay," she said around another laugh. "I'm finished. But," she slowly continued, "I don't recommend you and Henry kissing like that anywhere near your house."

Because my parents' heads would explode.

Alexis Evelyn Pfeiffer, good girls *don't behave like that in public.*

I faced my aunt. "I'm not stupid."

She frowned. "Sweetie, I know that." She closed the gap between us and wrapped me in a tight hug. "For the millionth time, I'm going to apologize for my uptight big sister *and* your dad," she muttered, "who is more uptight than she is."

I returned her squeeze, never wanting to let go or leave this studio.

"I have some news that I need to talk to you about before you change and the Ballerina Bears get here."

I smiled at the image of the dancing class made up of twelve enthusiastic, energetic, adorable five-year-old girls, who all wanted to be ballerinas—dancers—someday.

My aunt had been a professional dancer on the stage for fifteen years. Though to look at her slim, toned physique, most people would assume she still danced professionally.

Aunt Daphne led me to the metal chairs and we sat.

"I received a call today from Carolyn Chaplin." She folded her slender hands and placed them on her lap. "The choir teacher and musical director at your school?"

I nodded, though I knew her as Mrs. Chaplin, the Wicked Witch of Pacifica Academy. I'd never had her—thankfully—as a teacher, but so many of my friends were active in choir and theater that I'd heard too many not-so-nice stories about her.

"She asked me if I'd be interested in being the choreographer for the spring musical, *Crazy For You*. Strictly volunteer, of course."

I straightened.

That's right. *Crazy For You* was a George and Ira Gershwin review, dancing musical. Mostly tap dancing with a *big* chorus and equally big dancing numbers. It didn't occur to me until this second Mrs. Chaplin would need a fantastic choreographer used to working with kids. Someone like my aunt, though she—we—mostly worked with little girls.

"Did you say yes? And what about your classes?" I'd love seeing my aunt at school, but if she decided to take on such a huge job, she wouldn't be able to continue her evening dance classes until the show debuted in *late* April. Which meant I'd temporarily lose my job here with her. My sanctuary. My true home. Totally selfish, but I couldn't help it. I needed this place.

"I told her I had to think about it, but I want to do this," she admitted. "It would be a nice change." She winked. "Working with you *sassy* teenagers?"

I gave her a weak smile.

"It wouldn't affect my class schedule too much, since we're closed Sunday through Tuesday," she continued. "Carolyn told me rehearsals run Monday through Thursday until six. I could probably just push back class start times on Wednesday and Thursday."

I frowned. "Aunt Daphne, that would make for a really long day."

She shook her head. "I don't have to be at the school until 3:15, and it's only those two days that would be longer."

I slumped in the chair. "What about my schedule? You know my parents will never go for me working here any later than I already do. I can't lose this place." Yes, I was acting and had spoken like a Ballerina Bear having a rotten day. I'd also spoken the truth.

She, surprisingly, smiled. "What if you were my assistant choreographer for the show?"

I froze, then blinked twice.

"Carolyn agreed and ran it by your principal." Her smile deepened. "According to her, he said, 'A student working with and teaching other students for a great cause? Fine idea'." She laughed. "Carolyn said she put strong dancers in the lead roles, and good dancers in the chorus. The students are ready to begin dancing rehearsals. But it's going to take patience and stamina to corral and teach numerous teenagers to dance *together*. I could use your superb talent, my dear."

I released a steady breath. Working with—more like teaching—so many of my friends? To tap dance in unison? Would they even be okay with that? Was *I* okay with that?

I sifted through the pretty amazing cast list. I even knew who Noah had gotten. Pete, a largely secondary character who happened to be in the bigger dance numbers. And I knew this because I remembered Noah grumbling at lunch one day about getting the part he hadn't auditioned for. He'd said he could dance, but "tap dancing was Not. His thing."

I smiled softly at his often quirky way of ending his sentences.

"Does that smile mean you'll be my amazing assistant choreographer? For which you'll be paid," my aunt stressed.

"Like you are for helping with my classes. But that's between us."

I shoved my random Noah thought into the back of my mind and mentally buried it under memories of Henry's warm gazes and boyish grin.

"Lexi?"

I focused on my aunt. "It would be awesome to work with so many of my friends on this musical. And I really think they'd be okay with it." Well, maybe not one of them, but it's not like Noah and I hadn't been friendly since we came back from winter break. Just distant. Like the time we'd spent together helping Heather and Nicolas rehearse for the Christmas talent show had never happened.

"Of course they'd be okay with you sharing your God-given talent."

I sighed. "You know I'll have to clear this with my parents first. And I won't be able to help with the play *and* your classes." *Because school always came first and straight A's were mandatory since their alma mater, UC Berkeley, would accept nothing less.*

My aunt's smile vanished. "Sweetie, I'll manage with my classes. Do you want me to call them and explain everything?"

I opened my mouth to respond, but the street door opened, followed by high-pitched, five-year-old giggling. Seconds later the Randolph twins, wearing matching pink leotards and white tights, burst into the studio, their blonde hair pulled up into tight ponytails. Mrs. Randolph followed them and immediately shot us a weary smile.

The girls threw themselves as us and we each caught one.

I wrapped my arms around Jessica's tiny, wiggling body, stood, and caught my aunt's questioning eyes. "I'll call you if I need you?" I answered.

She sent me a quick nod and directed her full attention to

Jessica's fraternal twin, Kasey, who was talking at the speed of light about her day at school.

I'd miss the Ballerina Bears and my aunt's other classes. But working on the musical with several kids who'd become such close friends of mine in the last year or so would be beyond amazing. I could deal with Noah, too, since we'd always been friendly.

Hopefully my parents would agree to this, or I'd lose time with my aunt *and* this place until the end of April.

* * *

A long, tense silence fell around my parents and me as we sat at the dining room table.

With my fork, I poked at the grilled, garlic chicken breast on my plate. I actually hated garlic, but my parents always insisted I was being too sensitive.

Alexis, there's only enough garlic added for flavor.

Years ago, when they'd been younger and in love, they'd taken several cooking classes together. Dinnertime in my house, when they *didn't* work late, was just like this—at the dining room table set as if they were expecting royalty with food so perfect it looked like an ad in a magazine. Or picture in a cookbook.

I peeked at my dad, the deep frown lines around his mouth more noticeable than usual while he thought about what to say to my musical news. His turquoise eyes appeared, like usual, distant and dim from fatigue. His frown lines had once been from laughter, and I couldn't remember the last time I'd heard his deep laugh. Or seen him genuinely smile.

I dragged my eyes to my mom, sitting across the table from me. Same deep lines around her mouth. Same faraway, dim eyes, only hers were hazel. Smiles and laughter forgotten actions.

Nothing in their lives—careers, friends, this house, *each other*—made them happy.

Not even me.

I dropped my gaze to the plate of flawless food.

They now had nothing close to a perfect marriage, but that didn't stop them from making everything around them "perfect." Even me.

Dad dropped his fork with a *clatter* and sat back. "It would have been nice if your *sister* would have talked to us about this musical thing first before taking it to *our* daughter."

Mom calmly set her fork down and gave him an ice-cold stare. "I'll call *Daphne* after dinner and get all the details from her, then we'll talk about this. Will *that* be okay with you?"

He returned her icy stare. "I guess it'll have to be. But in case my opinion matters here, as her *dad*, I don't want Alexis doing this."

Tears burned my eyes, but I blinked until they cleared.

"This is her last semester," he continued. "She needs to be completely focused on her schoolwork and grades. She shouldn't even be working at that studio right now. *We* agreed when she started high school the dancing would be nothing more than a weekend hobby."

Yes. The first thing I loved most in this world had long been reduced to practically nothing by my parents, the success-ful, driven, *miserable* lawyers.

"But so much for that agreement," he muttered under his breath as he stood. He picked up his wine glass and focused on me. His gaze softened, but only by a fraction. "You obviously have decided to help your aunt on this musical, and I know what dancing means to you. But school comes first, Alexis." Our eyes locked. "*I'll* be watching your grades. And if I see any of them slip below a ninety-three percent, no more musical. No more working at the studio."

I slowly nodded. It's not like this rule wasn't already in

effect. But at least I had the musical, and still had my dancing and time with my aunt.

He tore his eyes from mine to look at Mom, still giving him her blood-chilling stare. "Can we at least agree on *that*?"

She pressed her lips together for a few seconds, then said, "Completely."

He stepped back. "Make sure to tell your sister all this, too." He turned and stalked from the dining room and in the direction of his office, the place I called *his* sanctuary.

But maybe escape was a much better word.

Mom tossed her napkin on her barely touched plate of perfectly made food and stood. "I need to get on the phone with your aunt." She grasped her wine glass. "I'll be in my office." Our eyes locked. "Alexis, you need to be a good girl and work ahead in *all* of your classes because of this musical. And I'll deal with the dishes later." She marched from the dining room, in the direction of the stairs since her office was the third-floor loft.

Years ago, when they'd been idealistic lawyers and in love, they'd shared an office.

I sighed, pushed away from the table, and also headed for the stairs. My bedroom—my other sanctuary—was on the second floor. A little ironic my room happened to be right in the middle of where my unhappy parents spent most of their home time.

I spent a lot of time between those two.

Chapter Three

I walked into my room, towel drying my hair, and kicked the door closed with my foot.

"*Hi, Lexi.*"

I looked over at my African grey parrot, patiently waiting for my reply of, "Hi, Coda." Because if I didn't greet him in return, he'd continue saying "*Hi, Lexi*" until I did.

I'd taught him that after he'd come into my life when I was twelve, through clients of my dad. They'd been going through an ugly divorce.

Coda, though that hadn't been his name at the time, had gotten caught between two people who he'd no longer made happy. I liked to think of him as my spirit animal.

He began to groom his feathers, and I continued drying my hair as I sat on my bed's edge.

Coda's permanent place in this house had been touch and go, namely with Mom, until I moved his cage into my room. He occasionally played with his toys a bit rambunctiously, went through phases where he'd repeat *everything* he heard, and I had to clean his cage every Sunday. But I still loved having him in here. A special, unique pet that was all mine.

My phone burst into the old-fashioned telephone ring.

I stood and headed for where I'd left it on my desk. It was probably Henry. We had plans to meet up at his place and walk his two, enormous black Labs to the Alta Plaza dog park.

A sweet, romantic Saturday afternoon. Very Henry—who wasn't calling me.

"Hi, Aunt Daphne." She had to be calling because of last night.

"*Hi, Aunt Daphne*," Coda squawked.

She laughed. "Hi, Coda." She paused, then asked, "What's it like around there this morning? And are you okay, Sweetie?"

I wandered over to Coda's cage in the corner of my room near the window. He'd gone back to grooming. "Just another day in paradise," I replied around a forced laugh. "They went into work early this morning. I guess they each have a lot of cases right now." At least, that's what Mom had written on the sticky note I'd found on the fridge door.

She released a heavy sigh. "I'm sorry, Lexi. Asking you to be my assistant choreographer for the musical was never supposed to start another dancing war between your parents."

"I know that," I murmured. "But I can help you and want to, and that's what's important. So what's next? Because I'm so excited about this." We needed to focus on the positive and forget last night ever happened.

"And I'm excited you're excited," she answered, and I could hear the smile in her voice. "Carolyn told me just now she wants us to ease the kids into the dancing on Monday."

I smiled at Coda. "Yay! This is going to be so much fun. Thank you, Aunt Daphne." Because I probably would have lost my sanity if I'd lost dancing, even temporarily.

"*Thank you, Aunt Daphne*."

I frowned at my pet.

"You're welcome, Sweetie," she softly said. "Do you have plans today? I have the music and want to start working on the choreography. I'm thinking we'll start with beginning tap steps and see how they do."

My shoulders fell forward. It totally made sense she wanted, and pretty much needed, to start on the choreography today. But I had plans with Henry.

"It's okay if you can't," she added. "You're a beautiful teenager with friends and a boyfriend, and a life—"

"What time do you want me at the studio?" Henry would totally understand. And it's not like walking his dogs to the park could be considered a formal date.

"Meet me there in an hour?"

"I'll be there with my tap shoes on." But first I had to dig them out of my closet. During my free dance time the last several months, I'd been focused on ballet, my first dancing love.

I stared at my bird. "Okay, Coda. It'll be laugher and smiles in here again." *I swear*.

"*I'm Coda.*"

I'd taught him that so he could shock my friends when they asked, "What's his name?" It had definitely shocked Henry the first time he'd been in my room. For only a few minutes.

Henry. I needed to call him. Yes. He'd understand all this, since he was learning what dancing meant to me.

"I Can't Be Bothered Now" blasted through my earbuds as I walked to school. It was the first big dance number in *Crazy For You*, and I mentally went through the tap number Aunt Daphne and I had worked on Saturday. It was a bit on the rough side, though I'd raved to my aunt about who'd been cast as Polly and Bobby, the main characters who danced the most in the musical. In fact, "I Can't Be Bothered Now" was

Bobby's number with the Follies Girls. But neither of us knew what Mrs. Chaplin considered "good dancers" when it came to the chorus.

That would change this afternoon. And after my parents' latest fight yesterday, thank *goodness* for the musical.

I focused on my excitement, mingled with a bit of nervousness, and allowed it to shoot through me. I'd never been a true assistant choreographer before today. I'd only worked with my aunt on her younger classes, like the Ballerina Bears, and helped keep the little girls as focused as possible while assisting them with the basic steps and posture.

I'd heard some adults say teenagers were just first graders in much bigger bodies. I'd never found that to be true or funny, but maybe I needed to keep that saying in mind to help with the nervousness. Since I *was* used to working with first graders.

"*Lexi*!"

I halted and squinted at the overcast sky. Then someone landed beside me.

I squealed, jumped back, and yanked out my earbuds. And my eyes locked with *his*.

"Sorry." Noah gave me a lopsided grin. "That's why you couldn't hear me shouting your name. Three *other* times." He pointed at my right hand, gripping the cord.

I peered at him. "Where'd you come from?" And was he here, willingly talking to me?

He turned and pointed at a building a few down from us. "I live there and saw you walking by as I came out." He faced me and tilted his head left. "Do you normally walk this way to school? If you do, it's weird we've never run into each other before."

Actually, my parents had a huge fight yesterday, my dad stormed out of the house, and stayed gone. The rest of the day and night.

I forced my mouth into a smile. "My mom or dad

normally drop me off at school, but they couldn't this morning. They had to be at work early." At least, Mom had fled to her actual office before I forced myself out of bed. She had left me a sticky note I'd, as usual, found on the fridge. I could only assume Dad had spent the night at his actual office.

"Hey," Noah said. "You okay?"

I blinked to find him giving me his piercing, trying-to-read-my-soul stare. I gave him a brighter smile. "I'm fine! Just talking to you on the sidewalk." I frowned. Why had he chased me down to begin with? "Did you need to talk to me about something?"

Guilt flashed through his eyes as he ran a hand through his thick, almost black hair.

Maybe my question had come out a tad snarkier than I'd intended.

"Yeah, I guess we haven't talked a whole lot since we've been back from the break." His arm fell to his side before he lifted his head. "So I heard you and your aunt are going to be our dance teachers for the show."

During my girls night out on Saturday, I'd told Natalie, Heather, and the rest of my girl crew, that included a couple of theater stars, the choreographer news. Based on their shrill and ecstatic reactions, I wasn't certain why I was still experiencing nervousness.

"Yep." I smiled. "The girls were so excited, but I'm sure within a few short weeks all of you will be *sick* of me and my aunt." I leaned toward him and caught a whiff of his cologne. Or maybe it was his soap. Clean. Fresh. Simple. *Hot.* Just like him. I straightened as warmth exploded inside me and reached my face. "Um...we can be dancing drill sergeants."

Oh, my *goodness.*

I stepped back as inconspicuously as possible.

His lopsided grin returned. "No one will get sick of you.

Or your aunt." He cleared his throat. "You're a really good teacher. And dancer. I think Nicolas learned a lot from you."

Our eyes snapped together. The air around us crackled. Or maybe it was my insides.

I broke our gaze. "Thanks. But he already knew a lot."

I turned from him and began walking. We needed to get to school where I'm sure my *boyfriend* was waiting for me. My boyfriend, who I hadn't seen since Friday afternoon. My boyfriend, who had no idea what was going on with my parents. Because Henry still didn't feel like a *boyfriend*. But we were still getting to know each other. So I shoved that first thought, and last night's rottenness, into a box and mentally buried it.

Noah fell into step beside me. "I also caught you because I want to apologize."

I whipped my head in his direction. Could he be regretting not asking me to Snowflake Formal? Not taking a chance—

"My tap dancing skills fall right around a Big. Fat. Zero."

I turned my head left, away from him, and swallowed a Big. Fat. Sigh.

"In my defense," he continued, "I auditioned for Lank Hawkins. One of the few guys in the musical who doesn't dance. But you know that part went to Shane." He paused, then grumbled, "I guess Mrs. Chaplin wanted a senior to play Lank."

I turned my head and peeked at him, his forehead stuck in a deep frown. But I knew it wasn't because he'd lost the part he wanted to Shane. They were good friends. Most of Noah's friends were seniors, though he was a junior. And it occurred to me for the first time he had to be, on some level, dreading May. Graduation month. Eventually having to say goodbye and watch us—well, his close friends—move on. Not many of them had applied to schools in the Bay Area. And Liam, one of his closest theater buddies, would be leaving to become a Marine.

Something deep within me ached at what Noah would be facing in a handful of months.

"Anyway," he said with a shrug, "I wanted to give you fair warning about my dancing."

I fought a smile. "I appreciate that. But you *can* dance, right?" I know he'd said that.

He eyed me. "Does head banging count?"

I stopped us at the intersection diagonal from the school, faced him, and blinked twice.

He angled his head toward me. "Lexi, I'm joking."

I nodded and said, "Oh. Right." I released a quick laugh and pointed at him. "You really got me there." Still, there was something about all of this I didn't understand. "How did you end up with a dancing part when you didn't audition for it?" A sliver of apprehension spiraled within me as I imagined an entire chorus of kids who'd been cast as dancers. Who shouldn't have been.

He sighed. "After my audition, Mrs. Chaplin asked me if I could dance. She probably asked most of us that."

"And you lied?"

He straightened and shot me a dirty look. "I was telling her the complete truth when I said" —he cleared his throat— "yeah. Sure. '*I got rhy-thm...*'" he sang while smiling and flourishing his left hand in my direction.

I laughed. "That's pretty clever." *And ridiculously cute.* "You really did that?"

He unleashed a huge, mischievous smile so powerful my head blurred. "Just like that. It didn't make *her* laugh, but she did crack a smile. If you can believe it." He shook his head. "I almost didn't recognize her." Our eyes caught once more, and my tummy flipped at the humor making his dark eyes sparkle.

"So I guess that's how I ended up as Pete, the singing and tap dancing cowboy from Deadrock, Nevada."

I lifted my shoulders. "Well, since you have '*rhy-thm*' you should be fine."

"I hope so, because I'll be honest about something." His forehead formed that deep frown. "A bunch of us found and watched this amazing high school production of the show on YouTube. Those kids were perfect. I'm not even sure they *were* kids," he added under his breath. "Mrs. Chaplin will expect that from *us*. And I thought about backing out of the musical. Tap dancing to Gershwin? Not. My thing." He sighed. "But it's the last show I'll get to do with so many of my friends. Our friends," he corrected. "I couldn't walk away."

I reached out, grasped his left hand, and squeezed. "Noah, I understand. And I promise by the time the show runs, you'll be a better tap dancer than the eight-year-olds I work with."

My strongly spoken statement dangled between us for several seconds before I winced.

Maybe not a good idea implying third graders were better tap dancers than him.

He peered at me as he said, "I guess that's something to look forward to."

I released his hand, turned from him—that's when I spotted Henry, waiting outside the school, probably for me. And watching us.

I mentally moaned. Noah and I hadn't been doing anything wrong. Just talking like the friends we'd been before Snowflake Formal. But we'd also been doing *a lot* of smiling and laughing. I'd also grasped his hand. From where Henry sat, it had probably looked like flirting.

Some if it *had been* flirting. Just like before Snowflake Formal.

I stepped closer to the curb. "Henry's waiting for me. I'll see you later."

Noah's expression transformed into an emotionless mask. "Yeah. Totally." He lowered his head and lightly kicked a rock aside.

I speed walked across the street and headed right for Henry, who stood. When I reached him, he wrapped me in his arms and pressed his lips to mine. For several seconds.

"What was that for?" I asked.

He turned us from the school's entrance, and we walked several steps. "I haven't seen you since Friday afternoon."

Yes. True. But it's not like that hadn't happened before, and he'd *never* kissed me like that in front of school. Which meant only one thing.

"What were you and Noah talking about?"

Sweet, likable, typically easygoing Henry Callaghan was jealous. And though it was an awful, useless emotion, he had every right to feel that way.

Henry deserved better than this. I had to clear everything up. Damage control.

I gave him my brightest smile. "Just the show. He got a big dancing part and is feeling nervous since that rehearsing starts today." *Absolutely not lies.*

Henry tucked a lock of hair behind my right ear. "Okay." His eyes caught mine. "But you know he *likes* you, right?"

I stared at him while blinking rapidly. I then swallowed my snotty comeback of *Well, if Noah Sanchez does like me, he has a rotten way of showing it.*

"I've seen the way he looks at you," Henry continued. "Like you're the girl who will...save him. It's weird." He shivered. "And kind've creepy. You've really never noticed it?"

I had caught many of Noah's piercing stares. But he'd always looked away the moment our eyes met. Then his face would turn scarlet. Yet another reason I thought he would ask me out. And it's not like I hadn't been staring at him.

"Nope. I haven't noticed any of that. I just see my friend."

I'd also never thought of his stares as "creepy." Noah seemed to love being active in theater, but his first love was his guitar. Henry, like so many kids at school, didn't know Noah Sanchez, the musician. Heather had once told me in private he'd written a few songs, though he'd never shown them to her. Still, that made him a poet in my eyes. And poets, like artists, were observers of their world. *Not* creepers.

Henry, being so analytical, would probably never meet creativity. It wasn't his fault. Just the way his brain was wired.

I withdrew from his arms. "You ready to go in?"

He sighed. "Lex, I'm sorry. I like Noah. He's a cool, funny guy."

I waited for the inevitable.

"But I *know* he likes you." He shot me a soft grin. "I'm throwing it out there, because you're so nice to everyone. And trusting."

Yes. Super sweet. Perfect. A *good girl*. Alexis Evelyn Pfeiffer in a nutshell.

"You're nice to everyone, too. And trusting." I went up on my tiptoes to kiss his cheek. "And I'm with *you*. So can we go inside now?"

He clasped my hand and we strolled toward the school's entrance.

And if Noah Sanchez really did like me, he'd blown it last month.

Chapter Four

"Lexi, what's up with you today?" Natalie asked as we joined the 3:00 swarm of students jogging down the stairs. "You can't be nervous about working on the musical."

At this moment, her boyfriend and many of our friends were heading for the auditorium for Day One of *Crazy For You* dancing rehearsals.

Jitters were making my tummy flutter, and so not for the reason she'd stated.

Once we cleared the stairs, she veered left with me and stopped us.

She angled her head to catch my eyes. "*Everyone* loves the fact you and your aunt are the choreographers for the show. They're excited." She frowned. "But you'd know that if you and Henry had sat with us today at lunch."

I smiled brightly. "I know that."

She crossed her arms. "Then why aren't *you* excited? And why didn't you sit with us?"

Because of Henry, Noah, and keeping as much distance

from Noah as possible. Especially now that I'll be seeing so much of him from now until April.

I shrugged. "Henry and I wanted to have lunch in the library. What's the big deal?"

"We missed you. And you're doing that more and more. So is it Henry?

I held my bright smile in place. "No. Of course not. Henry loves you guys."

She raised her eyebrows. "Don't take this the wrong way, but all of us have noticed Henry always seems a little...uncomfortable and out of place around us."

I'd noticed that, too. But his closest friends were like him. Into math, science, computers. Totally analytical without a creative gene between them. "I know he doesn't always get the jokes or everyone's sense of humor," I slowly said. "But I swear he's fine." And he was. Outside of Noah, though he had called him a "cool, funny guy."

Her eyes were still filled with doubt. "Then is it your parents?"

Wasn't going there. Not right now. Not even with Natalie.

"They're the same," I mumbled. "Nat, nothing's up with me, okay?"

She sighed. "Fine. Promise me two things?"

"Sure."

Her mouth inched into a wistful smile. "Have a fantastic time, okay? You're an amazing dancer." I laughed, and she added, "This is the first time since Shane and I have been together that I actually feel like it'd be cool to be in a show with all of them and *not* working on the set."

My mouth fell open. Because this Natalie Carlisle, who'd become my closest friend in the last several months, in no way resembled the Natalie Carlisle from our time together in the Anti-Love Club as juniors. And boy did *that* feel like forever and a day ago.

She squinted at a spot behind me, then shook her head. "And the feeling's gone."

I nodded once. "What's the second promise I need to make?"

"FaceTime me when you get home to tell me how it went?"

"Absolutely." But my smile vanished when I clearly envisioned what I'd be going home to in just a few short hours.

Nope. All of that needed to stay in the box and buried where it belonged.

"Can you also do me a favor?" she asked with a hint of irritation.

I blinked twice and grinned.

"Please tell my boyfriend to leave his southern accent in the auditorium?" She moaned. "I love him, but he's driving me *nutso* talking like that. Almost nonstop."

I giggled. Seconds later, she joined me.

"I'll try my best," I solemnly said. "But *all* the boys do seem pretty attached to their accents for the show."

"And it's only January." She rolled her eyes. "It's going to be a long few months if they don't stop practicing." She shot me a soft smile. "Say hi to your aunt for me." She turned and fell into step behind some kids sauntering toward the doors to leave.

I headed in the opposite direction, toward the auditorium. The closer I got to the place in school I'd spent the least amount of time, the jitters caused me to tremble. But then I remembered what Noah had said to me that morning.

You're a really good teacher.

I'd learned from the best teacher, who had to also be in the auditorium by now, and waiting for me. Her assistant choreographer. Then I remembered what Natalie had just told me.

You're an amazing dancer.

The ugliness at home, Henry, Noah, nothing else mattered

at this moment except helping to teach what I loved for the next few hours. Something I was pretty perfect at, too.

* * *

From my front row seat, I watched Liam, or Bobby Child, on stage with Barrett Wagner, also known as Bela Zangler. Under Heather's stage-management direction, and at my aunt's request, we'd started at the musical's beginning. And it was already time for Bobby to break out his tap dancing skills for the first time.

"Okay," Aunt Daphne said to Liam. "I'd like to see *your* dancing skills first."

Liam definitely had rhythm, but her question made him freeze and fall silent for several seconds. Until he started humming and dancing to the *Macarena*?

Aunt Daphne burst into laughter, along with me and everyone else in the auditorium. It was only us, Heather, the two boys, and the eight Follies Girls made up of freshmen and sophomores. Mrs. Chaplin had taken the rest of the cast into the choir room to rehearse other scenes. Which, of course, included Noah. And definitely a good thing.

Liam finished his "dancing" with a quick, flawless spin, then stopped with his left leg bent, the toe of his shoe on pointe. And he held his hands out in a *ta-da*!

Once Barrett stopped laughing, he threw his right arm toward Liam. "That was truly terrible dancing," he said, but in his Hungarian-Zangler accent that was on the rough side.

Liam faced him. "That was a truly terrible accent," he said in his much better Hungarian voice. That'd *he'd* been practicing—almost nonstop—since he spent a good portion of the play impersonating Zangler. "Are you sure you are Hungarian?" he added. With the accent.

The two continued laughing, which was actually nice to see. Things between Liam, his girlfriend, Maddie, and Barrett had been *pretty* tense after Liam and Maddie became a couple in the fall. Because Barrett had liked Maddie. But Barrett now had a girlfriend he seemed crazy about, though she went to a different private high school, and the three had eased back into friendship the last month or so.

"*Enough,*" Heather groaned from where she sat near stage left. She shook her thick script at them. "Focus. Especially you," she added, pointing at Liam.

"Believe it or not," Aunt Daphne said, still smiling from their—his—antics, "I'm already seeing *lots* of potential with our Bobby Child."

Liam straightened, puffed out his chest, and shot Heather an exaggerated glare.

Aunt Daphne focused on Barrett. "And Mrs. Chaplin told me you're the Bobby understudy." He nodded, and she grinned. "Is your Macarena as good as his?"

The boys laughed before Barrett replied, "It's actually better."

Aunt Daphne clapped once. "Excellent. Let's get started." She glanced at me. "Can you work with the girls?"

I sprang from my seat. "Yep!"

The girls and I went to the back of the stage. The air around us pulsed with their excited chattering. But once I demonstrated the basic tap steps, their excitement and nerves smoothly transitioned into focused determination.

What felt like minutes later, I tore my eyes from the girls, dancing somewhat in unison, to glance at my aunt's progress with Liam and Barrett. They were as focused as they practiced a part of Bobby's audition—dancing in a slow, deliberate circle while wearing goofy smiles.

I smiled, too. And a bit on the goofy side.

I'd absolutely done the best thing for me, saying yes to my aunt. Being here was *right* where I belonged. It was also helping me forget everything beyond this auditorium.

30

Chapter Five

P*atience and stamina.*

With wide eyes, I stood near the stage right stairs.

Almost the entire cast was now on stage and rehearsing what little Aunt Daphne and I taught them for the "Slap That Bass" number, the first *big* dance scene in the show. Kids "tap dancing" in their Vans or Converse or Nikes had made the auditorium sound like a herd of horses had taken over the stage.

Some of the cast, like the Follies Girls, had learned the steps pretty quickly. Even now, the girls were demonstrating the steps to others who seemed to be struggling. But there'd been almost no actual dancing in unison—at that moment, one of the Deadrock cowboys spun and collided with a cowboy to his left. The two staggered several steps, as if they really were drunk cowboys, then burst into laughter.

Maybe starting to rehearse this number had been a *tad* too ambitious for Day One.

My eyes drifted to Aunt Daphne, where she stood close to stage left. She'd been working almost exclusively with a few boys struggling quite a bit. A small group that included Noah.

I focused on him—yet again—his face stuck in a deep frown while he watched my aunt demonstrate the pretty basic tap steps. In fact, that's really all we'd taught everyone today.

He, along with the other boys, nodded once she finished. He then *slowly* did the steps...but ended up off balance during a turn. His head fell in frustration, and I cringed.

I guess he hadn't been exaggerating when he'd said his tap dancing skills fell "right around a Big. Fat. Zero." He *did* have rhythm, because he seemed to be picking up the steps. But doing the steps quickly and adding other movement was where he faltered.

He lifted his head, and our eyes came together. His face turned crimson, but I gave him an encouraging smile. He shook his head, then dragged his eyes back to my aunt.

I imagined my feet glued in place so I wouldn't go right for him and give him the hug he clearly needed. Because he was being way too hard on himself.

I sighed and dropped to the stage, the first time I'd sat since rehearsal began. I then angled my head toward the house where the few members of the cast *not* in this scene had been watching what could only be described as dancing chaos.

Kassidy, who'd been asked to take the small, non-singing and dancing role of Bobby's mother, caught my eyes and waved, which I returned. She sat in the front row of the section closest to me, between Shane and a boy named Michael I barely knew. The only other people sitting in the house were Mrs. Chaplin and her daughter, Sloane. They were in the front row of the center section.

Mrs. Chaplin had her narrowed blue eyes locked on the spectacle on stage. Sloane sat beside her, yawning, while focused on her phone.

I faced forward, smothering a smile at the fact Sloane Chaplin, a fellow senior, hadn't been handed the lead role of Polly Baker by her mom, the musical director. Though she *was* an amazing singer, my theater friends had told me her dancing ability fell around a Big. Fat. Zero.

"I swear the shows always look rough at this point in rehearsals." Maddie sat beside me.

At the same time those same two cowboys crashed into each other a second time.

She flinched. "Well, maybe not *this* rough. But in everyone's defense," she swiftly added, "this is our first *dancing* musical."

I gave her a bright smile. "It's been a great day. Really." *For the most part.* "And you and Liam are going to be *so* fantastic as Polly and Bobby."

She giggled. "Thanks." She huffed. "We've been running lines together since the day the cast list was posted, and I *still* can't believe we got the leads." Her eyes wandered to her boyfriend, standing just shy of stage left and talking to Barrett. "I keep pinching myself."

She and Liam danced together briefly in this number, and had picked up their routine pretty quickly. But Maddie, like me, had been dancing for years. And though Liam wasn't as strong a dancer as his girlfriend, they moved almost perfectly together. Because of their obvious chemistry, on and off the stage. The kind of chemistry that crackled and popped. The kind of chemistry Natalie and Shane shared. And my other girlfriends had with their boyfriends.

My eyes wandered to Noah, and my smile slipped at his continued frustration.

"Speaking of Bobby," Maddie continued, "how'd he do earlier? Before we came back?"

I blinked twice and glanced her way. "Great." I laughed. "My aunt was really impressed with his mean Macarena."

She frowned, and I explained how he broke out his "dance" moves.

"He's such a dork." She rolled her eyes, but with a grin.

"He's also lucky he's cute." Her frown came back. "Noah seems to be *really* struggling."

I nodded, but said, "He'll get it, though. It's only the first day. My aunt is the best dance teacher and will never let him give up." Which was how he looked now with his hands folded on top of his shaking head while he again watched Aunt Daphne demonstrate the steps.

"Okay everyone," Mrs. Chaplin loudly said, now standing. "I think that's enough for today. Starting tomorrow, Daphne and I would like you to bring clothes to change into since the dancing rehearsals have officially begun. Thank you."

Maddie and I stood, and she threw her arms around me.

"I'm so excited you're here," she murmured as I squeezed her back. "Noah said you were awesome in November. When you were helping Heather and Nicolas?"

We released each other, but then I froze at her words.

"I'm looking forward to you teaching *me* to be a better dancer." She smiled.

My insides swelled at her compliment. At Noah's compliments. And I lost my voice.

"I'll see you tomorrow!" she chirped before sprinting toward her real-life hero.

I stayed still, absorbing her words via Noah Sanchez's praise. Then I slid my eyes to him, now in the house. He stood talking with Kassidy and Shane, still wearing a mask of defeat.

I jogged down the stage right stairs and headed for him.

Our eyes caught during my approach. But then he looked down at his feet. I could only imagine what he had to be mentally saying to them.

"Hey." I flashed Kassidy and Shane quick smiles, then concentrated on Noah. "Can we talk for a sec?"

He shrug-nodded.

Kassidy and Shane glanced at me, grimaced, and quietly walked away.

"You weren't that bad, okay?"

He raised his head and sighed. "Lexi, you don't have to be nice." He shoved his hands into his pants pockets. "I. Sucked. You can say that. You won't hurt my feelings."

I leaned forward. "You Didn't. Suck. You were picking up the steps."

"At the pace of a *sloth* learning to tap dance."

A laugh escaped before I could stop it. And he cracked a smile.

"You'll get faster once you get comfortable with the steps. I *promise*." I lifted my shoulders. "Today was only Day One. Did you expect to be tap dancing out of the auditorium?"

His smile grew, followed by a quick laugh. "No. But that would've been seriously cool."

My insides swelled to near explosion at the fact that I'd put a smile on his face and made him laugh; his first since we'd started the rehearsal for "Slap That Bass."

His smile became a tad shy. "Thanks for the pep talk." He paused, then quietly added, "I'm really glad you're here, Lexi."

I froze, then blinked twice.

He turned, picked up his backpack, and all but fled the auditorium.

My breath left my lungs in a frustrated, confused puff. And for the millionth time since December, a question appeared—what was going *on* with Noah Sanchez?

"So that's the infamous Noah I heard so much about there for a while."

My face became hot at Aunt Daphne's teasing.

She stood beside me, and that's when I noticed the near silence. Everyone but us, and Mrs. Chaplin and Sloane, had left. But those two were strolling up the aisle toward the doors.

"I can see why you liked him," she continued. "He's...what did *you* call him? A hottie?"

"*Aunt Daphne*," I groaned above her laughter, "please

stop. And I'm with Henry." But I couldn't be certain who really needed to be reminded of that fact; me or my aunt.

"Yes, Sweetie, I know that." She shook her head. "In any case, Noah seems like a very sweet, respectful boy." She cringed. "But his dancing skills…"

I straightened. "He'll get better and you know it."

She nodded. "You're right. He was working extremely hard today. Always a good sign." She adjusted her purse strap and concern flashed through her eyes. "You ready, my dear?"

I picked up my backpack and flung it over my right shoulder. "Yeah."

She grasped my hand. "Call me if you need me tonight."

We walked up the nearest aisle, though I'd left my heart and soul on the stage.

Back to reality. Or more like the Pfeiffer war zone.

* * *

I walked into my house, closed the door behind me, and paused.

Silence penetrated the air. I breathed the peace into my lungs. And caught a whiff of cheesy yumminess and grilled bread, which meant *one* of my parents wasn't working late.

My tummy rumbled. I hadn't eaten anything since lunchtime in the library with Henry.

Thinking of him, followed closely by Noah, made me drop my backpack with a sigh.

Stuck between two boys I liked at school. Stuck between two parents I loved at home.

It seemed the only place in this world I wasn't stuck between anyone happened to be my aunt's dance studio; the one place I'd now be spending the least amount of time. Still, helping with the choreography today had provided me with escape. The auditorium wasn't my aunt's studio, but it would be a fantastic second place, based on how much I'd laughed and smiled during Day One of dancing rehearsals.

I held on to that fact as I forced myself to head for the kitchen, located at the back of the downstairs. The living room flowed right into the dining room that hooked onto the kitchen—I stopped when I registered Dad flipping a grilled cheese sandwich in a pan at the stove.

I hadn't seen him since long before he'd stormed out of the house yesterday afternoon.

"Hi."

He looked up and flashed a distracted smile.

Years ago, when he'd loved our life and being a dad, his turquoise eyes, that I'd inherited from him, would always light up the moment he saw me, followed by the deepest, affectionate smile. The kind of smile that made me feel safe. *Loved.*

I pushed my hair behind my ears and dragged my feet toward the island counter. "Where's Mom?"

His mouth hardened for a second, then formed a line of concentration while he flipped the second grilled cheese sandwich. That looked like something out of a cookbook recipe. Thick, golden bread with different types of cheeses oozing out the sides.

"Working late," he flatly replied.

Yes. Because that's how my parents escaped each other, this house, and even me. But would *I* be in this rotten place right now unless I had to be?

I sat on one of the barstools, folded my hands tightly in my lap, and asked, "Where have you been since yesterday afternoon?" I wasn't certain I wanted to know the answer. And would he even tell me the truth?

He picked up his nearby bottle of beer and took a long swallow. "Working. Important client going through a divorce and child custody battle." He set down his beer and went back to staring at the sandwiches being grilled to perfection.

It sounded like the truth, considering his—their—depressing jobs. And I had no interest in becoming a lawyer like my parents. But even if I did, I'd never in a million years choose family law like they had years ago. When they'd been completely different people. Before their law careers had crushed their positivity and their souls.

I watched Dad wiggle the spatula under a sandwich and place it on a plate, decorated with leafy lettuce, a perfectly sliced tomato, and dill pickle spear.

Something about yet another meal looking like a cookbook photograph made me ask, "You were working all night, too?"

Frustration and guilt flashed through his eyes as he handed me the plate. Then he straightened and stared at me. "It's a big case, Alexis. And that's all you need to know."

Of course.

He pointed at my plate. "Eat your dinner so you can get started on your homework." He picked up his plate and beer. "I'm expecting a call from my client. I'll be in my office if you need me."

Not likely.

I frowned at the snarky jab that had appeared in my mind out of nowhere. Or maybe the jab wasn't out of nowhere. He hadn't asked me about my school day *or* my first day as an assistant choreographer. Then again, he'd made it clear last week what he thought of me getting involved with the school musical. What he thought of my dancing.

I gripped the plate, holding perfect food, to stop myself from turning it into a frisbee. From where I sat, and with the right aim, it would land in the sink and shatter. I then tried to remember the last time he—they—had actually *asked* me about my school day. Or what was going on in my life, for that matter.

Tears blurred my vision when I failed to find the memory.

Chapter Six

Natalie shoved an orange slice into Shane's mouth. "I'm going to start carrying duct tape if you don't stop talking like that, *Lank*."

Snickering filled our packed table in the noisy cafeteria.

I eyed Shane, sitting on his girlfriend's left side, and fought a smile as he chewed the slice, then swallowed. But when he, grinning as if he were Satan's son, turned toward Noah right beside him, I cringed.

"Noah," he said, continuing his Lank Hawkins accent, "what'd she do that fer?"

I pressed my lips together at the same time Natalie's head fell back on her shoulders.

Noah picked up his red apple. "Well there, Shane, I don't right know," he replied, and in his Pete-the-cowboy accent. Followed by a lazy shrug and huge bite of his apple.

I glanced at Maddie and Kassidy, across the table from me, and they rolled their eyes. Though their boyfriends, Liam and J.R., continued their Satan-worthy snickering.

I sat between Natalie and Henry, who'd been quietly eating his lunch. When my eyes met his, he gave me a soft smile that I returned. But something in his actions and look spelled discomfort. Because he really *didn't* have anything in common with my friends, an odd combo of theater techs, actors, singers, musicians, dancers, and athletes who shared an unexplainable bond with undeniable chemistry. At the same time, I had nothing in common with his friends, a group of mostly boys who loved math, science, *Marvel* movies, and *Star Wars*.

My school social world had become *The Big Bang Theory* meets *Glee*.

But I'd made a commitment to myself and Henry when he asked me out. And it's not like opposites didn't work in real life. I just had to give him—us—a chance. While staying far from Noah, who'd acknowledged Henry and I with nothing more than a "Hey" and nod when we sat down with everyone. Then again, it'd been foolish of me to expect anything else from him.

Natalie looked at me with her wicked smile, then faced her boyfriend. "I meant to ask you last night how your scenes are going with Sloane."

Shane's evil grin vanished.

The girls, including Heather, sitting between Liam and Nicolas, began their own devilish giggling.

"Ouch, Sunshine," Shane said in his voice. "Right for the *jugular.*" He shot her an exaggerated scowl that I knew she returned, having spent so much time with them.

Sloane *had* been given the next biggest female role in the musical, Irene, Bobby's fiancée. Who falls in love with Lank, which comes out in a big singing number with him. But not before the characters spend most of the show hurling insults at each other.

"You deserved that," Heather threw at Shane.

Natalie's wicked smile doubled in size.

"Yeah." Maddie wrinkled her nose at Shane, Noah, and

Liam. "It's you guys acting like complete *dorks* that give theater kids a bad name." She focused on Henry. "Right?"

Henry froze as everyone else looked up and over at him. He clearly hadn't expected to be included in the conversation. He may not have even been listening, based on the fact his face, ears, and neck turned pink. Almost the shade of neon due to his pale skin.

I reached under the table and grasped his hand. That was cold and clammy.

Henry coughed once and shrugged.

I mentally winced. Because my friends weren't hard to be around. Not even a little bit.

Liam put his arm around Maddie, hugged her to him, and unleashed his dimpled smile. "Madeline, my love," he cooed, and in his Zangler-Hungarian accent, "why do you say such cruel things to us?"

All the boys' laughter broke the tension. Well, Henry didn't laugh, but I still released a quick breath at Liam's perfect timing.

Maddie glared at her boyfriend, and he slowly withdrew his arm.

"Right," Liam stated in his real voice. He held up his hands. "Got it."

She went back to her lunch.

Maybe Henry I needed to talk about my friends and his? Yes. Communication. Necessary in all relationships, especially romantic. Something I'd learned the hard way hearing my parents discuss bits of their cases. And while watching their marriage break, piece by agonizing piece.

"What are we going to be rehearsing today, Miss Choreographer?"

Liam's question slammed into my brain.

I'd talk to Henry the first chance I could.

I gave Liam a bright smile. "Same stuff as yesterday." I paused, then added, "I don't think anyone's ready for more."

Liam and Maddie nodded as Shane said, "It did look rough from what we saw."

He pointed at Kassidy, and she flinched her agreement.

I chanced a glance at Noah, concentrating on the apple he'd nearly eaten. "Guys, yesterday was only Day One." I waved my hand in the air as if shooing Shane's words. "That stage will be full of tap dancing experts by April."

Everyone agreed with me but two boys. One who had no idea what we were talking about, and one in the process of investing *every* part of himself into his role and the musical.

Probably not the smartest choice, but I had to do everything in my power to help Noah Sanchez believe. And become Pete, the tap dancing cowboy from Deadrock, Nevada.

* * *

I kept my eyes trained on Noah, specifically his feet.

Aunt Daphne and Mrs. Chaplin had taken a huge leap of faith by deciding to play the "Slap That Bass" music for Day Four of dancing rehearsals, since Days Two and Three had gone pretty well. For the most part.

Noah, however, was two or so seconds behind the music. And most of his fellow dancers.

His sharp features were once again tight with frustration, and my heart gasped at the sight. Up until adding the music today, he'd been in sync with the steps and everyone else. He'd also been smiling the last couple days. Easing into confidence.

He suddenly stopped dancing and stood there, staring at the stage. Everyone else slowly stopped, too, while trying not to stare at *him*.

"He's a good dancer," Heather mumbled from beside me from where we sat in the center sections's front row. "I've danced with him." She huffed. "He isn't like Nicolas, but he still knows what he's doing." She shook her head. "I'm the one at the dances who looks like he does now. So I don't understand why he's not catching on faster."

Because dancing in that situation is nothing like learning any kind of choreography.

A couple of cowboys and a Follies Girl began talking to him. From the looks on their faces, it seemed they were trying to encourage him. But his face remained set in darkness.

I said, "He needs to relax and stop overthinking the steps."

"Hmm..." She glanced at me. "That reminds me of something Nicolas told me about his dancing." Her round, green eyes wandered back to Noah. "It doesn't work for him unless he can feel the music. Get it into his bloodstream." She propped her elbow on the armrest and rested her chin on her fist. "Maybe that's what Noah needs. Real time with the music? He is a musician."

I straightened and blinked twice.

Yes. That's *exactly* what Noah the musician needed. Why had I never thought of that? He also needed extra time with the choreography, but one thing at a time. Him, being a seventeen-year-old boy who played the guitar, probably didn't keep Gershwin music in his library. He may not have even heard most of these songs—like "Slap That Bass"—before this musical. Though he'd seemed familiar with "I Got Rhythm." But that could be due to preparing for his audition. Still, I had an idea on how to inspire Noah's inner tap dancer that wanted to break free, considering how hard he was working.

"Heather, you and your boyfriend are brilliant!" I leapt from my seat.

Mrs. Chaplin had stopped the music, and she and Aunt Daphne were dismissing kids from the stage. That meant rehearsal had ended. Now I just had to catch Noah long enough to run my idea by him. Which might be tricky since he'd been staying away from me all week.

Heather laughed. "I think so, too. But what did we do?"

Noah rushed off the stage, down the stage right stairs, and went directly for his backpack.

Aunt Daphne strolled up to me with wide, glazed eyes. "How'd it look from here?"

Noah shrugged into his backpack and barreled up the nearest aisle. Not at all like him, either. All week he'd stayed behind to chat with our friends and walk out with them.

"I'll be right back," I tossed at my aunt while I moved around her.

I raced after him. My much shorter legs had nothing on his long, swift strides.

He jerked open an auditorium door that I barely caught as it closed.

"Noah, wait!" I called after him the moment I stepped into the lobby.

His fast steps slowed to a stop inches from entering the school.

I approached him, his shoulders moving up and falling in a deep breath. He then faced me, and I halted at the irritation and defeat in his narrowed eyes.

"Lexi, I know why you're here and I'm not in the mood, okay?"

I opened my mouth, but him defiantly crossing his arms made me lose my voice.

Why was he so angry? The rehearsal hadn't been *that* bad.

"I don't want to hear your sunshine and rainbows and pink unicorns opinion on rehearsal today. Or my *lousy* dancing."

I frowned. That's how he interpreted my encouragement? As if he were listening to a five-year-old girl's view of the world?

He looked away. "I know you mean well. And the fact you can look at everything the way you do is awesome." He released a soft laugh. "I've never met anyone like you." He raised his head, and our eyes came together. Like super-strength magnets.

Electricity ripped through me. My heart hammered my chest when his gaze transitioned into piercing. Familiar. The real Noah Sanchez.

"Most people need the bright side." He walked toward me and stopped when we were in touching distance. "But I don't work like that." He leaned forward. "I need *honesty*. The kind that brings me to my knees." He pointed at his chest. "The pain from hearing the honesty so excruciating it makes my heart stop beating long enough to make me breathless."

My breath stalled in my chest from his quietly spoken, *honest* words. And from the way he was looking at me like we were the only two people on the planet.

He held our stare for a handful of seconds, then stepped back. "That's not what you do." He shrugged. "I'm not saying it's a bad thing, either. This world needs more Lexi Pfeiffers."

The auditorium doors flew open, and I jumped.

The cast...our friends...went by us in a blur of chit-chat. I even caught Heather eyeing us closely as she passed. Because she knew Noah and I had a spark between us. That all of a sudden had flared into a southern California wildfire inside of me at what he *thought* he knew.

When we were once again alone, I defiantly crossed my arms. "You don't know anything about me, Noah Sanchez." But you would if you'd had the guts—*no*.

He tilted his head left. "I know what I see and hear because I'm Not. Blind. Or deaf."

Something about that, the way he said it, and him basically admitting he *knew* me based on how I acted at school, made me snap, "You're right. You. Totally. *Suck!*"

His eyes widened, and I laughed.

"In fact, you're the worst tap dancer I've ever seen in My. Life." I narrowed my eyes. "And I teach five-year-olds."

My harsh words echoed throughout the lobby for a few seconds, followed by silence.

His shock transitioned into a blank expression.

I dropped my arms to my sides as guilt spiraled through me. I'd never spoken to anyone that way. Where had that even come from? He'd definitely pushed a button, but I wasn't a mean person. And what I'd said had been the definition of nasty.

Alexis Evelyn Pfeiffer, good girls don't raise their voices in anger.

"Finally, some honesty." He slipped his hands into his pockets. "How do you feel?"

I glared at him. "Like a horrible person." Actually, the weight on my shoulders had lightened a fraction. But from the physical act of snapping and letting it all out. I certainly wasn't going to admit that to him, though.

He nodded once. "You'll get over it." The corner of his mouth barely lifted in what could have been his lopsided grin. "Because what you said was the truth."

I shook my head. "Noah, I *know* you'll get there. It's only the first week." Which reminded me of why I'd chased after him in the first place. But so much for that conversation.

He took another step back. "And I needed to hear from someone how awful I am because *that's* what'll push me to be the best tap dancer you've ever seen in Your. Life." He paused long enough to give me his trying-to-read-my-soul stare, then turned and headed into the school.

As I watched him amble down the hallway, I clenched my hands to the point I felt my nails. A way to stop myself from screaming the frustration coursing through my veins.

Chapter Seven

I marched into my room, turned on the light, and slammed the door behind me.

"*Hi, Lexi.*"

I sighed and grumbled, "Hi, Coda."

He spread his wings and gave himself a hard shake. Probably his way of saying he didn't like me slamming the door. If my parents had been home, I'd be hearing about my "unlady-like behavior" from them, too. But they—thankfully—were working late. So I shrugged out of my backpack and hurled it onto my bed. It didn't even bounce because the dumb thing was so heavy.

I eyed my bird, cautiously peering at me, and I walked to his cage.

"I'm sorry." I opened his cage door and used my right fore-finger to lightly pet the back of his neck. "But Noah Sanchez is the most *infuriating* boy I've ever known." Coda gently nipped at my finger, his way of saying stop. "Noah's so *stupid!*" I muttered through my teeth. "You can remember that, too."

I closed his door and went straight for my bed. After I

shoved my backpack to the floor, where it landed with a *thud*, I dropped onto my thick, fluffy, *pink* comforter.

Sunshine and rainbows and pink unicorns.

I glared at the ceiling.

He'd made me sound like a naïve, brainless, blondie. Just because I preferred building people up instead of...bringing them to their knees with harsh honesty. Why would anyone want to hear they suck that bad at something? How could that possibly be helpful?

I need honesty. *The kind that brings me to my knees.*

Remembering his unexpected honesty, and the way he'd been looking at me, caused my irritation and frustration to leave me in a long breath. My body sank deeper into the comforter.

The pain from hearing the honesty so excruciating it makes my heart stop beating long enough to make me breathless.

How'd Noah end up with that kind of need? There'd been an unmistakable darkness to his words. He'd obviously experienced that kind of brutal honesty at some point. And it had forever changed him—he thought for the better.

I guess I understood what he'd said about the honesty pushing him toward better. Stronger. Extraordinary. After losing dance competitions or not getting the grade I wanted in a class, I'd always done whatever was in my power to fix it. Make it extraordinary for the next time. I couldn't exactly hold his need for honesty against him. But something about the intensity mingled with his words and radiating from his eyes made all that seem much deeper than simply failing at something in his past.

Noah wasn't stupid. He also had at least one big demon impacting his choices.

I grabbed a pillow and hugged it to my chest.

What did I even know about him? Outside of him being a musician, the obvious school stuff, and that his parents were together and he had an older sister. He wore mystery in a brooding, poetic, solitary musician sort of way. At the same time, he could get on a stage and become whatever character he'd been given.

I'd first noticed him during *Romeo and Juliet* when he'd played the small part of Count Paris, but smiled when I remembered him as the nerd, Eugene, in *Grease*.

He'd stumbled across the stage, usually after being shoved by a T-Bird, dropped books and papers, pushed his fake, black glasses up his nose, and pulled up his pants that were a little too big for him. It'd been during the school matinee, watching him make a complete fool out of himself, that he'd caught my undivided attention. The fact a boy who totally qualified as a dark, mysterious *hottie* could convincingly play that character had hooked me, and for the first time since my humiliating experience with Cam Jenkins, my last boyfriend. Who'd also been into boys. I'd just been too dumb...and maybe naïve...to see the signs.

I squeezed my eyes shut and replaced Cam's face with Noah's.

Why hadn't he asked me to Snowflake Formal?

Our chemistry had been just as fiery as Heather and Nicolas. And Natalie and Shane. And Maddie and Liam. And all of our other friends who were couples. I should've, like Natalie told me, gone after him. But once we'd finished helping Heather and Nicolas, he'd distanced himself from me. What teenage girl would ask a boy to a formal dance in a confusing situation like that?

So I'd ended up going with Henry. A cute, sweet boy who didn't turn any part of me into mush with his gazes. Or lopsided grins. Or touches. Still, no relationship was perfect. Especially in this house.

I'd made my choices. So had Noah. And I genuinely liked Henry. No, we didn't have a whole lot in common. That didn't mean the answer was breaking up. Right? We simply needed to try a little harder. Or maybe *I* needed to try a little harder. With the exception of becoming mute while we sat with my friends at lunch, Henry was a pretty great boyfriend. That's when I remembered I wanted to talk to him about his awkwardness with my friends.

I rolled onto my stomach, since I'd left my phone in my backpack.

He'd, as usual, texted me about rehearsal.

I replied, *Everyone's getting there. Feel like having lunch alone tomorrow?*

Our relationship was nowhere near perfect, but we could be better than my *parents*.

As I waited for Henry's reply, I rolled onto my back, closed my eyes, and let the house's peacefulness surround me.

* * *

I leaned back and lifted my eyes from the complex math problems filling the page in my notebook. Henry sat across from me at our table buried at the back of the silent library. He'd decided to tackle his Calculus homework since he had Mathletes after school.

I had one more extra credit problem left, but we still needed to talk.

I didn't need the bonus math points. At this early point in the semester, my Trig grade sat at around a ninety-five percent. But my overachieving parents had long ago drilled into my brain to always do the extra credit a teacher offered, even if I didn't need it. Still, the concepts were already getting tougher. So it wasn't a bad thing to cushion my grade.

Henry dropped his pencil, slouched in his chair, and rubbed his eyes. "I can't figure out this stupid problem." He lowered his hand and looked at me. "How's the extra credit going?"

"Fine." And now that we'd stopped working on math, I could bring up the friends conversation. I inhaled and quietly released the air. "Can I ask you something? It's been on my mind for a while now."

He sat up and grinned. "Lex, you should know you can ask me anything."

I tried to return his grin as I began twirling a lock of hair around my index finger.

He pointed at me. "You do that thing with your hair when you're in serious mode."

I blinked twice, stopped, and folded my hands tightly in my lap. For some reason, it bugged me he'd already picked up on my quirky habits.

He laughed. "You don't have to stop. It's cute." His smile turned affectionate. "Like every single part of you."

"Thanks." Though being an eighteen-year-old young woman, I really didn't like being called "cute" anymore. But I had a feeling because of my petite size and blonde hair, I'd never escape the word that should be used only to describe boys like Henry and baby animals.

"What's up?"

Yes. Time for communication on an important subject.

"Do you like my friends?"

He stared at me a few seconds, then frowned. "Yeah. Why?"

I shrugged. "It's just you seem so uncomfortable when we sit with them at lunch. Like on Monday?"

He looked away, picked his pencil back up, and rolled it between his fingers.

This quirky habit of his didn't seem like a good sign. But I continued with, "I know they're nothing like your friends, but I swear they're *amazing*."

"I know that. Honestly."

I held my breath and waited, since he clearly *did* have a problem with them.

"But most of the time, all of you are talking about stuff I don't know anything about."

Just like I figured. At the same time, that's how I felt when we sat with *his* friends.

"Sports and theater." He slowly tapped the pencil's eraser on his notebook. "Mostly theater." He paused, then added, "And it seems like the guys are always performing. Like with the accents? It was funny the *first* couple times, you know?"

Okay. I could grudgingly give him that one. Though Henry had seen the girls were just as tired of their silliness and had, finally, stopped them.

"And Liam's the worst one. I mean, does he ever talk in his real voice?"

I straightened at the way he'd grumbled his words. Full of clear judgment.

"Is he ever serious about anything?" Henry shook his head. "I can't believe he's going to be a Marine."

His words stung my insides, and I lifted my chin. "Henry, you don't even know Liam." I didn't know Liam extremely well, either. But I'd heard, via Natalie, he'd barely left Maddie's side after her grandpa passed away in the fall; the definition of a boy who loved his girlfriend. I also knew one reason he'd enlisted in the Marines was following in his parents' footsteps.

Henry cautiously eyed me.

"And just because he likes to make people smile and laugh, doesn't mean he won't be an extraordinary Marine." I lifted my shoulders. "Seems to me his ability to do that will make him pretty popular during...rotten times." Where was his judgment coming from, anyway? Because his guy friends were certainly not easy to be around. At least mine were cute and funny.

He angled his head back. "You asked. And I answered honestly. Was I supposed to lie?" He frowned. "Nothing I said means I can't stand the guy. Or any of your friends."

But nothing he'd said sounded as if he truly liked them, either.

He dropped the pencil and leaned forward. "Well, Noah bugs me. But I told you why."

Yes. He had told me his feelings about Noah. I couldn't really blame him for that one, either. That's when Noah's honesty from yesterday after rehearsal filled my mind. Henry had just used that word, too.

Honesty.

Was I the only person on this planet who liked to spare people's feelings? I'd never thought of it as lying, though. Natalie could be brutally honest, too. Like Noah's honesty last night and Henry's right now about my friends, hers occasionally stung and reached my soul.

"Don't take what I said personally. I know my friends aren't perfect."

"No! They're not." My snarky, but true, comeback had slipped out before the words even registered in my brain.

Henry stared at me, and I dragged my eyes to the nearby stacks.

What was wrong with me? Snapping at Henry like that had eased my irritation with him and given him a taste of *my* honesty. But freeing my feelings like that, and twice in less than twenty-four hours, was not the way Alexis Evelyn Pfeiffer handled things.

The silence continued until he sighed.

"Lexi, we're dating each other. Not each other's friends."

I guess I could give him that one, too. Though it was obviously a good thing I was closer to Natalie and Shane than Maddie and Liam. But I wanted to be better friends with them.

"And I really like you," he quietly added.

I forced myself to glance his way and found him giving me an apologetic smile.

"So I promise I'll make more of an effort with your friends." He hesitated before saying, "Even Noah."

Even him. Who I refused to think about with Henry's words dangling between us; his statements the action of a boy who *wanted* to be with me. I couldn't fault him for that. And the tension left me in an exhale that relaxed my shoulders. Then I said, "Okay. Me, too."

He sent me a playful grin. "I think you and I need some serious alone time."

Yes. Maybe that's exactly what we needed, since I couldn't remember the last time we'd had such a thing. Between both of us being busy with school and homework and after school stuff, it sometimes felt like I didn't have a boyfriend.

I leaned forward and crossed my arms on the table. "What are you thinking?"

His grin eased into naughty, which made me laugh.

When Henry Callaghan grinned like that, he was pretty adorable.

"My parents are going out tomorrow night with some friends."

I fought a smile. "So pizza and Netflix?"

He reached out and pushed a lock of hair behind my right ear. "Sure. We can watch a movie, too." He winked at me.

I nodded. "It's a date." I'd give him nothing but my undivided attention, since I was *determined* to have what my friends had with their boyfriends.

Chemistry. Warmth. Love. I deserved and wanted those things, too. It's not like I received a whole lot of that home, either.

Chapter Eight

One by one, the Follies Girls returned my high fives as they filed off the stage. A little, fun thing we'd started that made me smile, while feeling like I was a part of something amazing.

We'd just finished another day of rehearsing "Slap That Bass" with the music. It had gone well, too, despite Aunt Daphne having to unexpectedly miss Day Five. But everyone had worked super hard as if she had been here. Then again, Mrs. Chaplin seemed to run rehearsals like an actual drill sergeant.

The cowboys followed the girls and also gave me high fives. And the line ended with *him*, who stopped in front of me instead of raising his hand.

My smile slipped.

We hadn't spoken or looked at each other since Thursday after that rehearsal. So I stood there on the stage, everyone's chattering in the house filling the small gap between us. I also tried not to notice how *good* he looked in his rehearsal clothes of a black T-shirt and black basketball shorts. His forehead and hairline still glistened with working his tail off from the moment we started rehearsing that number.

Noah wore hard work well, too, and I frowned.

Was there anything on this planet he *didn't* wear well?

He ran a hand through his hair, which made the thick locks stand up in a way that made me imagine him rolling out of bed early in the morning. Without a shirt.

Heat burst inside of me at the completely *unladylike* and inappropriate thought.

I lowered my head to stare at the stage. Then guilt rushed through me with the force of a tidal wave when Henry's sweet, smiling face appeared in my mind. And the way he'd looked at me Saturday night, in between too many long kisses to count. Affectionate. Totally into me—us—and our rare night alone on his couch, *not* watching the Netflix movie we'd chosen.

"So I'm here to tell you a secret," Noah quietly said.

I paused long enough to find my bright smile before lifting my head.

Our eyes caught, but I kept my smile in place. Despite his trying-to-read-my-soul stare that made me begin trembling.

"I can be a real asshole."

I blinked twice.

His face became hot pink. "I was being honest with you Thursday after rehearsal. But I could've been way nicer about it." He sighed. "I was having a bad day and took it out on you." He cringed. "I'm sorry, Lexi. Really."

I stared at him, since I couldn't remember a time any boy had apologized to me for acting badly. Even Henry hadn't really apologized for his unnecessary harshness toward Liam.

Noah's mouth curved into his lopsided grin, and my insides buzzed.

"But I heard what you said to me." He huffed. "Loud. And clear."

I mentally shook off the ridiculous buzzing and stepped toward him. "I didn't mean it."

He laughed. "Sure you did." He gestured toward his feet. "It helped, right?"

Yes. He had been noticeably better and more confident today. He definitely would have impressed Aunt Daphne, considering how he'd looked Thursday. I still said, "You looked *awesome* today, but what I said to you was more...mean than critical. Noah, I'm—"

"Don't. Apologize." He shrugged. "And I deserved more mean than critical."

Silence fell between us, and I tore my eyes away from him to glance at the house, now empty except for Mrs. Chaplin, who was talking on her phone, and Sloane, texting on hers.

"We should go before she *commands* us to leave," Noah grumbled.

I smiled, and we jogged down the stage left stairs.

After he flung his backpack over his right shoulder, he faced me. "Don't you normally get a ride home with your aunt?"

I nodded as I picked up my backpack.

"Does that mean your mom or dad are waiting for you outside?"

We headed up the nearest aisle.

No. Because they had no idea Aunt Daphne had to miss rehearsal today due to a plumbing emergency at her condo. And would either of my miserable parents drag themselves from their miserable work to pick me up from something they didn't support?

I shot him a quick smile. "I'm walking home tonight. No big deal."

He stopped us when we reached the auditorium's lobby. "But it's dark outside. And it's not like we live in suburbia."

Though his concern for my safety gave me a burst of

buzzing combined with tingling, I said, "I may be small, but that doesn't mean I can't take care myself. I also live on *this* side of the park, which means I don't have far to go."

He held up his hands. "Okay. Small but mighty?" His grin came back.

"Yes," I threw at him before I turned to head into the school. I needed to move. Something about his concern and irresistible grinning and *him* was making me jittery.

He easily caught up with me. "Well, since you're small but mighty, maybe you can walk me home?"

My determined steps faltered, and I whipped my head in his direction. To find him trying to give me a blank stare; the mischief brightening his penetrating eyes gave him away.

"I'll tell you another secret," he whispered. "I'm afraid of the dark."

I shook my head, then giggled. At the same time, where had *this* Noah Sanchez come from all of a sudden? Relaxed. Funny. *Flirty*. All traces of Thursday's darkness long gone. Which made me say, "You're in a really good mood."

He opened the first door of the school's main entrance and exit for me, followed by the second. He then adjusted his backpack. "I feel like I might conquer tap dancing after all."

At that moment, I remembered why I'd gone after him on Thursday, which led to our unexpected *honest* conversation. "Did you rehearse on your own over the weekend?"

We jogged down the steps and veered left.

"Yep." He smiled. "In the privacy of my room behind a locked door."

He had the kind of smile that reminded me of sunshine and rainbows after a hard rain—no. We were finally talking about the dancing, and I needed to stay focused. "Good," I stated. "With or without the music?"

He glanced at me. "Without, because I don't have the

music." He used his index finger to tap his left temple. "But it's in here. Music has a way of branding itself to my brain."

We reached the intersection, and I stopped us. "That's great. It's not good enough, though. Especially since you're a musician." I froze at my strongly spoken, *honest* words.

He tilted his head right and gave me that stare of his, mingled with a hint of surprise. "So what are you saying?"

I took a quick breath and lifted my chin. "Honestly?"

Without breaking our eye contact, he said, "Absolutely."

I leaned toward him. "Get the music to your numbers and listen to it until you can *feel* it." Our eyes stayed locked, and I saw something inside his spark. I straightened. "Heather told me it's what Nicolas does with his dancing. And with you being a musician…" My voice trailed into silence while he slowly nodded.

"He's right. Wow." He released a quick laugh and shook his head. "It never occurred to me to do that. But then" —he shrugged— "I've never had a role like this before." He unleashed his lopsided grin. "And Gershwin isn't exactly my type of music."

I faced forward, away from him. Namely that grin. And I suddenly and surely wanted to know his type of music. "I get it. But maybe make an exception until the show runs?"

He groaned, but had the good grace to follow it up with, "You're right."

We crossed the street, but when he continued walking beside me instead of crossing the street to where his building was located, I stopped us. Again. "What are you doing?"

He narrowed his eyes. "I'm not letting you walk home by yourself. I don't care if you're Small. But mighty."

I opened my mouth to protest, but he turned and continued walking.

Frustration, mixed with a tad too much excitement, rocketed through me and I jogged toward him. I sometimes despised people with long legs. "Fine." I barely fell into step beside him. "Since we still seem to be on this honesty streak, I think you could use real, extra rehearsals with the music." I eyed him. "Meaning not in your room behind a locked door."

Surprisingly, he nodded. "It would probably be helpful to have someone around to make sure I'm doing the steps right. Especially with the 'I Got Rhythm' number still ahead of us," he muttered under his breath. He then eyed me. "You offering to be that someone?"

The way he asked his question stole my voice. Relaxed. Interested. *Flirty*.

"You are a great teacher," he added, but seriousness had replaced the flirtatiousness.

Warmth shrouded me at him saying that a second time, and I peeked at him, but his attention was now directed straight ahead, on the dark, quiet street. That seemed a little too dark and quiet for—I had no idea what time it was. Around 6:30? Still, maybe it was a good thing he'd insisted on walking me home.

"So I'm up for the extra rehearsals with the music." He sent me a contrite smile. "But I should warn you, I'm not always the best student."

Between the smile and his words, something told me we were talking about more than him as a tap dancing student. *Brooding, dark mystery*. Who was this boy, walking beside me?

"Lexi?"

I smiled. "You don't scare me. I teach five-year-olds."

He laughed. "Well, my sister loves to point out when I'm acting like a five-year-old." He stopped us, and we faced each other. "Sounds like we'll start rehearsing this weekend? After I get the songs and spend the whole week listening to Gershwin instead of my go-to music."

This decision to help him master the tap dancing would probably come back to bite me. I mentally cringed at what

Henry might say when he found out *who* I'd be spending extra time with. Then again, he had told me he'd make the extra effort with my friends, including Noah, who needed me. The musical—and Mrs. Chaplin—definitely needed him to be perfect. Extraordinary. He had it in him. He just needed more time with the choreography.

Noah waved his hand in front of my face. "It's the thought of taking on these *fantastic* feet of mine that's making you quiet all of a sudden."

I pressed my lips together to stop my smile, then said, "We'll start Saturday, 11:00, at the studio if you tell me what your 'go-to music' is." That time wouldn't interfere with Aunt Daphne's two Saturday classes. And Henry, being Henry, would have to understand.

Noah's eyes brightened and he straightened. "I can do that. But it means you and I need to start over." He dramatically shook his head, stopped, held out his hand, then gave me a huge, mischievous smile. "I'm Noah Luis Sanchez. And you're..." He raised his eyebrows.

My mouth drifted open, and he thrust his hand closer to me.

I cautiously took—oh. His hand was warm, despite the cool, humid air. We squeezed each other's fingers as I absently said, "Alexis Evelyn Pfeiffer."

He held my hand, giving me that stare, as he said, "I can't believe I didn't know Lexi was short for Alexis." He gave my hand a quick squeeze and released my fingers. "Well, Alexis, when I'm not working my ass off at school or doing home-work or learning lines...or tap dancing behind my locked bedroom door—"

I burst into laughter.

"I can still be found in my room," he continued above my laughter, "spending important alone time with Eddie."

My remaining laughter died in my throat, and he froze. Until he kicked a rock aside.

"Yeah, that didn't sound right," he mumbled. "To clarify, Eddie's my electric guitar."

Wow. He had two guitars?

I stared at him. "You named one of your guitars *Eddie*? Why?"

We again started walking.

"I heard somewhere people name things that are important to them." He glanced at me. "Girls name their dolls and stuffed animals, right? At least, my sister did."

I nodded and shrugged, since I did have a couple of stuffed animals with names. Stuffed animals my dad had given me years ago. When he'd been a real dad.

I pushed that thought into the back of my mind and asked, "But why the name Eddie?"

"My go-to music is and always has been rock." He frowned. "And not the so-called rock music that's produced nowadays."

I made us pause at an intersection, then we jogged left once it was clear.

"So you like classic rock," I stated. But I knew nothing about that kind of music.

"Yeah. And that's how Eddie got his name." He looked at me. "As in Eddie Van Halen?"

The name sounded sort of familiar, but I stayed silent.

"As in one of the greatest guitarists of all time who co-founded the band Van Halen?" he tried again. At my continued silence, he groaned. "Seriously? You have to know the songs 'Jump'? Or 'Panama'? Or 'Hot for Teacher'?"

"I'm sure I'd recognize the songs if I heard them," I interjected, and a tad defensively. "I listen to all kinds of music." Even the occasional Taylor Swift and Shawn Mendes song.

But Noah the musician and rock music snob did *not* need to know that.

He released a long, low whistle. "I need tap dancing lessons, and *you* need lessons in badass rock music." He flashed me a devil-worthy grin. "No offense to Gershwin, but rock like I'm talking about is the kind of music that gets inside of you and Never. Leaves."

My pulse slowed at not only his grin, but the way he spoke about his "go-to music" that clearly was so much more than that to him. "You offering to be that someone to give me the badass rock music lessons?"

His eyes widened, and I gasped.

Had that flirty, almost naughty question come out of *my* mouth? Oh, what was wrong with me? And what was it about Noah Luis Sanchez that made me forget Alexis Evelyn Pfeiffer, my parents' *good girl?* Not that making out with Henry Saturday night would ever classify me that way. At the same time, being a normal, teenage girl could never be considered a crime.

Unless hot, guitar-playing Noah was involved with anything *teenage-girl related.*

"Okay," he answered. "That's fair."

I frowned. "What do you mean?"

"You're going to help me master Gershwin and tap dancing, and I'll help you learn what I mean about rock music."

I blinked twice at his conviction. Still, I could only blame myself for our newest deal. A deal I had zero interest in challenging. Once again, Noah had hooked me.

"So," he slowly began, "Henry's going to be okay with you helping me out, right?"

I jolted at his question. That felt like he'd doused me with a gallon of ocean water.

"He doesn't seem like the psycho, jealous type," he softly

continued, "but I don't know him very well. He doesn't say much."

I shook my head, as if a gallon of ocean water had hit me. "He'll be fine." *Hopefully.* "You're my friend, I want to help you, and it's for a good cause." Those truths would be exactly what I'd say to Henry tomorrow.

"Yeah." He nodded. "Totally."

We lapsed into silence that seemed a tad filled with tension compared to how *honest* our conversation had been. Until he'd asked about Henry.

I kept a long, frustrated sigh with myself and Noah in check. Since the moment he'd walked up to me on stage, he'd been acting like the Noah from November. Times two. And, of course, followed up with the "we're only friends" attitude. Too. *Weird.* And confusing.

So when my dark house came into view, I heard myself mutter, "My house is right there. Thanks for walking me home." Though it hadn't sounded anything like gratitude. Or like me.

We stopped at the stoop that led to the front door.

He frowned at my house. "Your parents still aren't home?"

"No." I gave him my back. "They're lawyers and work late a lot. I'll see you tomorrow." I marched up the stairs, not certain what or who was upsetting me the most at this moment.

"Um...Alexis Evelyn Pfeiffer, if I have homework this week, then so do you."

Homework?

I halted, slowly faced him, and narrowed my eyes.

He flinched. "Ouch. I can't believe you, of all people, are giving me the I-hope-you-drop-dead stare right now." He shivered.

I crossed my arms. "I'm tired." *Mostly of you and your*

confusing, maddening behavior. "What homework are you talking about?" *I also hope I don't regret helping you.*

He grinned up at me, and I swallowed a snarl. Also not like me.

"My homework is to listen to the Gershwin music all week. Until I *feel* it?"

I gave him a curt nod.

"And your homework," he said while taking a step backward, "is to listen to all the music from Van Halen's *1984.* Just Google it." He paused, then added, "Pay close attention to 'Hot for Teacher'." His devil-worthy smile returned. "Totally. Badass. Guitar playing." He pointed at the front door. "I'll wait to leave until you're inside."

I turned from him and pulled out my house keys. Once I was inside my dark, silent house, I released the long sigh I'd managed to keep inside.

"Hot for Teacher."

Cool song title. Unfortunately, I could relate to it a Little. Too. Well—oh, my *goodness.*

What had I been thinking, agreeing to all of this?

Chapter Nine

Henry closed his locker door before facing me. "Lexi, what are you doing?"

Other lockers opening and closing mixed with loud chatter and sporadic laughter as we stared at one another. His eyes were filled with the same disappointment and frustration I'd heard in his voice, despite the morning, hallway chaos surrounding us.

I stepped closer to him. "Noah's my friend and needs my help. This isn't a big deal." *And it wouldn't be.*

"You're too nice. And trusting." He moaned. "How can you not see he *likes* you?"

I raised my chin at the way he said that. Like I was a poor, little simpleton.

Noah did give me that soul-tingling look of his and occasionally said cute, funny things. But after last night, I couldn't help but feel those two things were simply Noah Luis Sanchez being himself. Shedding his thick, dark armor for a brief moment in time. Treating me the way I'd seen him act with Heather and Maddie. Minus those penetrating looks of his. And some of his comments had been cute, funny, *and* flirty.

Still, he liked to banter with all of his closest friends. Which meant last night had meant nothing, and Henry's attitude was based on one thing.

"When it comes to Noah, I'm a Heather or Maddie. So let that go!"

He drew back at my razor-sharp words, and I dropped my gaze to the floor.

Guilt and confusion and irritation wrapped itself around my core. I wanted to transport myself to my aunt's studio and get lost in feeling *my* dancing. Something I hadn't done since winter break and the only thing on this planet that righted everything inside of me.

Henry crossed his arms. "I'm your boyfriend, and I don't like the way he looks at you. Sorry if that makes me the *bad* guy," he muttered, not sounding at all apologetic. "And why is he in that play if he can't dance?"

I lifted my head to find him frowning at me.

"I can't even picture him tap dancing." He released a quick laugh that held no humor. "Liam and some of those guys, yeah. But Noah, the tall, dark, *creepy* guy? No. It's weird."

I clenched my teeth at the judgment and jealousy oozing from his voice.

Who was *this* boy, standing in front of me?

"Henry, stop saying that about Noah. You don't even know him—"

"That's the second time you've said that to me about one of your friends."

I leaned forward. "Because it's the truth. And you said on *Friday* you'd give all of them—even Noah—a chance."

A group of boys burst into obnoxious laughter as they passed us, but I kept my determined stare on Henry, whose shoulders slumped forward.

Triumph replaced some of my irritation with him, but I

managed to keep a smirk in check. Yet another action that wasn't at all like me. In fact, this confrontational girl standing in front of her boyfriend wasn't someone I recognized. But loyalty to *all* of my friends, who I adored, made this Alexis Evelyn Pfeiffer press her heels into the hallway floor.

"Fine," he grumbled. "I did say that." He expelled a long breath and straightened. "I can't be a total ass about this, since helping people—your friends—is what you do." He cracked a half smile. "It's one of the things I like most about you."

I relaxed my shoulders and posture at seeing and hearing the real Henry. "Thank you."

He angled his head left to catch my eyes. "I don't mean to act and sound like *that* kind've boyfriend. And Noah seems like a nice enough guy, but unlike your other friends, he bugs me."

Because of the way he looks at me. And maybe, just maybe, Henry sensed that spark between Noah and I that had started in November. That spark I couldn't shake.

The guilt returned so strongly I trembled.

"I don't trust him," Henry continued. "But I trust *you*. And I don't want to fight with you about this. Or him. He's not worth it." He grasped my hands and pulled me a step closer. "So do what you need to do." He looked all around us, then placed a quick kiss on my forehead. He leaned back, and our eyes met. "I swear I'll do my best at keeping my promise about giving him a chance. Because I really want to be with you," he softly added. "Our friends shouldn't get between that, either. Okay?"

I nodded and forced my mouth into a bright smile. Hopefully, what he'd just said would be the real end to the uncomfortable Noah conversations. I'd also come up with the perfect plan to keep the Noah-and-me sparks buried deep where they belonged. An idea that jumped into my brain last night while listening to Van Halen's "Jump." For around the hundredth time.

"There's another part to this I need to tell you." Something that would probably make him feel *loads* better, too. And as he eyed me warily, I added, "I'm going to ask for guy help." I then launched into my plan.

* * *

I spotted Heather and Nicolas together at his locker and wound my way toward them. Rehearsal started soon, and though she didn't need to be there when I begged her boyfriend for help, her stage manager opinion would back me up. Plus, she was one of Noah's closest friends.

Nicolas shoved a book into his backpack while he and his girlfriend chatted about something making them smile. They looked just the way Henry and I should have this morning. The way we should have *most* mornings. But we were still missing the connections that bound a girl and boy together. Something I'd never experienced. After this morning, and despite his encouraging words, I couldn't help but wonder if we *would* ever get there. But being with Henry was better than being single for more than a year and watching my friends become parts of something beautiful.

Watching my parents fall into hate, I'd needed to see that kind of beauty, too.

I plastered a smile on my face, and landed beside Heather and Nicolas.

They turned their heads in unison; their faces flushed from something beautiful.

"Hey!" Heather returned my smile. "We missed you at lunch today."

Being the good, loyal girlfriend I was determined to be

with Henry, especially after his three-sixty on the topic of Noah, we'd sat with his friends at lunch.

"Thanks. I missed you guys, too." All of me meant it, but I'd promised Henry I'd also give *his* friends a chance. Even though they'd been talking about some Marvel, superhero movie. Or video game. Or maybe it had been a superhero video game?

"You ready for another day of *slapping that bass*?" Heather added, then giggled. "The opening lines of that song always get stuck in my head."

Nicolas shot me a pained look. "Mine, too, because she hums the song."

She batted her eyes at him. "Just wait until we start rehearsing 'I Got Rhythm'."

He sent her a huge, toothy grin. "You definitely have rhythm, Santa *Baby*."

Heather's face turned scarlet as he completed his compliment by giving her a quick wink.

"Speaking of rhythm," I interjected, while trying *not* to begrudge them their crazy-in-love cuteness, "I need your help, Nicolas."

I quickly told them about my helping Noah Saturday mornings with the tap dancing and my idea to, hopefully, make him feel more comfortable, since he really didn't know me that well. Henry had *fully* supported this idea, too.

Nicolas frowned while Heather stared at me with wide, skeptical eyes. Because she knew.

He shut his locker door. "Have you talked to Noah about this?"

I shrugged. "No. But you're friends. And it's not like he's a silly *alpha male*."

Heather remained silent, still watching me while Nicolas nodded.

"No, but he's *Noah*." He shook his head. "Not the easiest

guy to get to know. And I'd say we're more friendly than friends." He glanced at Heather, and she gave him a weak smile.

More friendly than friends. Maybe that better described Noah and me, as well.

"I get it," I persisted, "but it would be so helpful to me and him if I had a co-teacher. Someone to dance with him. Someone to watch him." I smiled. "You know it's hard to do both. Even with the mirrors." Nicolas *had* to agree to this. And it's not like what I'd said wasn't true. I also couldn't expect my aunt to be my co-teacher for this. She had enough going on right now.

I focused on Heather. "What do you think? You've seen Noah at rehearsals."

She cringed. "Yeah. Although he looked good yesterday," she swiftly added.

Because he'd practiced over the weekend in his locked bedroom. But they didn't need to know that.

"He could use the extra help," she continued, glancing at her boyfriend. "Your help absolutely wouldn't hurt anything." She gave him a sassy grin. "You are a *hot* dancer."

He laughed. "I don't think I'll ever get tired of hearing you say that."

I cleared my throat. And not just because Heather and I had to get to rehearsal.

"Sorry." Nicolas faced me. "Yeah. Sure. I'll help you out. You were awesome back in November and December." He grasped Heather's hand, and we headed for the stairs. "Actually, the *four* of us made a fucking awesome team."

I smiled, but a tad wistfully since he'd said nothing but the truth.

We joined the mass of other students rushing down the stairs. When we reached the bottom, Nicolas went left with us, toward the auditorium.

"I'd still run this by Noah." Nicolas looked at me. "To make sure he'll be cool with the idea of a guy helping another guy with dancing?"

"Will *you* be okay? And Henry?" This, of course, from Heather.

I gave her—them—my bright smile. "Yes! Why wouldn't I be? Or Henry?"

Her eyes again filled with skepticism, but I kept my smile in place.

"Noah and I are friends, and he needs our help. Not a big deal." *And it wouldn't be.*

Chapter Ten

"Okay," Mrs. Chaplin said in a raised voice while she stood in front of the stage, "I want to start at the beginning like we did yesterday and run through it so Daphne can see how it looks. Then we'll only focus on 'Slap That Bass'."

Everyone in the opening scene, and in the first Deadrock scene, filed onto the stage in a rush of enthusiastic chatter. A good sign no one was burned out yet on rehearsing the same scenes, especially "Slap That Bass."

I settled into a spot in the center section behind and to the left of my aunt, then leaned forward and folded my arms on the seat back in front of me. But my eyes widened as Noah ambled toward us.

He dropped into the seat beside me and copied how I was sitting. "Hi, again."

I fought a smile and said, "Hi. What are you doing?" He wasn't in the first Deadrock scene, but he was in the next one.

"I have an answer to what you and Heather brought up."

Yes. My—our—insistence on having Nicolas help during the extra dancing rehearsals. He hadn't been able to reply, though, since Mrs. Chaplin had ordered everyone to go change.

As the cast in the opening scene got into their places, Aunt Daphne turned left. And gave us a questioning smile.

"Hi, Aunt Daphne," Noah said, followed by his lopsided grin.

I tore my eyes away from him and that grin of his that tickled my tummy Way. Too—*no*.

Her smile grew. "Hi, Noah." She glanced at me and back at him. "I hear you're going to be spending a lot of time at my dance studio, starting this Saturday."

She'd been surprised by the extra rehearsals news, but, like others, thought it would be best for him and the musical. Of course, she'd asked me the same questions Heather had before we walked into the auditorium. Because Aunt Daphne also knew. But I'd told her the same things I'd told Heather. No one needed to know the truth. And Henry *had* come around pretty quickly.

Noah nodded. "Yep." His cheeks turned a tad pink. "At some point, me and my feet will stop making you, and everyone else in here, cringe. I really do have rhythm," he quickly added.

She laughed. "I promise I see it. Learning to tap dance, particularly in these big Gershwin numbers, takes time." She focused on me. "But my niece is gifted. She'll get you there."

I felt my cheeks turn the temp Noah's had looked seconds ago.

"I know that," he murmured.

And at that my body turned the temp of a wildfire.

He leaned toward me, to the point our shoulders touched. Which didn't help the burning.

"Can I talk to you?" he whispered so close to me I felt his breath on my cheek.

I straightened and gave him a blinding smile. "Sure!"

Aunt Daphne faced forward to continue watching the rehearsal.

Noah sat back and slouched in his seat until his head rested on the back.

Not knowing what else to do, I copied *his* actions.

He rolled his head right, and our eyes locked. "If you think having Nicolas there will help you and me, and me in the show, then okay." His stare turned into that oh-so familiar one. "He's a cool guy. I trust him. And I" —he cleared his throat and rolled his head forward— "had a lot of fun back in November and December with all of you."

Then why didn't you ask me to—I really needed to let that go. Especially now.

"So," he softly continued, "I'll be at the studio Saturday, at 11:00, if you tell me what you thought of *1984*." He eyed me as his mouth curved into that grin. "I know you listened to it."

I tried to smother a smile as I asked, "How could you possibly know that?"

He laughed. "Between that smile you're *trying* to hide and not denying it, you just proved me right." He again rolled his head toward me. "What'd you think?"

Liam-Bobby started his tap dancing audition for Barrett-Zangler at the same time I stopped fighting my smile.

"Honestly?"

"Always."

I paused, then said, "I loved it."

His eyes brightened with appreciation. And a hint of arrogance.

"Don't look at me like that," I quietly scolded. "Because my favorite song wasn't 'Hot for Teacher'. But..." I shrugged. "The guitar playing in that song was pretty cool."

He squinted at me. "I believe the word I used was *badass*."

I giggled. "Fine." I leaned toward him and whispered, "It was Totally. Badass."

We laughed as Liam-Bobby finished his audition.

"What was your favorite song?" Noah asked.

I started to twirl a lock of hair around my index finger. "I loved 'Jump'." But he didn't need to know how many times I'd listened to it. "The lyrics make you want to—"

"*Jump!*" he said in an exaggerated whisper.

I rolled my eyes, then laughed and released my hair. "Yes. But into something that will change your life." *Something like love*. A deep message for a high-energy rock song.

"Yeah. That song's one of my favorites, too," he added, though he'd turned serious.

"And it does have some cool guitar playing."

He shot me a pretend dirty look.

"I mean, *badass*."

He sat up, fully faced me, and held out his hand.

I stared at it, then lifted my eyes to his. "Are we introducing ourselves again?"

He, now fighting his own smile, tilted his head right. "Did that smartass question come from *the* Alexis Evelyn Pfeiffer?"

I guess I deserved that. But what was it about him that brought out this side of me? Without thinking.

"With the exception of calling Eddie Van Halen's guitar playing '*cool*'," he continued, "I liked all of your answers about *1984*." He flashed his devil-worthy grin. "And the fact you listened to it right away. So we officially have a deal. You and me and Nicolas and Gershwin Saturday mornings until I master tap dancing." He cringed. "I can't believe I Just. Said. that."

I frowned. "If you turn into a silly alpha male about all of this, we *won't* have a deal."

He sighed. "Okay. Fine. You win." He then replaced his frown with a goofy, exaggerated grin. "I can do this. Now shake my hand, because I should get back there on stage."

The opening notes of "I Can't Be Bothered Now" burst

from the sound system. Mr. Lowry, the tech theater teacher, was already working with a few of his best seniors up in the sound booth. They'd eventually be in charge of everything sound related.

Liam's smooth, yet powerful singing easily blended with the music.

I faced Noah. "I'll shake your hand if I like *your* answer to *my* question."

He raised his eyebrows.

"Did you do your homework last night?"

"Yep." He stood and again held out his hand.

"And?" I persisted.

"And...what?" He shook his head. "Lexi, you can't expect Gershwin music to get inside of *this* guy in one night. And I warned you I'm not always the best student."

He had warned me. And what he'd said about Gershwin music was fair enough. So I grasped his *warm* fingers and we shared a firm handshake.

"But you..." His voice trailed off as he continued holding my hand. While giving me his familiar stare. "You're a great student and can move to the next rock music lesson." He released my hand and sauntered toward the stage right stairs.

Aunt Daphne slowly angled her head left and caught my eyes.

Yes. She'd been sitting there the whole time and had probably heard most of our conversation. That had been a tad flirty a few times. At least. But it didn't stop me from giving her a bright smile. "He's just ready for Saturday," I said in an idiotic rush of words.

She nodded once. "I'm sure he is," she murmured before turning forward.

I again began twirling that same lock of hair around my finger.

He'd seemed so relaxed. Comfortable in his own skin.

Totally opposite of the boy from last week. But then, music seemed to be the gateway to Noah Luis Sanchez. Suggesting he connect with the Gershwin music had, ultimately, started us down the rock music path. A pretty fun, exhilarating path. And even though it was incredibly wrong, considering Henry and the way Aunt Daphne had just looked at me, I couldn't wait until Noah's next lesson.

* * *

I walked into my house and closed the door.

"Denise, this is an important case and needs my full attention. And I'm not the only one who hasn't been around here lately!"

My dad's sharp tone and words, coming from the direction of the kitchen, felt like a slap across the face. My high from being around my friends, my aunt, all the dancing, evaporated with the speed of water landing on a scalding sidewalk.

I couldn't hear my mom's reply. Because ladies never raised their voices in anger. I still closed my eyes and leaned against the door. And just when I'd started savoring the fact they were choosing to work late instead of being here to demolish the peace. My peace.

"I never said your cases weren't as important as mine. But I'm not her only parent."

I opened my eyes as Mom said something that was probably nasty.

Even better. They were fighting about me.

"What the hell does that mean? If she has a favorite in this *family*, it's your sister."

Yes. For some reason, Dad had never warmed to Aunt Daphne; the person who'd brought dancing into my life. And Mom probably did think I preferred Dad to her because, years ago when we'd actually been a *family*, I'd been a bit of a daddy's girl.

"I'm not talking about this anymore," Dad declared. "She's eighteen and already has a life of her own. She knows if she needs me, I'm here. Can she say the same thing about you?"

And that was my cue to escape to my bedroom.

Within seconds, I was behind my closed door. Which I locked.

"*Hi, Lexi.*"

I dropped my backpack next to my desk. "Hi, Coda." I walked toward his cage, like I always did when I came in here after school, just as Dad's raised voice reached my room. But I couldn't make out what had to be another nasty remark thrown at Mom.

Totally. Fine. With—I sighed and focused on Coda.

"So how long have the *hate birds* been at it tonight?"

He vigorously shook his body, which made his feathers go *poof*.

"That long?"

His head bobbed up and down, and I couldn't help but smile. In moments like these, he really did feel like my spirit animal.

Dad's voice found me where I stood, and I groaned.

"This is so *stupid*," I muttered. "I can't listen to this—him—all night."

"*Noah's so stupid.*"

I froze, then blinked twice.

Coda gave me that funny, sideways look; the one only birds could give.

"Noah's *not* stupid," I enunciated. Well, not *completely* stupid.

Coda continued staring at me, and I repeated what I'd said.

"Noah's so stupid."

I frowned. "Fine. But you can't say that when Henry's around. Okay?" I couldn't imagine what his reaction would be if he found out I'd been talking about Noah to my *parrot*. I absolutely didn't need any more drama in my life.

Coda shuffled to his water dish, and I tried not to be discouraged by the fact he hadn't bobbed his head in agreement with me.

More yelling filtered through the hardwood floor. And this time it sounded like my mom.

I guess ladies did raise their voices when guys pushed their buttons.

I went for my backpack. I needed my phone and earbuds. I also needed some high-energy rock music to drown the voices of two miserable people who stayed together. But why? Because of me? They weren't doing me any favors. And they certainly weren't helping each other.

Their love had long since shriveled after a slow, excruciating death.

I pulled my phone from the front pocket of my backpack, followed by my earbuds.

Henry had texted, but not about rehearsal.

What'd Nicolas say?

Yes. I did need to get him caught up.

We're all good and start Saturday morning.

That news would make him happy, which was good news for me.

I sat on my bed and plugged the earbuds into my phone.

Cool. How'd rehearsal go?

Another round of mutual hate came from below. As if replacing the text message *ding*.

Great. Everyone's really starting to get the moves. Even Noah, in spite of a few minor missteps here and there. And something he'd said twice drifted through my now tight head.

I'm not always the best student.

Why did he keep saying that about himself? From what I'd seen, he worked *hard*. He already knew most of his lines and the song lyrics, too. And he was willing to give up a few hours of his Saturdays to "master" Gershwin and tap dancing.

All of that equaled being the *best* student.

It also seemed like he'd be a fun, super knowledgeable teacher of his favorite music. The type of music he played and wrote?

I stared blankly at my phone as I imagined him in his room right now, spending time with Eddie. I'd heard him play his acoustic guitar many times while we helped Heather and Nicolas. He'd been amazing, too. Had made guitar playing look effortless. Still, that hadn't been Noah playing *his* kind of music.

Nice. About to start your homework?

It's what I normally did after rehearsal, but stupid extra credit problems and an English paper, and other horrible homework, could wait.

I texted him, *Yeah. See you tomorrow.*

Maybe a little abrupt, but I wanted to crawl under my covers and forget *everything* in this world while I listened to some Totally. Badass. Guitar playing.

Chapter Eleven

I picked at my little container of pasta salad as I, again, slid my eyes across the cafeteria.

My friends were together, chatting, while smiling, followed by bursts of laughter. Natalie sat between Shane and Noah, who was in my usual spot. I hadn't sat with them all week, because of Henry's discomfort with Noah. And I'd spent the week convincing myself it was better this way, sitting with Henry's friends. Better for Henry and me, especially since I'd soon be spending extra time with Noah on Saturdays. But watching all of them, the obvious chemistry and deep connections, tugged my soul.

I'd said yes to Henry in December. There hadn't been a reason to say no to him. At the same time, I'd probably said yes for the wrong reasons, one of them being I'd been lonely. Tired of being surrounded by blissful couples who only had eyes for each other.

Watching and hearing my parents' continued fall into a black, dismal hole had probably made me want to be a part of something blissful, too. Another escape. Like dancing. And being alone with Henry, away from school, did feel like a break from reality. But—the Noah confusion aside—I missed *my* friends and their ability to make me laugh when I needed it. Like right now.

"Lex?" Henry placed his *cold* hand on my knee and gently squeezed.

I sat up, faced him, and gave him a bright smile.

"You okay?" he asked, frowning. "You've been really quiet today. And distracted."

I glanced at his closest friends, peering at me, and said, "Yeah. Why?"

Tyler, our student council president, pushed his glasses up his nose. "Curtis and I were talking about that paper in Washburn's class, and asked you what your topic is."

They had?

I looked at Curtis, sitting beside his girlfriend Isabel. His almost black eyes, a tad lighter than his skin, were wide open with interest. I did like Henry's friends, though Tyler could be more socially awkward than Curtis and Isabel. Who were another blissful couple.

"Oh. Sorry!" I shook my head. "I'm going to write about how dancing requires as much mental and physical dedication as a professional sport, and years of practice, but dancers only make a fraction of what athletes do. And deserve better than that."

Curtis nodded his approval.

Isabel laughed. "That's so awesome. It'll probably be easy for you to write, too."

I shrugged, smiled, and went back to my pasta salad. Then I saw, from the corners of my eyes, my friends at the other table, mostly the boys, shaking with laughter.

I kept a sigh in check and forked some pasta.

"I'm writing about *Star Wars*," Curtis announced, "and making the argument that all nine movies are the best theatrical depictions of the hero's journey."

Yes. Of course.

"You're such a nerd," Isabel teased her boyfriend while humor lit up her dark eyes.

"And you love it," Curtis threw back before taking a huge bite of his sandwich.

She giggled, and Henry angled his heard toward me and rolled his eyes. He then fully faced me, giving his friends his back.

He lowered his head toward mine. "Seriously, Lex. What's going on? Between being so distracted today and how you said goodbye last night..." He nudged me. "You know you can talk to me, right?"

Guilt pummeled me at his concern and kind words; the actions of a boyfriend who cared about his girlfriend. What was wrong with me? Outside of his weirdness when it came to Noah and around my friends, Henry had been nothing but *this* boy sitting beside me.

I gave him a soft smile. "I know that." A good, devoted girl-friend would have mentioned the nasty state of her parents' marriage by now. But I didn't see the purpose of letting him into that depressing drama. And none of that was his problem. I could, however, be honest with him about something else. "I've just missed sitting with my friends this week," I murmured, since I didn't want to risk hurting Curtis, Isabel, or Tyler's feelings.

Henry frowned. "But *you're* the one who's been saying we should sit here."

I returned his frown. "Because I know how you feel about my friends." *Namely Noah.*

He released an exasperated sigh. "I never said I didn't like —" He stopped, took a quick breath, then said, "We've talked about this way too much already. So I suggest, to keep things peaceful and fair, we sit with them one day and mine the next. Take turns, you know?"

I clenched my teeth at his snarky tone and nodded once.

"Hey!" Isabel chirped. "What are you two planning for your *first* Valentine's Day?"

Henry faced forward and picked up his soda. "Not sure. We haven't talked about it."

Yes. I guess Valentine's Day was next week.

The school used to have a dance, but the activities committee cut it out of the schedule after our sophomore year. Between planning and decorating for the fall dance, Snowflake Formal, and prom, the students and the advisor had felt the Valentine's Day dance made for "almost back-to-back dances."

Henry eyed me and tried on a grin. "Maybe we can talk about it this weekend?"

I forced my mouth into a not-so bright smile. "Sure."

He went back to his lunch, and my eyes went right. To smiles, laughter, chemistry, connections. It all equaled love. And not just the kind of love associated with Valentine's Day, a so-called holiday I hadn't celebrated in two years and really couldn't get excited about now.

Alexis Evelyn Pfeiffer, good girls are grateful for everything they have.

But what if I was getting sick and tired of being a *good* girl? And it could be why a different Alexis Evelyn Pfeiffer came out when Noah Luis Sanchez was around.

* * *

Natalie flung her backpack on the table with a *thud* and dropped into a chair beside me.

Mrs. Ferguson shot her—us—a dark look, and I turned and stared at my friend.

She rolled her eyes, then leaned toward me. "I wasn't that

loud," she whispered, since it was study hall. "And it just so happens I'm pissed at *you*."

I frowned and angled my head back.

"First, you haven't sat with us at lunch all week." Her expression softened. "And I've missed you."

My shoulders fell from the weight of guilt and frustration and sadness.

"I also can't believe you never told me about helping Noah with his dancing."

My eyes widened. I hadn't told anyone about that but Henry, Heather, and Nicolas, because I didn't think he would have wanted *everyone* to know about the tap dancing help. So that made me ask, "How'd you find out about that?"

Irritation flashed through her eyes. "So you didn't tell me on purpose. Why? And Noah, Nicolas, and Heather were talking about it at lunch. Because you're starting *this* weekend?"

I nodded and shrugged. "Yeah, but it's not a big deal." *And it wouldn't be.* She remained silent, and I asked, "How did Noah seem about the whole thing?" If I found out he was acting like a big baby about it behind my back, I *wouldn't* help him. Just like I'd told him yesterday.

"He seemed fine." She paused, then added, "Maybe a little embarrassed that he needs the extra practice." She smiled. "It's kind've hard picturing him tap dancing. He has this dark, brooding thing going on. So the opposite of Shane and Liam."

Yes. But she'd left out the words Totally. Hot—*no*.

"It must be a musician thing." She shook her head.

"I guess." I concentrated on my notes for my research paper. "I've never really thought about it." I somehow managed not to cringe at that fat lie rolling right out of my mouth.

"Is that why you and Henry haven't sat with us all week? Lexi, be honest."

I lifted my head and gave her a confused smile. "What are you talking about?"

Her eyes narrowed into slits, which meant she didn't believe my confusion.

"Don't do that." She crossed her arms. "Just talk to me."

I sat back and angled myself toward her. "Nat, Henry's fine with everything." *And he was. For the most part.*

"I don't believe you."

I sighed. She was being a good friend, but I had no interest in talking about Henry or Noah, especially since that meant lying to her. She didn't need to know the truth.

"You and Henry stopped sitting with us this week," she softly continued. "When I asked Noah when you two set all that up, he said Monday after rehearsal."

I began twirling a lock of hair around my index finger.

She scooted her chair closer to mine, glanced at Mrs. Ferguson, focused on her computer, and fully faced me. "And you can't tell me you haven't *noticed* Noah."

Heat the temperature of a desert in July surrounded me. To the point my sweater felt like wearing a winter coat in a sun-baked desert. I suddenly wanted to fan my hot cheeks and neck.

"Between his hotness and dark, musician thing—" She lifted her shoulders. "If I were Henry, I'd be jealous."

Of course Natalie would say exactly how she saw things. But strength from deep within made me mentally dig in my heels. The Henry-Noah drama *would* go away. "Henry's fine. And what would Shane say if he heard you talking about Noah—his good friend—like that?"

She squinted at me, then released a quiet laugh. "Wow. Where'd that come from?"

I suppose my question had been a little on the sassy side. I still raised my chin, waiting for her to answer.

She unleashed her wicked smile. "He knows he has absolutely *nothing* to worry about."

Because she and Shane were Totally. In—oh, my goodness.

Her smile slowly transitioned into a frown. "What's really weird about you being with Henry and helping out Noah, is that I thought for sure you and *Noah* liked each other. While you were helping Heather and Nicolas?"

Our eyes connected, and I blinked twice.

"The way you two were watching each other and smiling before Snowflake Formal?" Her frown deepened. "I wasn't the only one who noticed it, either. But I guess we were wrong."

Maybe we'd been a little more obvious than I thought.

Still, that brief moment in time had passed. Right? So I forced my mouth into a bright smile. "I have no idea what you're talking about." I released my hair, leaned forward, and went back to my notes. "We're friends. I'm helping him out because he needs it. No big deal."

Nicolas and I would help Noah "master" tap dancing. He'd give me rock music lessons. We'd continue being friends. Henry really would be fine. I'd get to spend quality time in my favorite place, far from my house and parents. That thought alone made me genuinely smile.

Chapter Twelve

I walked to the center of the studio, faced the mirrors, and went into fourth position.

Dreamy piano music drifted, and on the loud side, from my nearby bluetooth speaker via my phone, and surrounded me.

I held the basic ballet position for a few seconds, then did a plié, followed by going up on my left tip-toes, bending my right leg in passé, and completing a triple pirouette.

All in one *perfect*, fluid motion. Which made me smile at my reflection.

Back to fourth position. Plié. Up on my left tip-toes. But this time I extended my right leg, toes pointed. Triple pirouette. *Perfect*. In fact, this was the best way to start a Saturday. Really any day of the week.

Now for some chaîné turns; one of my other favorite ballet movements.

First position. Spread legs. Arms out at shoulder height. Up on toes. And I completed several fast turns across the length of the studio, then stopped in perfect epaulé position.

"That was. So. Cool."

I yelped and spun toward the oh-so familiar voice.

Noah leaned against the wall while giving me his lopsided grin.

I tore my eyes from his mouth—grin—and said, "I didn't hear you come in."

"Apparently. And I'm a little early." He pointed at my speaker. "That's pretty loud. What are you listening to? Gershwin?" He sauntered into the studio.

With his tousled hair, black hoodie, basketball shorts, and Nikes he looked so *good*. Which wasn't fair. And the black clothing only added to his dark, mysterious, musician thing.

I headed toward him. "No. Just a piano piece I really like."

Silence, except for the music, filled the space between us.

He shoved his hands into the front pocket of his hoodie and kicked at nothing on the hardwood floor. "You're a ballet dancer, too." He paused, then added, "And *really* good." He cleared his throat. "You look like a ballerina dressed like that."

Him noticing my pink leotard, black ballet skirt, and pink tights suddenly made me feel way underdressed. I fought the urge to sprint toward the chair where I'd dropped *my* hoodie.

My steps wobbled as I came to a gradual halt when I reached him, standing by the metal chairs that lined the studio's left wall. "Yeah. And thanks," I murmured, now fighting to suppress the heat from his compliments. "I was just warming up."

He nodded. "How long have you been dancing?"

"Since I was six."

"And that's why you make it look so easy."

I shrugged. "Just like you make guitar playing look easy. How long have *you* been playing?" If he was going to ask personal questions, then I would, too.

He smiled. "I was the ripe old age of *twelve* when I picked up my first guitar."

I giggled. "Is that also when you discovered Totally. Badass. Rock music?"

"Yep." He pulled on a mock serious expression. "It was love at first touch and sound. Especially after my first guitar lesson."

Fighting a smile, I leaned toward him. "It was that way for me and my first dance class. Which happened to be ballet." Our eyes locked. "Ballet is my first love."

His eyes held mine as he said, "Sounds like you want to be a dancer. Like your aunt?"

His words made me think of my parents. I straightened and broke our gaze. "It'll never happen." I gave him my back, and headed for my speaker and phone.

"Why's that?"

His voice sounded close, which meant he'd followed me.

I picked up my phone and paused the music. A thick silence descended. I then plastered a bright smile on my face and turned toward him. To find him standing steps from me and wearing a deep frown. "Dancing's only a hobby. That's all it's ever been."

He crossed his arms. "Between that and your smile I can see through, I call bullshit."

I narrowed my eyes and crossed my arms. "You have no idea what you're talking about."And why did he actually think he knew anything about me, outside of school?

He groaned. "Lexi, I'm not deaf, dumb, and blind. Just now wasn't the first time I've seen you dance. Well, it's the first time I've seen you do ballet," he quietly admitted. "Your aunt's right. You're gifted. And the way you talk about dancing..." He shook his head. "Collecting baseball cards is a hobby. So don't reduce your dancing to something like that."

A darkness deep inside me snapped with such force. I said, "Fine! I would *love* to be a professional dancer like my aunt was. But it will never happen because of my parents. Okay?"

My bitter words hung between us for several long seconds as we stared at each other.

Once again, Noah Sanchez had brought me to the place of being brutally honest. How did he *do* that? At the same time, some weight lifted off of my shoulders. My heart. My soul.

He sighed. "That sucks. Really. And I'm sorry." His deep frown returned. "For your parents and for being so pushy. I wasn't trying to be an asshole."

The studio's street door banged open and closed. Then Nicolas appeared.

"Sorry I'm late," he grumbled as he rushed toward us. "My sister is spending the day with her boyfriend and wouldn't get out of the bathroom."

Noah eyed him. "Sisters. I Totally. Get it."

Nicolas laughed and glanced at me—his smile slipped. "You okay?"

Yes, because I feel a bit lighter. No, because Noah had brought me to this point. But I guess I had to give him credit for the apology. I also believed he hadn't been *trying* to be a jerk.

I brought back my bright smile. "I'm great! And warmed up."

"Cool." Nicolas focused on Noah. "What about you?"

Noah gave him a blank stare. "I warmed up by tap dancing the entire way here. Even got some encouraging honks."

I pressed my lips together to stop my smile and swallowed my laughter.

It also wasn't fair he could say such super cute things after being so serious.

"I would *pay* to see something like that," Nicolas tossed at him. "But you really should warm up first, Guitar Hero."

Noah glared at him. "Your girlfriend is going to *pay* for that nickname."

Nicolas grinned, and the two strolled toward the chairs.

They removed their phones from their pockets, set them down, then pulled off their sweatshirts—I ripped my eyes from *him* and went into my phone to bring up the *Crazy For You* music. It was time to forget reality and focus on Gershwin, and helping Noah become Pete, the tap dancing cowboy from Deadrock, Nevada.

* * *

I danced alongside Noah in time with the music. We then stopped, faced each other, he took me in his arms, and we began the waltzing part of "Slap That Bass." But he was still—

"Noah, stop looking at your feet," Nicolas practically barked.

Because *we'd* told him that about a hundred times in the last few hours.

Noah looked up, our eyes caught—and his steps faltered. To the point I crashed into him.

"*Shit*," he muttered, releasing me.

He groaned. "I'm trying not to look at my feet, but I can't help it. I'm not used to dancing like this," he practically barked at us.

Nicolas walked up. "We know that," he calmly said. "But you have to learn to trust yourself *and* your feet."

Noah's expression became a mask of darkness, and I cringed.

Nicolas and I had been taking turns as teacher and dancing beside him. But I had a feeling hearing that advice from Nicolas, who'd *quickly* picked up the steps, wasn't helping Noah's attitude. Or ego.

I smiled at him. "You're doing much better."

He turned his dark expression on me.

My smile vanished. "Don't you dare look at me like that, because I know what you're thinking. I was completely serious. But Nicolas is right." I placed my hands on my hips. "You have to start trusting yourself or you'll *never* become dancing Pete."

Nicolas stared at me with wide eyes. Noah, on the other hand, peered at me.

"Who are you right now?" he asked, and with a fair amount of confusion.

I crossed my arms and lifted my chin. "I'm your teacher," I enunciated. "And I'm—we're—trying to help you. So you need to lose your nasty look and bad attitude by next Saturday."

He looked away, and it was in that moment I registered the music was still playing.

My arms fell to my sides before I turned and marched to my speaker and phone. Seconds later the studio became shrouded in silence. That lasted until Noah released a heavy sigh.

"Okay, Miss Pfeiffer." He faced me. "Done."

I gave him a curt nod. "Good."

Nicolas eyed us for several seconds before taking a sideways step toward the chairs. "So, I'm gonna go." Another step closer to the chairs. "I'm meeting up with Heather at her house, but I have to go home first." He glanced at Noah. "You'll get there. I swear." He focused on me and grinned. "You can be a little scary, *Miss Pfeiffer*."

"Only when I have to be."

Noah dropped his gaze to the floor.

Nicolas reached the chairs, and grabbed his phone and sweatshirt. "See you guys Monday." Then he was gone, followed by the street door opening and closing.

Leaving Noah and me alone, once again.

As I watched him concentrate on the floor, as if waiting for an answer to his tap dancing problems, a long, exhausted breath left my lungs.

"I told you I'm not always the best student."

I straightened my shoulders and stomped toward him. Because I was so sick and tired of hearing him say that. I stood in front of him. "No. *I* call bullshit."

He swiftly lifted and angled his head back. "Did you just—?"

"Yes. I did. Why do you keep saying that about yourself?" I frowned. "You're working your butt off. No, you don't always have the best attitude. But you're *such* a hard worker."

His expression eased into something I couldn't interpret. Surprise? Acceptance? Gratitude? Affection—*no*.

"Noah," I said in a kinder voice while pushing that thought aside, "you're being way too hard on yourself. I mean, you already know most of your lines, speaking and singing. You know where you're supposed to be on stage. And your dancing *has* gotten so much better."

A shy smile teased the corner of his mouth. "You've noticed all that? Really?"

Between his shy smile and almost boyishly asked questions, the fight left me as my shoulders drooped. I reached up to grasp—that's when I remembered my hair was pulled up into a tight bun. My face warmed as if I were in a sauna.

"Thanks for noticing." He shoved his hands into his pockets. "I know I'm too hard on myself. But" —he shrugged— "I have to be. *None* of this comes easily to me."

I squinted at him. "What are you talking about? The tap dancing?"

He laughed, but without humor. "That, too. For some reason." His eyes wandered back to mine. Then his face flushed. "I'm talking about learning my lines, keeping the blocking straight in my head, even memorizing song lyrics. Sometimes," he added. "Depends on the song."

I stayed silent, not certain what he was trying to tell me.

"I have to work twice as hard because...I have dyslexia."

I froze, then blinked twice.

"It was so bad," he muttered, "I had to repeat third grade."

My mouth drifted open. But that would mean—

"I *should* be in your class. I'll also be eighteen next week."

Oh, my *goodness*. And the bitterness mingled with his words sliced my insides.

"But dyslexia is one of the reasons I got into theater. To challenge myself." He tried to smile. "And because I like the adrenaline rush of being on stage, in front of a packed house."

I closed my eyes.

What was he talking about? Because I was still on the fact he'd confessed incredibly personal things to me. Things so incredible, the Noah Luis Sanchez puzzle pieces began to fall into place. And maybe, just maybe, being given the diagnosis of dyslexia, on top of being held back in third grade, were the reasons behind his need for brutal honesty. Maybe even his wall?

I opened my eyes to find him cautiously watching me. I reached out to grasp his hand.

He groaned and stepped backward. "Don't *you* look at me like that."

I gave him my bright smile. "Like what?"

"And don't smile like that, either. I can see right through it."

I kept a growl in check and leaned forward. "Noah, what do you want from me?"

He also leaned forward. "No. Bullshit. Which you're getting really good at. And I told you because I want and need you to understand why I'm *always* so hard on myself."

"Okay." I stepped closer to him, paused to slow my racing thoughts, and said, "I hate that you had to go through that when you were little and feel you have to be hard on yourself. I also hate...that you're not in our class and can't graduate with all of us." Darkness flashed through his eyes, which hurt my heart, but I kept going. "I hate that you have to work so much harder than everyone else in the plays. Have to work so hard to be *perfect*, which I totally get—" I gasped at such a personal piece of info tumbling from my mouth. Without thinking. Again.

I mentally groaned and took two steps away from him.

How did we almost always end up like this after these *honest* moments? At the same time, we didn't seem to have the guts to talk about not pursuing an us—*no*.

"Thank you for telling me," I mumbled. "It does help." *And explains so much*. A thought popped into my mind, and I asked, "Who else have you told?"

He shook his head. "Just you. My—our—friends don't need to know that about me."

But he'd told me, because he needed and wanted me to understand *him* better.

I pressed my lips together as that thought sank in, then said, "I promise you can trust me."

"Lexi," he quietly began, "I wouldn't have told you if I didn't trust you."

I lifted my eyes from the floor and they connected with his. *Magnets*.

"My sister and her boyfriend are picking me up, and they're probably here. But I have something for you." He closed the gap between us and withdrew a folded piece of white paper from his left pocket. "Lesson Two."

We stayed focused on each other as I pulled the paper from his fingertips.

His eyes warmed and became the trying-to-read-my-soul stare.

My breathing slowed.

"Keith Richards."

I remained silent, and his mouth eased into the grin that made my tummy melt.

"The iconic guitarist for The Rolling Stones. A band you *have* heard of, right?"

"Yes. Of course." The band's name did sound familiar.

"It's a short list of my favorite songs." He held our gaze for a breath before stepping around me.

"Noah, wait just a minute." I faced him. "What about you and *your* homework?"

He swiped his sweatshirt and phone off the chair. "I'm doing my homework, Miss Pfeiffer." He smiled. "But Gershwin was no Eddie Van Halen or Keith Richards."

I rolled my eyes. "You're not even trying, Mr. Rock Music Snob."

"Yes, I am. Do you want to walk out together?"

I wanted to do so much more with him than walk—I really needed to stop this.

"I'm going to stay and dance." *Until my feet ached.* Afterward, I'd take real time to process every personal, surprising thing he'd told me.

He strolled toward the doorway, then stopped and looked across his shoulder at me. "Listen to 'Start Me Up' first. It has a cool ass guitar riff...and lyrics."

I held up the paper. "Will do." *Without hesitation.* Which he had to know.

He tilted his head right. "Lexi, I always have to remind myself that no one's perfect."

So he had caught my slip.

"But you're pretty close." And he disappeared from view.

I sighed at his latest compliment. That's all I could do, since a *perfect* girl didn't pine for a pretty amazing, inspiring boy when she already had a boyfriend.

Chapter Thirteen

y eyes widened at the fact "approximately fourteen to forty-three million children and adults have dyslexia." I already knew it was a learning disability that affected reading, writing, and spelling. But, *wow*.

I continued scrolling through the site dedicated to learning disabilities on my laptop. I should have been researching my topic for my English research report. But Noah confessing such a personal challenge, on top of how deeply it had and currently affected him, had made me want to know more. Made me want to understand him even more.

I stopped when my eyes caught another mind-blowing, heartbreaking fact about dyslexia: "If untreated, kids were more likely to drop out of school, be unemployed or underemployed, or become incarcerated."

Noah didn't fall into these categories, since his dyslexia had been caught so early and obviously been treated all this time. He also went above and beyond to make sure none of it conquered him, and I smiled softly when I recalled what he'd said.

Dyslexia is one of the reasons I got into theater. To challenge myself.

Totally. Admirable.

Still, thinking of how much harder he had to work to memorize his lines and keep *everything* play-related straight in his head tugged my heart and soul.

My mouth formed a straight line.

It wasn't fair.

I then pictured him as an adorable little boy, struggling as a third grader to keep up with his classmates, yet falling short and it not being his fault. Followed by receiving the news he wouldn't be able to move to fourth grade with his friends. Based on what I'd read about the impact of dyslexia on kids, he probably hadn't fully understood what was happening and felt like *he'd* done something wrong. May have even felt "dumb." More parts of his wall?

I cringed.

No wonder he occasionally went to such a dark place and was so incredibly hard on himself. And all of this explained why he seemed more than a little bitter about being a junior, having to watch most of his friends graduate in a handful of months.

My tummy twisted when I recalled the darkness that flashed across his face when I'd told him I hated he wouldn't be graduating with us. Probably hadn't been the best thing to say.

I sighed. Then it occurred to me I'd only researched the "dark" part of dyslexia. So I went to the search bar and typed in *the strengths of dyslexia.*

A list immediately popped up, and I zeroed in on two words—highly creative.

I went to the list's actual site, and scanned "Seeing the bigger picture," which seemed to explain his big-time observant side, "Picture thinkers," "Sharper peripheral vision," then

"Highly creative." And I smiled again when I read many actors have dyslexia. The site even listed a few recognizable names. Apparently, the actor side of Noah wasn't at all alone. Even Picasso was thought to have dyslexia. Actors, artists...and Noah was a musician. A different type of artist, and gifted, too. The fact he wrote music had to be another way he challenged himself while expressing his creative side.

More Noah puzzle pieces snapped right into place. At the same time, knowing only this much about him made me want to know every *other* part of him, mysterious or not. That thought made my eyes drift to the piece of paper sitting beside my computer. Also known as Lesson Two, Keith Richards and The Rolling Stones.

Grinning, I reached for the paper. But then someone knocked on my door and it opened.

"*Hi, Mom,*" Coda squawked.

He'd picked that up on his own. She, per her usual, frowned at him. She also appeared fresh from the gym, between her exercise leggings and bra, a loose, white tank top, and tight ponytail with sweaty tendrils around her—also per the usual—unhappy face. Even spending time at the gym to keep her figure in *perfect* shape didn't bring her joy, despite the endorphins.

She looked at me. "Have you been keeping up with cleaning his cage?" She sniffed twice. "It's smelling a little dingy in here."

I sat back in my desk chair. "Every Sunday morning." *Like clockwork. And perfect.*

"Then I recommend opening your window. And air freshener."

I stayed focused on my computer as I mumbled, "Okay." But it wasn't as if Coda was a kitten or puppy, constantly having bathroom accidents in here.

"Where were you today? You were gone for quite a while."

How nice of you to notice.

I froze at the snarky thought that had come out of nowhere. Or maybe it had come from the personal, dark place I kept to myself. Except when around Noah and his constant push for honesty. Which really wasn't a bad thing when I remembered how much lighter I always felt after releasing my true thoughts and feelings.

I faced Mom. "I was at the studio with a couple friends from school." I hesitated, then added, "Noah, one of my friends, is in the musical and is struggling with the tap dancing."

"Noah's so stupid."

Mom's eyes flitted to Coda and back to me.

I tried to smile as I held on to a sigh. I guess I would have to work much harder at training him to stop saying that, especially since that word in *no way* described Noah.

"Another friend of ours and I will be helping him out Saturday mornings until he gets better with the moves."

She frowned. "Now you're giving dance lessons on top of helping with that musical?"

I straightened. "Mom, it's not a big a deal. Just a few hours on Saturdays."

"And school comes first, Alexis."

"I know that!" I snapped. Followed by pressing my lips together, since I'd never spoken to my mom that way.

Her mouth hardened. "Alexis Evelyn Pfeiffer, good girls don't talk like that."

I gritted my teeth and went back to staring at my computer.

"You have more than enough going on right now," she evenly continued. "You have school, friends, a boyfriend, and that musical. It's also your final semester. Giving some friend of yours Saturday dance lessons was *not* something you should have taken on." She sighed. "Your dad isn't going to be happy when he hears about this."

But like you, nothing *makes him happy.* So why should I even care? And unlike my last snarky thought, I let those sit in the center of my brain, and grow in size and strength.

"He needed my help."

"Just like Daphne needed your help with the musical."

A tense silence settled between us, and I slid my eyes to Lesson Two. I could almost hear the piece of paper calling my name. And I wanted nothing more than for her to leave me alone. Like she *and* my dad did most of the time.

"Now that you've taken something else on," she said, irritation dripping from her voice, "homework *will* come first Friday nights and Saturday afternoons after you come home."

I glared at her from the corners of my eyes.

"If that means giving up your social life, then fine. UC Berkeley is too important."

Too important to you and Dad.

She pointed at my computer. "I know you have a huge, important research paper to work on for Mr. Washburn's class."

Yes. And she must have found that out by stalking his class web page, which most of the teachers at P.A. had, probably because of parents like mine.

"Do you have plans with Henry tonight?"

I shook my head. "No." Thankfully, he'd made plans to go bowling with Tyler. And what kind of girlfriend did that make me when I felt relieved I didn't have to see my boyfriend?

I then remembered something Natalie had said to me about Henry a couple weeks ago in study hall, when she'd caught me working on my picture of Noah.

He's way more into you than you're into him.

"Good. Get to work on that paper. I'm meeting up with

Daphne for dinner after her last class. I went shopping before going to the gym, so there's food."

I absently nodded.

Henry deserved better than a girl like me.

"I have no idea when your dad will be home," she added. With an edge to her voice.

My parents, who drove me crazy, deserved better than what they had, too. Didn't everyone on this planet deserve better than...*settling*? Even if they couldn't have what—or who—they really wanted? Was being alone better?

Mom turned and closed the door behind her.

My dyslexia research still filled my computer's screen, and I closed the site.

I went into my backpack to pull out my English folder, filled with everything I'd need to work on my paper. But my sketchbook caught my attention.

I hadn't worked on *his* picture since Natalie caught me that day in study hall. I'd put it aside, because *good* girlfriends didn't draw pictures of other boys in her spare time.

Before I realized it, I held my sketchbook. I skipped the pages where I'd drawn ballerinas on pointe, dressed in beautiful, elaborate ballet costumes. Suddenly, my eyes were locked on his. Dark and mysterious. Though I needed to change mysterious to something like vulnerable. The way he'd been watching me when I opened my eyes, after he'd shared such personal information. Then I must have given him a look he'd interpreted as sympathy.

I pushed my laptop aside to make room on the desk for my sketchbook. I then picked up the piece of paper with my lesson, slowly unfolded it, and found—he'd typed the list of eight songs instead of writing them out. Perfectly typed, too. Which tugged my heart to the point I had to take a quick breath. But the first song was "Start Me Up." Between listing it first and telling me to listen to it, I wasted no time Googling the song. Now I just needed my earbuds and a pencil to continue my other creative outlet. It's not like my parents would be around to check on me. Henry was off...being Henry. And I had plenty of time to work on my stupid English paper.

* * *

I spotted Henry waiting for me when I reached the intersection that was only steps from Noah's building. The chorus of "(I Can't Get No) Satisfaction" blared through my earbuds as Henry stood and waved.

I shoved aside the weirdness of that timing, returned his wave, and headed toward him. I also squelched the guilt from that thought. And the fact I'd been *hoping* to run into another boy, so I could tell him how Lesson Two had gone. Was still going, actually. Because after listening to his favorite Rolling Stones' songs, and downloading a few of them, including "Start Me Up," I'd gone in search of more songs by the band. A couple of the songs he'd listed I'd recognized, like the one I had blasted right now. But the rest had been new to me and I'd wanted more.

He'd been right about this kind of rock music getting inside of you and Never. Leaving. A healthy drug. Addiction. I also wanted my Lesson Three *before* Saturday.

Henry pulled me into his arms the second I reached him and lowered his head, but I leaned back. He frowned, and I pointed at my earbuds. That I pulled out while casually stepping away from him. I then pulled my phone from my sweater pocket and paused the song that could have been my personal anthem.

He tried on a smile, though his eyes were filled with wariness. At me pulling away from him. A first, too. Which meant many things I didn't feel capable of dealing with at this moment.

"What are you listening to? You were walking kind've funny."

I gave him a bright smile. "'(I Can't Get No) Satisfaction'. The Rolling Stones?"

He peered at me. "I know the song. And band." He laughed. "I didn't know you listened to their music. I thought Natalie had you hooked on alternative rock."

I shrugged. "I like all kinds of music." I paused, then added, "I've really gotten into Van Halen, too. And though Eddie Van Halen's guitar playing was pretty badass, I think I like Keith Richards's playing better. There's an...edge to it. And his riffs that I *love*."

Henry angled his head back and squinted. "Where'd all that come from?"

Heat rushed through me and stopped at my face.

Yes. All that had been meant for another boy. But I guess I'd been so excited and pumped from all the music—Noah's lessons—I hadn't been able to contain my feelings.

I released a quick laugh. "Just discovering new music." *And loving every second of it.*

"More like discovering old music my *dad* likes." He shook his head. "But that's cool."

I stared at him. "What's wrong with liking old music your *dad* likes? There's worse music to like." I could think of a couple music genres I couldn't stand.

He sighed. "I just said it was cool. Don't get defensive. I like some of that music, too." He grasped my hands and pulled me toward him. "We need to talk about something way more important." He placed a quick kiss on my forehead, then turned us toward the stairs.

We followed a small group of kids into school. They

headed left, since they were freshmen or sophomores, and we went up the stairs.

"What do you want to do for Valentine's Day?" he asked.

I missed a step at his question, and Henry caught my right arm before I fell forward.

"Thanks," I grumbled as we continued up the stairs.

I'd completely spaced Valentine's Day was this week.

We cleared the steps and, like usual, went straight to pause and say goodbye. Our lockers were on opposite sides of the building.

He shot me a playful smile. "I already bought your present. Now you just have to tell me what you want to do and I'll do my best to make it happen."

Of course he'd already bought my present. Because that's what a *devoted* boyfriend did for his girlfriend for Valentine's Day.

"I'm thinking we'll have to go out and celebrate Friday night, though," he continued, "since Valentine's Day is Thursday and you have rehearsal. *And* it's a school night."

Yes. I could find time to buy him a present between now and Thursday. Right? And we would most definitely have to go out Friday—oh, my goodness. Friday nights were no longer mine, because I'd chosen to "take on" helping Noah with his tap dancing. I certainly couldn't tell Henry my mom's new rule, either. But I could work my butt off this week on my schoolwork and actually start my stupid English paper. I could also lie to my parents if absolutely necessary.

Alexis Evelyn Pfeiffer, good *girls don't*—did I care what *good* girls did or didn't do?

"Lex? Where'd you go?"

I blinked until Henry's concerned expression came into focus and I plastered a smile on my face. "Friday night sounds great."

He returned my smile. "Cool. You'll let me know what you want to do?"

"Sure!" I replied, probably a tad too enthusiastically.

He leaned toward me. "I'll still give you your present on Valentine's Day." He straightened. "And I know we're sitting with your friends today, so I'll see you then."

I turned right, and nearly dragged myself down the hallway and around students.

Maybe Aunt Daphne could take me...where? I had no idea what Henry would like or want for Valentine's Day. Maybe I'd find something at a comic book store? But what? I knew nothing about that kind of stuff, despite having been around him and his friends the last couple months. And I suddenly felt like the Penny character from *The Big Bang Theory*, with the exception of the fact she'd fallen for Leonard.

Something I now needed to except would never happen with Henry.

I wanted what all my friends had, but *settling* wasn't the answer. It's what my parents were doing, and they were miserable. I'd really settled for Cam, which had gotten me nowhere. I'd settled for Henry, *mostly* because I'd been tired of being alone.

I refused to think about Noah right now.

Henry. I couldn't keep stringing him along, but with Valentine's Day happening this week, I couldn't be totally heartless and break up with him. And it absolutely wouldn't be any better breaking up with him afterward.

I mentally moaned as I reached my locker, and now understood the phrase of being "caught between a rock and a hard place."

Chapter Fourteen

February 14th. Valentine's Day. A day for people—couples—to celebrate their love.

I frowned at the plastic bag on my lap that contained my gift for Henry.

"Sweetie," my aunt said from the driver's seat, "I'm sure Henry will love the shirt."

I gave her a tight smile.

He probably would love my gift. But I would feel like a total phony giving him the shirt in a few days. Valentine's Day. A silly, commercial "holiday." This time last year I'd been alone, and by choice after my Cam stupidity. As my friends and their boyfriends were making plans and buying gifts, I'd decided to research St. Valentine on my own time. One of the only reasons I found as to why he'd ended up associated with love and happy couples was the legend he'd secretly married Christian couples. Pretty cool and definitely brave. Still, he'd ultimately died for his bravery and love for his *faith*.

Cam had simply been my first boyfriend; my disastrous first relationship. I didn't love Henry. My parents didn't love each other anymore. My aunt hadn't been super lucky in love, either. It's why she was single. Love had gotten St. Valentine killed.

My blissfully happy friends aside, was love even *worth* it?

Aunt Daphne pulled into the driveway and the car's headlights illuminated my dark house. "Lexi," she quietly said, "with things being so tough and tense around this place" — she gestured at my house— "I want you to know my guest room is yours anytime you need it."

Between the love woven into her words and my dismal thoughts, tears blurred my vision. But I swiftly blinked them away, faced her, and sent her an affectionate smile. "Thanks." I huffed. "But you know if I did that, my parents' heads would explode." *Namely Dad's.*

Her mouth hardened. "And I don't give a crap. Not anymore." She sighed. "I tried, for the millionth time, to talk to your mom Saturday night about her and your dad getting into marriage counseling." She shook her head. "Your mom made it clear that topic is officially closed."

I nodded, then released a sad laugh. "It's too late for that." *Too late for them.* I glanced at her. "Why do they stay together when it's clear to *everyone* they're so unhappy?"

She reached across the console and grasped my hand. "Because, for some people, it's just easier to stay together." She frowned. "The thought of uprooting a life together is paralyzing. And overwhelming." She squeezed my hand. "They also have you to consider."

When in any of their misery *had* they considered me?

But I said, "I'll be gone soon." And could it be they were waiting for me to leave for college? It wasn't a hard leap to make.

"So you keep holding on to that thought," she softly continued as she released my hand. "Keep my offer in mind if you need it." She shooed my house. "I'll deal with your parents."

My affectionate smile grew. "I love you, Aunt Daphne." Every inch of me meant it, too.

This was the kind of love and devotion that had gotten St. Valentine killed. So the better question seemed to be, was romantic love worth it?

She returned my smile. "I love you, too, Sweetie. I'll see you tomorrow for more Gershwin fun." She laughed. "I meant to tell you Noah looked so much better today. Even Carolyn—Mrs. Chaplin—made a comment to me about it."

Yes. He had. Though he was still looking at his feet too much.

"You and your friend, Nicolas, need to keep up the hard work with him. It's showing."

"We will." Thank goodness I had the musical. And helping Noah. And my dancing.

A few minutes later I walked into my room and turned on the light.

"Hi, Lexi."

Smiling, I dropped my backpack and Henry's gift on my bed. "Hi, Coda." I then went into the pocket of my backpack where I put my phone.

Henry had probably texted me by now. Stopping to pick up his gift after rehearsal had made me later than usual, and since my parents *still* weren't home from work, one or both of them may have texted—I halted when I saw I had two messages from *him*. Along with a message from Henry and my mom. But I focused on Noah's.

This was the first time he'd ever texted *just* me, since we'd exchanged numbers back in November while helping Heather and Nicolas. We hadn't needed to text each other recently about the Saturday rehearsals; we'd figured everything out in person.

With shaky fingers, I chose his message.

Hey. You and your aunt left so fast after rehearsal, I didn't get a chance to check in with you. I felt like a tap dancing cowboy! What'd you think?

I grinned and read his second message.

Everything okay? You seemed a little distracted. At lunch and rehearsal.

My eyes widened at him noticing. Then again, Henry and I had kept to ourselves while sitting with all of them today. I couldn't even remember what they'd been talking and joking and laughing about. I'd been so focused on Henry and Valentine's Day and my complete phoniness.

Once again, I frowned at the plastic bag that contained a present I'd bought out of obligation. Because he'd already bought my gift. I was also supposed to be thinking of how I wanted to *celebrate* with him Friday night. But I really needed to be figuring out how to break up with him, without hurting his feelings.

Stuck between a rock and a hard place. With a useless Valentine's Day gift.

What had I been thinking? Exchange gifts, then break up with him and *sprint* in the opposite direction?

"Coda, what am I going to do?" I groaned. "I'm so *stupid.*"

"*Noah's so stupid.*"

I lifted my head and glared at Coda, staring at me. "You're not helping." On top of everything else going on in my life, I had to train him to stop saying that.

"*I'm Coda.*"

I sighed and quickly replied to Henry's normal, how'd-rehearsal-go message.

Mom had texted, *Meeting running late with clients. Eat dinner, then do your homework.*

I narrowed my eyes at her abrupt words before sitting on my bed's edge. I went back into the thread Noah had started and paused to think about what to write back.

I'd actually wanted to talk to him, too. About Lesson Two and getting Lesson Three from him. And those thoughts brought the grin back to my mouth.

You're definitely getting there, Pete the Cowboy. Still looking at your feet too much. And I'm fine! Just a long day. You should also know I'm beyond ready for Lesson 3.

I re-read the message that contained one little white lie, since I was the earth's distance away from the sun when it came to feeling fine. I still hit send and tossed my phone beside me.

My grin slipped when I pictured him in his room, probably being a good P.A. student and doing his homework. Working doubly hard, because that's what he had to do.

My eyes landed on my bulging backpack full of *yuck*. With the exception of my sketchbook. Listening to badass rock music and doing art, or homework? Also known as the yuck. Especially Trig extra credit and that dumb English paper I'd barely started writing. The Trig work was due tomorrow, but the paper wasn't due for another few weeks. Though I did feel a strong connection to my topic of professional dancers deserving to be paid as much as professional athletes, another subject area had caught my interest.

Maybe Mr. Washburn would let me change my research topic?

My phone began to incessantly vibrate, and I sighed. It had to be Henry calling. Or one of my parents—no, it was *him*.

I picked up my phone and stared at the screen as it continued to vibrate.

Now he was *calling* me?

I cautiously answered, "Hey."

"Okay, Miss Pfeiffer," Noah said with a hint of mischief. "Prove it."

I frowned. "Prove what?"

He groaned. "That you're 'beyond ready for Lesson Three'."

"Oh." I released a quick laugh. "Right." I pushed all thoughts of homework and Henry and Valentine's Day and my parents into the back of my mind. Then I launched into *everything* I'd accidentally said to Henry that morning about Keith Richards and The Rolling Stones, including preferring Keith's playing to Eddie's. "I searched for *more* of their songs," I breathlessly continued, "and discovered 'Happy' and 'Shattered,' which I really, really love. I loved all the songs on your list, too, but I just needed *more*. Does that make sense?"

Of course it made sense to him, but silence fell.

I flinched, since I probably had sounded like someone in the middle of a high.

"Whoa," he finally said. "Everything you said was Fucking. Awesome."

I smiled. "Even the part about liking Keith better than Eddie?"

He laughed. "Yeah. Because I get it. Richards is a master. A genius, really." He paused, then added, "And now *you* get it. I should've given you a longer list." He laughed again. "But it sounds like you found the songs I didn't include."

I grabbed a pillow and hugged it to me. "They have *way* too many badass songs to list."

"Agreed," he slowly said. "I'm sorry, am I talking to Alexis Evelyn Pfeiffer?"

Yes. But, no, I didn't sound like myself. Because I was talking to *him*. I still rolled my eyes. "I think I've proven I'm ready for Lesson Three, Mr. Sanchez."

"You're right, Miss Pfeiffer."

"And when will I get to see and hear *you* play?"

He again fell silent, and I gasped.

That question had tumbled out of my mouth. From the direction of deep within my soul.

"You've seen and heard me play."

I frowned. "Covering a Christmas song does *not* count." And after two rock music lessons inspired by his love and passion for guitar playing? He couldn't be serious.

"My concert schedule is a bit up in the air right now, because of school and *Crazy For You* rehearsals."

Now I groaned. "Noah, I'm being serious."

"*Noah's so stupid.*"

I froze, then blinked twice.

"Are you with someone?" Noah asked.

It sounded like he hadn't understood what Coda said. Totally a good thing, too.

"No." To my troublemaking bird, I called out, "Coda, be quiet!"

He shook himself and his feathers went *poof.*

"Then who's Coda?" Noah persisted.

"He's my African grey parrot." *Who had developed a* big *mouth.* Apparently, I also needed to stop saying Noah's name in front of him.

"That's so cool," he replied, and I heard the smile in his voice. "He sounds like a person. What have you taught him to say?"

Nice try, Noah Luis Sanchez.

"Many things. But we were talking about something else?"

He sighed. "Lexi, I'm flattered you want to hear my *real* playing. Really. But I'm not sure that would be a good idea. Okay?"

I swallowed a snarl. "No. I thought we were friends." And if he wanted and needed honesty, I would not hesitate to give him that. "You've played for your other friends, right?"

Silence, followed by, "A couple times. Yeah. But just acoustic guitar. They were here at my place for different reasons and asked if I would—"

"So, invite me over to study or help you run lines or...listen to some badass rock music. Like you would with your *other* friends. Then play your guitar for me." Maybe I had ulterior motives, but I did consider him a friend. Especially now.

"I've never invited Heather and Maddie over to listen to some badass rock music."

I freed my newest snarl and gripped my pillow. "You're. Infuriating. Will you give me Lesson Three? I have to go and do my homework." Because now I had no interest in working on my sketch of *him*.

"Lexi, there's no way Henry would be okay with me inviting *just his girlfriend* over to my place to study or help me run lines or listen to some badass rock music."

Yes. Henry. My *boyfriend* who I wanted to break up with.

"I don't know any guy who'd be okay with that," he muttered.

Fine. I guess I could grudgingly give him that point. But maybe, just maybe, he'd let me further into his life if I wasn't with Henry? And oh, my goodness. What kind of person did that make me?

"But I promise someday you'll hear my *real* playing," he quietly continued. "Maybe it can be my graduation present to you."

Something about the defeat and sadness in his voice caused my irritation with him to leave in a long, quiet breath. All I could think to say was, "I won't forget you said that."

He huffed. "I know. Trust. Me."

I loosened my grip on the pillow. "So what's Lesson Three?"

"You'll see."

I straightened. "Are you serious? I wanted my lesson now."

"Well, Alexis," he answered, and I could clearly picture his devil-worthy grin, "in the spirit of The Rolling Stones...'*You Can't Always Get What You Want*'," he sang. Perfectly, too. As if the music had been playing with his singing.

I wanted to growl, but a giggle escaped.

How did he go from so serious to seriously cute in a matter of seconds? It wasn't fair.

"Now I have to go and listen to that song," I threw at him. *Among so many others, including "(I Can't Get No) Satisfaction."*

"Me, too," he admitted. "Happy listening. And home...working?"

We shared a quick laugh and hung up.

My eyes again fell to my backpack.

He'd irritated me there for a bit, but had somehow managed to bring the conversation back to the lighter side. And remind me he could be incredibly adorable when he wanted to be.

So, listening to badass rock music and doing art, or homework?

I tugged my backpack toward me and the first thing I pulled out was my earbuds.

Chapter Fifteen

atalie appeared at my locker, and I gave her a bright smile.

She pointed at the gift bag I'd hung on the hook. "Your Valentine's Day present for Henry?"

I nodded and kept a sigh in check.

Today was February 14th. Valentine's Day. And all I wanted to do was walk out of this building, go back home, and bury myself under the covers on my bed with my phone, rock music, and earbuds. Especially since this school seemed to be bursting with the excitement of this silly "holiday." Happy, crazy-in-love couples up and down the hallway. Holding hands. Giggling together. I'd even seen some, after making sure there wasn't a teacher or other adult in sight, sneak quick kisses.

I frowned at Henry's gift.

"Where is he?" she asked. "I thought for sure he'd be right here, plastered to your side."

I shoved a notebook into my backpack. "His mom is running late. I probably won't see him until lunch. We're eating in the library today." *Because he wanted to be "alone" with me.*

She giggled. "Shane and I are going up to the rooftop for lunch, since the weather's not awful." She leaned against the locker next to mine. "I can't believe it's already Valentine's Day." Her smile slipped. "This year is *flying* by."

"Yeah," I murmured as I zipped up my bag. But I didn't want to think about what she was *really* saying. I just needed to get through today, then...what?

Inevitable heartbreak.

I lowered my head. How had I let things with Henry get this far? All the way to Valentine's Day? That had to make me an agent of Satan. Especially since I wanted another boy.

The memory of Noah singing *"You Can't Always Get What You Want"* filled my head.

Natalie snapped her fingers in my face, and I blinked twice.

"Lexi, where are you right now? Did you hear my question?"

I closed my locker door and faced her. While wearing my go-to, I'm-perfectly-fine smile; the same smile Noah saw through. "Right here. What's up?"

She peered at me for a few seconds, then said, "What do you and Henry have planned for Valentine's Day? Since you can't go out tonight?"

"Nothing. Why?"

She angled her head back. "No plans for your first Valentine's Day together?"

I shook my head.

Her expression softened. "What's going on? You've been a little...distant."

I shrugged. "It's been a long week. That's all." Even as I said those words, a huge part of me wanted to pull her into an empty classroom and spill everything. From my parents to

Henry *and* to Noah. But now wasn't the time for that conversation. So I kept my phony smile in place.

"I don't believe you."

Of course she didn't. I still remained silent.

She released a loud, frustrated sigh. "Because we're at school, I'm going to let this go. *For now*," she emphasized. "And the reason I'm asking about your plans with Henry is that Noah's birthday is today and all of us are planning—"

"Wait, his birthday is *today*?" I nearly shrieked.

"Yes," Natalie slowly replied, watching me closely.

I crossed my arms. "I can't believe he didn't tell me." Though he had mentioned last Saturday he'd be turning eighteen this week. Right after he'd told me other personal things.

"Lexi, Noah's not exactly an open book."

Yes. A true statement. But I now had a better understanding of why he was that way.

"*Anyway*," she continued, "we decided to throw him a surprise party tomorrow night. My parents' place." She unleashed her wicked smile. "They'll be out of town this weekend. Unexpected business trip." She lifted her shoulders. "I know all of this is a little last minute. It was the boys against the girls on doing this for him. Because Noah's...well...*Noah*." She laughed. "But the girls won. My parents going out of town only helped our case, too." She straightened. "Since you and Henry still don't have Valentine's Day plans, you *have* to come to the party."

I looked at the floor.

As much as I would absolutely love to go to his surprise party, and hang out with my friends I adored, it would never happen—I froze. Friday nights weren't mine anymore. My mom had said they were now for schoolwork. Something I had completely forgotten about, being lost in other things this week. Like the musical rehearsals. And the yuck that surrounded me at home. And how to break up with Henry without crushing him into a million pieces.

And way too much badass rock music.

"So talk to Henry about it at lunch and let me know *immediately*."

I absently nodded.

As she started to leave, my phone buzzed in my sweater pocket. It had to be Henry, letting me know he was here and maybe wanting to meet up before—no, it was *him*.

My mouth eased into a huge, genuine smile.

"Who texted you?" Natalie asked. "Because I can't remember the last time I saw you *really* smile."

I glanced at her. I guess my everything-is-perfectly-fine smile didn't fool her, either.

"And don't you dare say it's Henry."

I shook my head. "My aunt." Oh, my *goodness*.

Natalie gave me a soft smile. "Let's hang out this weekend. Sunday? Just you and me." She paused, then added, "Because I also can't remember the last time we *really* talked."

I returned her smile as her love and friendship hugged my insides. "Yes. Absolutely."

She started to leave again, but stopped and flashed her Natalie smile. "Say hi to your *aunt* for me."

Between the smile she'd caught, knowing I wasn't truly into Henry, and catching me drawing a boy she knew *wasn't* my celebrity crush, her comment didn't surprise me.

I needed to tell her everything on Sunday. Before all of it caused me to explode. But right now, I needed—wanted—to read his message. Especially since we'd barely seen or talked to each other since our unexpected phone chat on Monday night.

Lesson 3. Jimmy Page from Led Zeppelin. Listen to "Heart-breaker" and "Dazed and Confused." His guitar playing will blow your mind.

I smiled and replied, *Took you long enough. But thanks. I can't wait.* I hit send, then decided to say, *By the way, Happy Birthday.*

Now I wanted to run home, as fast as my short legs could go, and focus on Lesson Three. Like the other bands he'd led me to, Led Zeppelin sounded familiar. But that was it. I had a feeling I'd love this newest lesson, too. I'd *loved* all his previous lessons. He definitely knew his rock music and badass guitarists. Which made me want to hear his *real* playing even more.

Thanks. But who told you? One of our friends may not live to see tomorrow.

I burst into laughter and typed, *In that case, I'll never tell.*

The 8:00 bell exploded, and I jolted. We only had five more minutes to get to our first periods or we'd be considered tardy.

How did I lose track of life whenever Noah Luis Sanchez was involved?

Figures. But I'll still find out. See you later.

I closed out of text messaging, shoved my phone back into my sweater pocket, and sprinted down the hallway, in the direction of first period.

Today was February 14th. Valentine's Day. A day for celebrating love and romance. Or, in Noah's case, his eighteenth birthday. Or, in my case, facing inevitable heartbreak.

Despite the terrible timing, I knew what I needed to do at lunch, for myself and Henry.

I had no idea what I'd do about my feelings for Noah. But Henry deserved an actual good girl. A description that fit me, *Lexi Pfeiffer*, less and less every day.

* * *

My entire body trembled as I headed to the back of the library to meet Henry.

I tightly gripped the gift-bag's red, thin rope. Ridiculous, really, to still be giving him the present, considering how the next several minutes would be going. He probably wouldn't even want the gift, but I had nothing to lose by offering it to him. I could also return the shirt if he refused to accept it. After I told him everything I'd been rehearsing in my head all morning.

Breaking up with a boy on Valentine's Day had to classify me as the *lowest* of the low. Worse than pond scum. But would it have been any better breaking up with him yesterday or tomorrow, or the day after that? And I knew in my heart, mind, and soul this is what had to be done. My feelings for Noah aside, Henry and I never would have lasted. We actually never should have lasted *this* long.

Me, boys, and stupidity seemed to fit way too well together. So it was probably a good thing Noah was perfectly okay with us being friends. I also had distractions to help me through all of this. Noah *was* involved in those distractions, but nothing I wasn't used to at this point.

I emerged from the stacks into an open back area filled with tables and spotted Henry at one by the windows. Students—more like couples—sat at tables throughout the area, while whispering and smiling and—I sighed.

I tightened my grip on the bag I held and forced my wobbly legs toward him.

He looked up and sent me a huge, genuine, blinding smile.

I was officially an Agent. Of. Satan.

When I reached the table, he pulled out the chair next to him, clasped my free hand, and tugged me down beside him. He then leaned toward me, clearly wanting a quick kiss.

I turned my head slightly away and placed his gift on the table.

He frowned. "What's wrong?"

I managed to not give him my phony, blinding smile. "We're in the library?"

"So?" He shrugged. "I've seen kids sneaking kisses all morning. And I haven't seen you since after school yesterday."

That wasn't anything new.

But I said, "I'm not comfortable with stuff like that at school." *Not a total lie, either.* He'd also never, until today, tried to sneak a kiss while we were in the building.

His frown deepened. "Okay." He stared at me a few more seconds, then reached down and picked up a pink and white gift bag that was bigger than mine for him. "Happy Valentine's Day." He brought back his smile. "This gift had you and your cuteness written all over it."

Yes. That was me. The cute, little blonde, who'd probably still look twelve years old in ten years. Another description I didn't want. Just like *good girl.*

"Open it," he added. With the enthusiasm of a boyfriend excited to see the reaction to his first Valentine's Day gift for his girlfriend.

How was I going to do this? Get through the next several moments?

My hands visibly shook as I reached into the bag and withdrew—a good-sized, bright white teddy bear wearing a pink tiara, ballet tutu, and "pointe" shoes.

I stared at the bear, blinked twice, then lifted my gaze to Henry.

His smile doubled in size. "If you were a stuffed bear, I *know* that's how you'd look as a ballerina. Do you like her?"

I suppressed a Big. Fat. Sigh.

She *was* cute and super soft, and he had captured my love for ballet. But I'd never really been into stuffed animals. This also seemed like a gift more appropriate for the little girls in my aunt's Ballerina Bears dance class.

"This isn't working," I blurted out, followed by a gasp. Because that's not exactly how I'd planned to start the inevitable heartbreak.

His smile vanished. As if he'd taken an eraser to his mouth. "You don't like the bear? She's a ballerina. Just like—"

"It's not the bear," I interjected, followed by placing her back in the bag. "It's...us." I somehow stopped myself from releasing an enormous breath of relief. "*We're* not working."

His deep frown returned and he leaned back. "What are you talking about?" His eyes widened. "Wait a minute. Are you...breaking up with me? On *Valentine's Day?*"

And here we go.

I took a shaky breath and said, "Henry, I know my timing is awful. Maybe even cruel—"

"So that is what you're doing." His mouth hardened. "I knew something was going on with you. You've been snapping at me over dumb stuff. And distant. Almost cold."

I stared at him. Because most of what he said was true, all I could say was, "I'm sorry for all of that. But I've realized the last couple weeks that we have almost nothing in common. You also don't like my friends—"

"I never said that," he harshly whispered. "I just don't *get* them all the time. There's nothing wrong with that. I'm sure you don't get my friends all the time, either."

"No, I don't!" I whispered back. "But at least I *talked* to your friends. And you actually made it clear many times you don't like Noah. Though you never gave him a chance." Or any of my other friends, though he obviously saw things way differently than I did.

He narrowed his eyes. "This is really about him. Noah. Isn't it? Because you started to change after you agreed to help your aunt on that stupid musical. That he's in." He shook his head. "Then you agreed to help him on Saturdays. *Supposedly* with his dancing. And the way he looks at you?" He smirked.

"None of that ever felt right. But I let it go because I trusted *you*."

I straightened as anger flared within my stomach, reached my eyes, and blurred my vision. "The musical isn't stupid. You have no idea how hard everyone works on the shows. And I haven't done anything wrong but help Noah." *For the most part.* And the rock music lessons didn't count as doing anything wrong. "Nicolas was also there on Saturday. Remember?"

Henry pushed his chair away from the table. "Like I'd trust anything that guy would say. *All* of you are friends." He stood and punished me with a glare so dark I leaned backward.

He totally deserved his feelings, but *wow*. And I now understood the phrase, "everybody has a dark side."

He swiped the gift bag with the ballerina bear off my lap. "Before you said a word, I could tell you didn't like my present. But my...heart was in the right place."

I looked away as his words pressed my shoulders down. Then my stomach twisted into a knot so tight it physically hurt.

I'd never in my life treated anyone the way I'd treated Henry today or the last couple weeks. No, we weren't meant to be a couple. Still, what was *wrong* with me?

"You can return your gift for me." He turned, then stopped and said over his shoulder, "I really liked you, Lexi. I thought you liked me, too." He sighed. "I guess all this makes *me* stupid." His eyes caught mine. "It took me days to work up the courage to ask you to Snowflake Formal. And when you said yes, I couldn't believe it. I was so excited." He raised his chin. "But now I wish I could take it all back."

Tears hit my eyes as he stalked away and out of sight. My lower lip quivered while I rapidly blinked, but a couple tears still escaped.

I sniffed and wiped my cheeks.

This morning, all I'd wanted was to walk out of the building, go home, and bury myself in bed with my phone, rock music, and earbuds.

I slowly stood and picked up my former gift for Henry.

Between my knotted stomach and overall feeling of ickiness, I didn't feel an ounce of guilt about going to the office to have my aunt pick me up and take me home. I also didn't care what my parents would say about their *good girl* leaving school for the rest of the day.

Chapter Sixteen

My steps faltered the moment I saw Noah waiting outside the studio. But it was only 10:30. What was he doing here so early?

I continued heading toward him, while trying to stop my tummy flutters.

He casually glanced up from his phone and in my direction, then did a double take.

Our eyes locked, and he sent me his lopsided grin.

I released a quick breath and gave him a tentative smile. "Hi. You're really early."

He slipped his phone into his pocket. "Thought it'd be cool if we warmed up together. Is that okay?"

I stopped when I reached the studio's door, and Noah stepped to his right. "Sure." Though I'd really been looking forward to having the studio to myself for the next half hour. After the last day and a half, I'd so wanted and needed alone time with my dancing.

"You must be feeling better, since you didn't cancel our rehearsal."

I pulled the keys from the pocket of my hoodie. "I am.

Thanks." But not really. I'd managed to get away with "playing sick" since leaving school Thursday afternoon. My parents had relented, but with the *order* I was to do schoolwork. And I had done some work.

"We missed you at rehearsal Thursday." Noah kicked at nothing on the sidewalk. "And at school yesterday."

My mouth eased into a soft grin as I unlocked the door. "I missed you guys, too." Which I had, even while buried in bed with my phone, earbuds, and Led Zeppelin music. The songs he'd told me to listen to had also been eerily appropriate. Especially "Heartbreaker."

He followed me into the studio, and I paused long enough to flip on the light switch. When we reached the row of metal chairs, I faced him. "Did you have fun at your party?" But I held on to the fact I'd seen many pics on Snapchat of him, with all of our friends, having a fantastic time. A party I should have been at, too.

The tug—more like heartbreak—of seeing them in the pics, with huge smiles and laughing, had been so intense last night I'd logged out of Snapchat as a way to stop the torture.

He laughed and shook his head. "Yeah, they definitely shocked the hell out of me." He shrugged. "It was cool. And fun. But I'm...sorry you weren't there," he added in a rush of words.

I glanced at him and fought a smile at his flushed cheeks. Funny, though, he hadn't mentioned Henry. Because one of the reasons I'd "played sick" yesterday was to avoid dealing with what I'd done to him on Valentine's Day. His friends probably knew by now; knew I was, in fact, an agent of Satan. But I hadn't said a word to anyone in my circle. Not my aunt or even Natalie. Still, she and I had plans to meet up tomorrow.

"I'm sorry I missed it," I murmured. "But I'm glad you were surprised and had fun."

He gave me his trying-to-read-my-soul stare that I couldn't break. "You sure you're feeling better? You seem a little" —he tilted his head right— "less than mighty today."

I broke our gaze. "I'm okay. Really." I pulled off my sweatshirt to reveal a somewhat loose t-shirt over an exercise bra. I'd also chosen to wear gym shorts, still under my sweat pants, instead of ballet tights or exercise leggings. These rehearsals had nothing to do with ballet, so no reason to wear that kind of clothing. "I usually use ballet as my way of warming up—"

"Okay." He nodded. "Bring. It. On." He quickly removed his hoodie to reveal what had to be considered a vintage, black Led Zeppelin t-shirt.

Smiling at what he'd said and his shirt, I pointed at his *nicely* lean chest. "Nice shirt. And I'm not sure you're quite ready to take on ballet."

"Thanks." He shot me a fake hurt expression. "But what happened to the *you-can-do-anything-if-you-put-your-mind-to-it* Lexi Pfeiffer?"

I fought a grin. "Oh, she's right here. But you and ballet are *not* going together in my head." I then giggled at the image of his feet and legs in fifth position; arms above his head.

He crossed his arms. "You know, I might look pretty cute trying to do ballet."

Very true. But his pretty flirty comment caught me sideways, then made my head buzz.

What was up with him? Because if any of my friends— namely Natalie—had heard about Henry and me, I know she and they would have caused my phone to blow up by now.

I pushed that thought aside and said, "I'm thinking the better word is ridiculous."

He smiled. "That, too. But I'm getting the feeling you could use a good laugh."

Also very true. And every part of me tingled at him noticing such a thing.

I still crossed my arms. "I told you I'm fine." He held my stare, and something he'd said a couple times filled my mind. "You've told me you have *rhy-thm*." I leaned forward. "Prove it, Mr. Sanchez. That can be our warm up. After stretching."

Humor and determination flashed through his penetrating eyes. "It's on, Miss Pfeiffer."

I nodded, and we headed to the middle of the studio.

As we quietly stretched, I tried not to look at him in the mirrors. Specifically every time his t-shirt lifted just enough to show a glimpse of his *nicely* lean stomach—oh, my goodness.

I forced myself to focus extremely hard on every long stretch of my arms, legs, and back.

Once we were finished, he faced me while wearing his tummy fluttering grin.

"I'm ready." He paused, then added, "Any music but Gershwin."

"Okay," I replied. "Fine with me." We would be listening to him the rest of the day.

Within less than a minute, I had my bluetooth speaker ready to go and was scrolling through my music, that now included too many badass rock songs to count. A couple of them could work—a *pop* song caught my eye, sung by a certain guy singer and his current girlfriend.

What had to be an evil grin played with the corners of my mouth when I imagined the rock snob's reaction. So I tapped the song and pressed my lips together as its super catchy, opening notes exploded from my speaker.

I watched him, fighting my giggles.

He frowned, then his eyes widened, followed by a death glare.

"Oh, *hell* no. Shawn Mendes? Not. Happening."

I laughed until I could say, "Wow. The rock music snob actually knows this song."

He groaned. "Only because my sister loves him. And plays

and sings this, at the top of her lungs, from her bedroom across the hall from mine. Just to piss me off."

I laughed harder.

"It's not funny," he tossed at me. "And the fact *you* like this song is making me rethink giving you Lesson Four."

I stopped laughing and gave him the best somber expression I could manage. "I just wanted to see your reaction. I'll turn it off." I started to hit pause, but he stepped toward me.

"Wait a minute." He took a deep breath. "You've blown my mind, listening to every song and band I've thrown at you the last week or so. And really *getting* it." Our eyes snapped together. "I can handle dancing to this for three minutes of my life."

He leaned toward me, and I breathed in his right-out-of-the-shower yumminess—*no*.

"But if you tell anybody about this, I'll deny it and never speak to you again." He straightened. "Which would suck, since I consider you a...really good friend."

I kept a frustrated sigh in check as I set my phone on the floor. Then I held out my hand. "I'll take this To. My. Grave."

He smiled, grasped my hand, but led me away from the speaker and phone. When we again reached the middle of the studio, he stopped, faced me, and twirled me three times.

With wide eyes, I glided toward him. "Wow. Where'd *that* come from?"

We moved perfectly together in time with the catchy music. I followed *his* lead, too, which was a nice change. And during just the right moment in the song, he released me, twirled me twice—something I was ready for this time—and again smoothly pulled me close.

"I told you '*I've Got Rhy-thm*'," he sang while wearing his grin.

I swallowed, suddenly feeling like I was dressed to hike

across Antarctica during their winter months. I could only hope he wouldn't notice my hands had turned sweaty.

His grin fell. "But not when it comes to tap dancing."

We fell into smooth swaying that matched the song's rhythm.

"I promise you looked so much better this week."

"I felt stronger, too." His eyes wandered to mine. "Thanks to you. And Nicolas," he swiftly added.

Silence, outside of the music, descended between us. And he again, at just the right moment in the song, released and effortlessly twirled me three times.

When we were back together, I asked, "Have you ever called a girl 'señorita'?" Then I gasped at asking him a question about his personal life. Even though I was curious.

He wore his mystery close to him. Bundled up in it, with barely *him* showing.

He raised his eyebrows. "Nope. And I never will because of this song."

I giggled. "You're such a music snob."

"And proud of it."

We continued our smooth swaying.

"Do you speak Spanish?"

He shrugged. "Not much." He frowned. "I had enough trouble with school when I was little. My parents, who are fluent, didn't want to...overwhelm me."

My smile faded as I again pictured him as a cute little boy, working so hard on his schoolwork. That made me say, "I know you said you still have to work harder than everyone else. But everything you say, and write in your texts, is so clear. It must have gotten better as you've grown up?"

He hesitated, then said, "My teachers had to *accommodate* me. My parents also found me great tutors." His face turned a heartbreaking shade of pink. Because he was clearly embarrassed by his reality. "Texting automatically recognizes the word you want—for the most part—and has autocorrect. It's like typing something up in a computer doc."

I wanted to stop dancing and pull him toward me for a hug.

"But the accommodations and tutoring stopped when we moved here my sophomore year." He gave me his penetrating stare. "I wanted to prove to my family and myself I didn't need the extra help anymore." He cracked a smile. "That's one reason I have to work so hard. But I also want to." He huffed. "I know what my parents are paying to send me to P.A. I'm not going to blow it. They have really tough jobs and work hard."

Our dancing transitioned into a slower sway.

I angled my head toward him, and his eyes caught mine. "I think you're pretty close to perfect, too." What else could I think about him or say? He was doing everything in his power to make sure dyslexia didn't conquer or define him, when it would probably be so much easier for him to give up. Or use it as an excuse to *not* do his best in school.

He looked away at the same time his face became cherry red. "Thanks."

We fell silent once more, but he seemed to be in such an open, *honest* place, I asked, "What do your parents do?"

Another release, double twirl, and back together.

"My mom's a trauma nurse and my dad's an agent with the FBI."

I stopped, which caused him to stop, and my mouth fell open.

He groaned. "Everyone looks at me like that when I mention my dad's job. But it's almost *nothing* like the movies and shows on T.V." He cringed. "Well, his specialty is undercover work, but it's still nothing like Hollywood's version of the FBI."

I narrowed my eyes. "So you're saying it's *not* a dangerous job?"

He sighed. "Of course any job in law enforcement is dangerous. But shows and movies have a way of glamorizing working for the FBI. And it's not. Trust me," he muttered.

Something about the way he said those last two sentences told me he'd just revealed another reason he kept himself behind his wall called mystery.

He squinted at me as the song neared its end. "How do you do that?"

I frowned. "Do what?"

"Get me to talk about stuff I hate talking about."

The music stopped, though we were still holding our dancing pose as if it hadn't. The air between and around us sizzled while we kept our eyes on each other.

The corner of his mouth lifted in that grin of his. And I imagined going up on my tiptoes, leaning forward, and kissing That. Very. Spot.

"Because I've been doing all the talking," he softly said, "which is weird, I haven't had a chance to ask you what you thought of Lesson Three."

I blinked twice.

Yes. Jimmy Page and Led Zeppelin. A much better thing to focus on; *not* his mouth.

I started to answer. But then Nicolas came bounding into the studio.

"Right on time!" He stopped when he noticed how we were standing. And the closeness. "What are *you two* doing?" he teased, but with his deep voice it came out a tad naughty.

We released each other and stepped backward.

"Just warming up," Noah smoothly answered.

"Right." Nicolas didn't bother hiding his smile. "So what, exactly, *was* the warm up?"

Noah shot him a withering stare. "Will you shut the hell up and move it along? We're ready whenever you are."

Nicolas laughed, shook his head, and mumbled something under his breath while he went toward the chairs. The only words I could make out were "Heather" and "love."

Noah and I glanced at each other, and he rolled his eyes.

"I'll tell you how Lesson Three went later," I quietly assured him. I also couldn't wait for that conversation, either.

"I'm counting on it," he just as quietly answered. "But now it's time to show you and Nicolas I've been doing *my* homework."

I smiled. "Getting Gershwin into your blood?"

"Lexi, that'll never happen." He returned my smile. "But I'm definitely starting to feel the music."

"Oh, yeah?"

"*Hell* yeah."

I leaned forward. "Prove it."

His smile grew. "And it's on. Again."

Chapter Seventeen

I sat with my back facing the mirrors and kept my eyes trained on Noah. He danced beside Nicolas in time with "Slap That Bass" blaring from the speaker.

He'd proven the entire rehearsal he "felt" the music. His dancing had been more confident. Almost no missteps. He also wasn't looking at his feet as much. More progress.

Pride at the fact I'd helped him get to this point, and in two Saturdays, shimmied through me. I'd always loved helping my aunt with her classes, but working with Noah was so different. Because I—with Nicolas's help—was the actual teacher, doing what I loved most in the world.

I grinned and lifted my eyes from his feet to focus on his face. That was set in a deep frown of concentration. Also known as our next dancing hurdle, which made my grin fade.

He needed to relax. Find the fun. This number was all about the cowboys of Deadrock, Nevada, realizing they could dance and sing, and *have* fun in the process.

The song—for what seemed like the millionth time today—neared its end.

Noah kept up with the music and Nicolas, who was grinning, and the two stopped right as the song ended.

Silence filled the studio, and Noah's eyes found mine.

"Nailed it, Miss Pfeiffer." He finally smiled. "*Again.*"

Nicolas laughed. "That was really good. Have you been practicing outside of these rehearsals?"

Noah lowered his head and kicked at nothing on the floor. "Maybe."

Nicolas nodded while fighting a grin. "It's showing. So keep doing that."

I stood and headed for them. "Agreed. And you did look pretty good today."

Noah's mouth fell open in genuine shock. "'*Pretty good*'?" He frowned. "I was *in* the music. And felt like Pete for the first time since day one of rehearsals," he quietly added. "What did I do wrong?"

He sounded so frustrated that I gave him an encouraging smile. "You're getting the steps. You're not looking at your feet as much. All of that's awesome."

He crossed his arms. "*But?*"

I leaned forward. "*But* you need to lighten up. Smile. You're supposed to be having fun?"

His eyes flitted to Nicolas, who nodded and shrugged, and back to me.

I gestured at his feet. "You're concentrating so hard on the steps that you almost look...angry. And you're not Pete, the *angry*, tap dancing cowboy from Deadrock, Nevada."

He released a huge sigh. "Fine. So what do you suggest?"

I thumbed the mirrors behind me. "Use those more next week. It's what they're for." I angled my head down and left to catch his eyes. "You'll see what I'm—we're—talking about."

He shoved his hands into his pockets. "Okay."

Nicolas stepped toward him. "*But* you've come a long way in one week."

Noah cracked a smile.

Nicolas glanced at me. "I guess we're gonna call it a day?"

I nodded, and he and Noah walked to the chairs. I went right, to grab my phone and speaker.

The silence seemed so heavy with Noah's frustration, I felt the need to—and probably out of guilt for causing his change in mood—lighten the air around us. So I asked Nicolas when I reached them at the chairs, "What are you and Heather up to tonight?"

He gave us a huge, toothy grin before pulling on his hoodie. "Celebrating Valentine's Day. We couldn't last night because of this guy's party. Which was so cool."

I eyed Noah, still unsmiling, as he grabbed his phone and sweatshirt.

A tiny sigh escaped as he went into his phone.

I hadn't meant to burst his tap dancing bubble. Especially since he had looked so much better today. I'd just been giving him the *honesty* he wanted and needed.

"What are you and Henry doing?" Nicolas asked.

I froze, then blinked twice.

Now wasn't the time to confess what I'd done to Henry on Valentine's Day. And if Natalie heard about all of that from someone else first, I'd never hear the end of it.

Noah's eyes wandered to me for a couple seconds and back to his phone.

"Nothing. I'm drowning in homework right now." *And not a lie.*

That caught Noah's attention again, and he and Nicolas frowned at me.

I looked away and busied myself with putting on my sweatshirt, and placing the speaker back in my pink and black backpack purse. When I finished, I faced them. "Ready to go?" I headed for the light switch where I waited for them to catch up.

"My mom let me borrow her car today," Nicolas said once we were outside. "I'm parked around the block." He glanced at me. "Have fun doing homework tonight?"

I plastered a smile on my face. "I'm living the dream." *More like my parents' dream.*

He stepped backward and pointed at Noah. "And I guess you'll have fun doing whatever is *you* do, Mr. Guitar Hero."

Nicolas's eyes bounced between us, and he seemed unfazed by Noah's death glare.

As he sauntered off, Noah faced me.

"Now Heather has her boyfriend calling me that." He shot me his devil-worthy grin. "But payback's going to be a real bitch."

I smiled. "Why don't you like that nickname?"

"Because it makes me sound like a guitar playing super-hero." He rolled his eyes. "I hate superheroes. *All* of them. Marvel versus DC Comics?" He groaned. "I. Don't. Care."

I burst into laughter, since I. Could. Relate.

"It sounds like we're in agreement on that, Miss Pfeiffer?"

I nodded once. "Yes we are, Mr. Sanchez."

He released a dramatic sigh of relief, then said, "Are you walking home, too?"

Sensing where he was going with that question, a spark ignited in my tummy. But I replied, "Yeah. You don't have to walk me home, though."

"Yeah. I do." His mouth curved into that grin of his. "We have unfinished business."

I tore my eyes from his irresistible—*no.* "Jimmy Page and Led Zeppelin." He also had made it clear earlier he'd come prepared to give me Lesson Four.

The spark in my tummy became a white hot flame.

I turned from him, and he fell into step beside me.

Where was *this* Noah coming from? Our unexpected

connection over the rock music lessons? And all the extra time together?

"*Soooo...*" he said. "You're killing me here. What'd you think?"

The fact he seemed so interested and excited about what I thought of Lesson Three did nothing but turn the flame into a full-blown fire. To the point I really didn't need my hoodie, even though the weather was, per the usual this time of year, cool, damp, and dreary.

"I can't say I like Led Zeppelin better than The Rolling Stones," I slowly began, watching his expression that had transitioned into serious. Focused and waiting for what I'd say next. "But Jimmy Page's playing on 'Dazed and Confused' and 'Heartbreaker' did blow my mind."

He smiled.

"His playing grabbed and pulled me into the song. And I got lost. In a good way." *Absolutely the truth, too.*

He glanced at me. "Excellent. Answer."

I returned his smile, then added, "You know, some of these badass guitar players you've been having me listen to seem to have this certain...sound. I don't know how to explain it."

He leaned toward me and angled his head down. "What you're most likely noticing is called *blues* music." He straightened. "But that's another series of lessons." He placed his hands in his hoodie's pocket. "Most badass rock guitarists were heavily influenced by blues guitar players. Like B.B. King and Buddy Guy and Chuck Berry, who's called the 'father of rock-and-roll'" —He laughed. "I can tell by your expression you have *no* idea who I'm talking about."

No, I didn't. But I playfully said, "So teach me about them, too."

His steps faltered at my pretty flirty response. That didn't cause me to gasp. He'd been just as flirty here and there throughout our last few hours together. And he did like *honesty*.

He stopped, then I did, and he gave me that piercing stare of his. "One music genre at a time, Miss Pfeiffer."

I lifted my shoulders. "But it's already more than one. Because of what you just said?"

Smiling, he shook his head. "Fair enough." He peered at me. "Okay. Now that I know you want the history of rock-and-roll, I'll rethink my next lessons." He paused, then said, "You may even be ready for another badass and fucking *brilliant* guitarist." His smile fell. "Who died way too young."

Anticipation shimmied through me as I asked, "Is he my next lesson?"

"Nope." He turned and started walking.

I nearly choked on my moan of frustration as I caught up with him. "You're killing *me*."

He grinned. "I know."

I shot him my death glare.

"So you said something last Saturday that's been kind've bugging me."

I frowned and hit my brain's rewind button. I had been hard on him a week ago, because of his bad attitude. But he'd bounced back pretty quickly, then and today—

"When you said you'll never be a dancer like your aunt because of your parents?"

My steps faltered, and I whipped my head in his direction.

We again stopped, but separated on the sidewalk to make room for an older couple power walking. Once they'd passed between us, we stayed apart.

Just like he felt about his dyslexia and dad's job, I hated talking about *this*. And them.

"Do they want you to be a lawyer, too?" he persisted.

I tore my eyes from his to focus on the parked car behind him. "I'm sure they'd love that," I grumbled. "But *that'll* never happen, either." *Never in a million years.* I raised my chin. "They want me to go to UC Berkeley like they did and pursue something *professional.* Like pre-law or pre-med or things like that." I shrugged. "And I love working with kids, so I could deal with being a pediatrician." Though the thought of committing myself to many *more* years of schooling made me shiver from Absolute. Dread.

Keeping his gaze trained on me, he tilted his head right. "Being a pediatrician is a *big* commitment. Shouldn't you feel more excited about it than 'I could deal'?"

Yes. I should. But I turned left and began walking. "It's complicated."

He caught up with me in one step. "I'm sorry," he mumbled. "Because what you want to do for the rest of *your* life shouldn't be that way." I felt his eyes as he asked, "Do you even want to go to Berkeley?"

I shot him my bright smile. "It's an excellent school."

He frowned. "I've told you I can see right through that smile. And you didn't answer my question."

A sigh escaped me in an agitated burst. "I don't know what I want, okay?" Why wouldn't he leave me—this—alone?

"Yes you do."

I gritted my teeth, then managed to say, "Well, in the spirit of The Rolling Stones, 'You Can't Always Get What You Want'."

He nodded. "Wise words. But you should when it comes to your life." He paused before adding, "You should rebel. Break the fucking rules. Just like these badass rock guitarists did."

I stopped and faced him, and he copied my actions.

A hint of defiance flashed through his penetrating, dark eyes.

Although the thought of rebelling like that made a flare go off inside and surge through me, I still crossed my arms. "Are we still talking about me?" Because something about that brief, defiant glint in his eyes had caught my mind.

He gave me a soft smile. "My parents are super cool with my guitar playing." He lifted his shoulders. "But they want me to do the city college thing. Like my sister. And I get it. Really. But I have no idea what the hell I'd major in. I've *never* liked school," he added under his breath.

Oh, my *goodness*. A part of me wanted to say I didn't know a kid who did like school. At the same time, I knew his dislike came from a completely different place.

I tried on a smile. "You seem to really like theater."

He kicked a rock aside. "Yeah. It's hard work. Challenging. And fun." He shook his head. "But that's all it is." Our eyes connected. "One of the other reasons I got involved with theater when I came to P.A. was to make friends."

I leaned forward. "And you've made *awesome* friends." Actually, both of us had through our different connections to the kids active in theater.

Sadness settled into his eyes and on his face. "Most of them are graduating in a few months." He cleared his throat. "Including you."

The sadness radiating from him, and that had been mingled with his words, reached inside of me, clutched my heart, and squeezed. Especially his comment, "Including you."

I forced myself to take a breath.

Something else about his last comment struck me a little sideways. It seemed as if he was trying to tell me more. Like I needed to read between his lines.

He ran a hand through his hair and released a quick laugh. "I don't know how I always end up doing all the talking when it's just you and me. Weren't we talking about *you*?"

We turned left in unison and our steps became more of a stroll.

I peeked at him. "I like you talking about yourself."

He peeked at me. "I like you taking about yourself, too."

I fought a ridiculous, girly grin.

He sighed. "I really am sorry your parents expect you to do what *they* want you to do."

I lost my grin and focused straight ahead. "I'm used to it." *Totally the truth*. But that didn't make it okay. Because he was right.

Silence, outside of passing traffic, fell between us.

Why couldn't I do what *I* wanted to do after graduation? I was already eighteen. Legally an adult. But they still treated me like a little girl who couldn't make her own decisions. A little girl who couldn't take care of herself.

I smirked at that thought.

They'd hardly been home for the last month or so, using their miserable jobs as a way to escape their misery with each other. Yes, they'd checked in with me mostly through texts, and made sure the fridge and pantry were filled. And I'm sure they'd been staying on top of my grades through the school's online grade system. But that's where their "parenting" the last several weeks began and ended.

They had no idea what was going on with me. With my life.

Moisture filled my eyes, and I swallowed and rapidly blinked.

Why did I care about what *they* wanted me to do next year?

Do you even want to go to Berkeley?

"Hey. You okay over there?"

His concerned voice broke apart my thoughts. And normally I'd turn and flash my bright, everything's-fine smile. But he'd made it clear, a few times, what he thought of that smile.

He groaned. "Did I say something I shouldn't have? I told

you I can be an asshole. But you have permission to tell me when I'm being one. Really."

I laughed, which made the remaining moisture evaporate. "You're not. I promise." I glanced his way to find him eyeing me. "You're just being honest. And I like it," I softly added.

His mouth curved into that lopsided, tummy-fluttering grin. "Feels good, right? Being honest?" His grin slipped. "Well, hearing the honesty isn't always cool. But I'd much rather hear the truth than have smoke blown up my you-know-what hole."

I giggled. "Noted, Mr. Sanchez."

His grin came back, and at full force.

I looked forward, trying to squash the fluttering as we again lapsed into silence.

Minutes later we stood outside my quiet-as-a-grave house. I swung my eyes between it and him, standing there kicking at nothing on the sidewalk.

I battled the near-overwhelming urge to suggest—more like beg?—that we continue this rare time together. See where the moment, the day, the night led us. Would that be so wrong? And would he really say no? Especially after I told him Henry and I were no longer together?

There'd be no reason for him to say no. Right?

I squared my shoulders, took a quick breath, and opened my mouth.

"David Gilmour from Pink Floyd."

I closed my mouth so hard my teeth clicked.

"He's your Lesson Four," Noah continued in a rush of words. "Check out 'Comfortably Numb' from *The Wall*. And *all* their music on *The Dark Side of the Moon*."

I blinked twice.

Yes. I'd been waiting for—wanting—Lesson Four.

He cleared his throat and kicked the sidewalk. "You can text or...call me later. To tell me what you think? I'll just be"

—he shrugged— "at home, too. Spending quality time with Eddie."

Despite my disappointment at the fact we clearly weren't on the same page when it came to letting *this* last for as long as possible, I still smiled. At his surprising, yet adorable shyness. "I'll do that."

He returned my smile. "I'll wait until you're in your house."

My smile grew as I turned and walked up the steps. But once inside, my smile vanished.

I leaned against my locked door and released the longest, whiniest moan of my teen life.

Why couldn't I get what I wanted when it came to Noah Luis Sanchez?

Chapter Eighteen

I inhaled in time with Pink Floyd's "Breathe (In the Air)," track two on *The Dark Side of the Moon,* as I colored *his* hair with a black pencil.

My sketch had definitely started to reveal more of him the last week or so. I'd finished drawing his oh-so perfect eyes, perfectly-shaped nose, and I'd finished his hair earlier. Thick and wavy on top, but short in the back and around his ears. *Perfect.*

He'd also led me to another badass rock guitarist and band. Pink Floyd didn't really have the "bluesy" influence of The Rolling Stones and Led Zeppelin. And didn't have the kind of in-your-face feel of Van Halen. But there was something...soothing...about most of the songs I'd been blasting through my earbuds. Like if I fell asleep while listening to their songs, I'd start to float. "Breathe (In the Air)" was one of them. And "Comfortably Numb," which also had some *serious* badass guitar playing.

The lyrics of these songs, like others he'd led me to since the lessons started, seemed to weirdly fit my life. I couldn't stop myself from wondering if they fit *his* life, too.

"Jump." "You Can't Always Get What You Want." "(I Can't Get No) Satisfaction." "Comfortably Numb." "Breathe (In the Air)." Just the beginning of the list, too.

I stopped coloring, stared into his eyes, and I remembered his earlier, brief moments of defiance and sadness. He didn't want to be left behind at the end of the school year. But there was *nothing* he could do, except watch his friends, including me, move on after graduation.

I released a Deep. Sad. Sigh.

Of course most of the songs he'd led me to also fit *his* life.

But he'd thrown in some other amazing songs. Like "Dazed and Confused" and "Heartbreaker," though those songs were about love not going so well. Which I understood. And then there were the totally-into-a-girl songs, like "Hot For Teacher," "Start Me Up," "Wild Horses"—I froze, then blinked twice.

Yes. His lessons had included too many songs to count. But what about those three? He'd *specifically* told me to listen to two of them, and "Wild Horses" he'd listed right after "Start Me Up." He also thought of me as his teacher. Miss Pfeiffer. And oh, my *goodness*.

I dropped my pencil, sat back, and gritted my teeth. I knew it and I'd known it all along. Noah *did* want to be with me. And not just the way two of those songs implied. Though it wasn't a bad mental image. Him, me, some badass rock music in the background, and—I needed to focus on one thing at a time right now.

The next song on Pink Floyd's *The Dark Side of the Moon* began to play.

I narrowed my eyes.

He'd said I could call and text him about Lesson Four, because he'd be at home tonight, "spending quality time with Eddie." So why not just talk in person about David Gilmour and Pink Floyd? And the other rock music lessons? And me breaking up with Henry? And why the heck hadn't he asked me to Snowflake Formal? After all, he did want and need *honesty*.

I closed my sketchbook and stood.

Within minutes, I jogged down the stairs, again wearing my hoodie from earlier and pink-and-black backpack purse. From the corner of my eye, I saw my parents in the living room, sitting and actually talking for a change. But past experiences had proven their talking could erupt into something totally different, and with the intensity of a volcano. Which meant I was leaving at just the right time.

"Alexis!"

I stopped at my dad's voice and forced myself to face him, now standing by the fireplace. My mom had stayed seated on the couch.

"We need to talk to you. Can you come in here?"

I pressed my lips together to stop another long, whiny moan from escaping. Of course they wanted to be real parents *now*. "I'm meeting up with a friend." I turned toward the door.

"Who are you meeting up with? Henry?" he persisted. "I didn't know about it. Did you?" He looked at Mom.

She barely shook her head.

I lifted my chin. "I'm not meeting up with Henry, and it just came up. Can I leave?" And I didn't flinch at my defiant tone, words, or stance.

Dad frowned. "No, you cannot leave." He paused, then added, "What we need to talk to you about can't wait. But your friend can."

I crossed my arms and marched into the living room.

"You've obviously been alone too much lately." My parents glared at each other before Dad added, "Yes. You're eighteen now. But coming and going as you please isn't the rule in this house. Or has that been changed without my knowledge?"

"No," Mom ground out. "It hasn't."

I glared at *them*.

You should rebel. Break the effing rules. Just like these badass rock guitarists did.

I inched backward.

"Alexis, please sit down." Mom patted the cushion beside her.

I halted, and my posture stiffened. They were about to tell me something huge that would change my life forever. Something huge that I'd been expecting for weeks. Even months.

"I'm fine right here."

Mom's eyes widened at my stubborn and still defiant tone.

Dad sighed and nodded. "Starting tonight, I'll *only* be staying at a hotel near my office." He paused, then added, "Until I find an apartment."

So that's where he'd been sleeping. Not his office.

I stared at them, watching me for a reaction. And I wanted to scream, *did they really think I hadn't noticed he'd been sleeping somewhere else since that last big fight I'd heard the second I walked into the house?* But I managed to swallow the words.

"We'll also be starting divorce proceedings Monday morning," Mom softly stated.

Yes. Of course they were. Finally. Still, hearing those words —that your parents who used to love each other—were calling it quits...giving up...stung deep, unknown parts of me.

I quietly inhaled through my nose as the lyrics of "Breathe (In the Air)" filled my head.

"I know I won't be here anymore," Dad continued, "but you can call or text me anytime."

Nothing new there.

"I'm also hoping to spend a Saturday or Sunday with you?" he asked. "If you're not busy with school."

Because school comes first, Alexis Evelyn Pfeiffer. Being your dad isn't even important.

The stinging multiplied to the point my skin felt as if I'd set it on fire. I needed to get out of this house, and away from them and his business-as-usual attitude.

"Alexis?" Mom focused on me. "I know we just threw a lot at you, but—"

"No, you didn't." I took a huge step backward. "I have somewhere to be." I then turned, left the house, and slammed the door behind me.

I all but ran in the direction of school. Also known as Noah's building. But even his place wouldn't be far enough away from that stupid, *miserable* house and them—well, I guess now it would officially be only my mom and me, stuck in a broken home. Or would it?

I veered right to avoid a jogger, and my fast steps became heavier.

Mom's life, or Dad's for that matter, wouldn't change One. Bit. They'd continue to use their jobs as an escape like they'd been doing. Which would leave me stuck in that now broken home and dealing with the shattered pieces. From a catastrophic break I didn't cause.

Anger and resentment exploded inside me, and I clenched my hands.

None of this was fair. I wanted to punish him for being able to permanently leave. Move out. I wanted to punish her for losing herself in her job, yet still expecting me to be a *good girl*. The perfect student. They actually both expected that, but she'd been the one enforcing it. When she was actually at home, being a mom.

I continued my swift stomping, pausing only for traffic at intersections. And barely pausing for that. All around me the

Pacific Heights neighborhood buzzed with Saturday evening electricity, despite the cool, wet, gloomy weather. Humidity filled the air with a recent rainfall and smelled of another one building in the gray sky.

I'd long since freed my hair of the ponytail I'd pulled it into during rehearsal, so I could feel the damp air clinging to the ends, making the thick locks wavier and heavier.

A small part of me wanted to pause long enough to pull my hair back up and off my neck, but I refused to stop. I had to keep moving and breathing as a way to release my anger and resentment. I also needed to prepare myself for what I was about to do when I saw Noah.

Yes. One thing at a time. The reality of a broken home life could wait.

The lyrics from Van Halen's "Jump" now filled my head. And I quietly hummed the music as a way to lose myself in the inspiring, badass song.

But would Noah "Jump" with me? All the signs and even some rock songs pointed to him wanting to do just that. Still, the question caused me to tremble as I approached his building. In that moment, I realized I didn't know where he lived in the building. Hopefully their last name was near the button I'd have to push?

I stopped at the stoop; the toes of my Vans against the first step.

"Breathe (In the Air)."

I did just that, then squared my shoulders.

"Jump."

My legs wobbled as I headed up the stairs.

Chapter Nineteen

The door opened and there stood Noah. With two tan, fluffy, yapping Pomeranians at his ankles. I'd actually heard them through the intercom when I was explaining who I was to his sister, now standing behind him.

"What's wrong?" Noah asked above the rambunctious barking.

His curt question caught me off guard, but there'd been definite concern behind it.

"Francis and Michael, *enough*!" Noah's sister yelled at the two dogs.

They finally fell silent. But not before whining their displeasure.

She shoved Noah aside, took my hand, and pulled me into their apartment. Or condo?

Francis and Michael began anxiously sniffing my shoes while she closed the door.

"We've never officially met," Noah's sister began. "I'm Eden. And you're Lexi."

I returned her wide, genuine smile.

We'd only ever seen each other from her car in November and December during *those* rehearsals. I'd noticed then she was pretty, but standing inches from her, striking was a much better word. She wasn't as tall as her brother, but shared his slimness, deep dark eyes, and black hair that she wore short, but with purple streaks. She also had a silver nose ring.

"And I'm sorry my little brother is a complete *ass*." she continued, shooting him the death glare that I totally recognized. "'*What's wrong*'? That's the way you say hi to a girl who's here to see you?" She snorted. "No wonder you're single."

He narrowed his eyes into his full-blown death glare. "I said it out of *concern*?" He shook his head and faced me. "Seriously. What's going on?"

Before I could answer, a tall, older, really handsome man with an older, shorter, curvier, really pretty woman appeared in the hallway from another room and headed toward us.

Noah quietly groaned.

They stopped to my right and gave me warm, yet tentative smiles.

"Mom and Dad, this is Lexi," he mumbled. "Lexi, my parents." He frowned. "And it's not like I've *never* had a friend from school over," he muttered.

Eden gave him what could only be called an are-you-kidding-me look. And something about the exchange between sister and brother fueled the power I'd found before walking into the building.

Noah's mom waved him off and said to me, "It's nice to finally meet you." She laughed. "You must possess the patience of Job to be teaching *my* son to tap dance. And to *Gershwin*."

Noah's face turned tomato red, and I shot him my devil-worthy grin.

"Well, I am used to working with five-year-olds."

His parents and sister burst into laughter. While he glared at me.

Noah's dad eyed him. "Wow. Enough said." He focused on me. "So how's he doing?"

I smiled at him, then Noah, still glaring. "He definitely has *rhy-thm*."

Noah crossed his arms. "Thank you. And did it kill you to say that?"

Eden leaned forward. "Not yet. But she could drop at any—"

"Shut. Up." He clasped my hand, stepped backward, and pulled me with him. "Do you mind if Lexi and I go talk now? Is that okay?" He turned right without waiting for an answer.

With our hands tightly and so rightly joined, I went with him down the hallway, but waved goodbye to his parents and sister watching us. And not bothering to stop their smiles.

Yes. Noah Luis Sanchez *definitely* wanted to be with me.

"Francis and Michael Go. Away," Noah told the two excited dogs at our heels. He led me into what had to be his room and closed the door before the dogs could trot inside. "*Fuck*," he mumbled. "I love my family, but they're acting ridiculous."

The dogs started whining and scratching his door. To the point it vibrated.

"And my mom named those two after saints" —our eyes connected— "but I call them Beelzebub and Lucifer when she's not around."

A giggle escaped; my first since I'd been with him earlier in the day.

Had that really only been a few hours ago?

"They're so spoiled because of her and my sister."

I smiled. "Do you have to walk them?"

He frowned. "Yeah. And I'd rather not talk about it."

I giggled again at the mental image of him walking the two, fluffy, "ferocious" dogs.

His face relaxed a fraction as the scratching and vibrating stopped. "When I opened the door, I didn't expect you to walk into insanity." He subjected me to his reading-my-soul stare. "What are you doing here?" He cringed. "I'm not trying to be an ass. But this isn't like you."

Yes. Very true. I wasn't used to "jumping." But where to begin? *A lot* had happened since he'd, in his gentlemanly way, watched me walk into my house hours earlier.

"Hey. I know something must've happened." He cleared his throat. "And I have no idea what, but...shouldn't you be at your boyfriend's house?"

I burst into laughter that sounded like hysteria had consumed me.

His forehead formed a deep V. "Lexi, now you're *really* worrying me."

I somehow reigned in *my* insanity and blurted out, "I broke up with Henry on Valentine's Day." I continued laughing for a few seconds, then said, "I guess that means you can call *me* Beelzebub or Lucifer. But I think I like Lucifer better. Because of the cat from *Cinderella?* He was evil." And what the heck was I babbling about? Based on his wide eyes, I sounded crazy.

I was also crazy for *him*...oh, I needed to stop and breathe. *"Breathe (In the Air)."*

Noah led me to his bed, placed his hands on my shoulders, and gently pressed me to the edge. He went for—of course—his chair at his desk, located to my immediate left, and rolled it toward me. He sat, his knees barely brushing against mine, but I let my eyes wander around his room. Actually, there was something I specifically wanted to—and there *they* were. To my right and just behind me in the corner. His acoustic guitar that had to be in its case and

Eddie. A black, shiny electric guitar, leaning against an amplifier, hooked up to electronics equipment situated on black shelving. Nothing else in his corner but what he loved, with fancy-looking headphones, and a black-and-white area rug.

"Black must be your favorite color," I stated, noticing *all* of his furniture was black. He also wore black quite a bit, too.

"It goes with everything."

"So does white," I challenged while taking in his black comforter.

"And I like white, too. It goes with black."

I whipped my head in his direction to find him not trying super hard to fight his tummy-fluttering grin. But I still said, "You're. Infuriating."

"So you've told me," he threw back. "But you didn't come over here to inspect my room and give me decorating advice."

No. That was most certainly *not* the reason I'd come over.

"And I'm not surprised you and Henry aren't together anymore," he nearly whispered.

"I'm sure no one will be surprised." I flinched. "Well, they may be surprised by *when* I broke up with him."

"Yeah." He peeked at me. "Valentine's Day. *Ouch.*"

I sighed. "It was either then, or right before or after. Would that have been any better?"

He shook his head. "Nope."

"So, I did the right thing."

He held up his hands. "Lexi, you did what you had to do. Okay, *not* great timing. But I don't understand why you went out with him to begin with, since you two—" He closed his mouth, focused on the floor, and turned that spectacular shade of tomato red.

And he'd given me the Perfect. Opening.

Time to "Jump."

I leaned forward. "I went out with him because he asked

me to Snowflake Formal." My eyes found his. "Even though I'd been so hoping *another* boy would ask me."

A huge breath of relief burst from my lungs at having finally said that to him. And I didn't care one bit about the surprise and discomfort and guilt merging within his eyes and on his face. "You need and want honesty, so there you go."

He looked away. "Lexi, I don't want to talk about this. And is it why you came over here?" He ran a hand through his hair. "Because you should've called or texted first. I could've saved you the walk."

Something dark inside me exploded with nuclear-level force at his snarky tone and attitude. And his refusal to admit the truth. Ironic coming from him. "So much for *honesty*!" I snapped. "Why can't you admit you like and want to be with me? And that *you* should've been the one who asked me to Snowflake Formal."

He stayed silent for several seconds before slouching back in his chair.

"Okay. You're right." He released a defeated sigh. "You win, Alexis Evelyn Pfeiffer."

I froze, then blinked twice.

Yes. Of course I'd won. But what exactly did that mean?

"If things were different," he quietly, almost sadly continued, "I would've asked you, you obviously would've said yes, and" —he huffed— "we'd probably be doing other, *way* more fun stuff right now, than sitting here like this. Frustrated and...pissed."

I'd liked—loved—everything he'd said but the "if things were different." Because I now understood why he'd emphasized "including you" from earlier. He had been wanting me to read between his lines. "You haven't asked me out because I'm a senior and you're a junior." And the me graduating that went with being a senior.

His eyes drifted to mine. "It's better this way."

"Why?" I persisted, and with the power of *honesty* fueling my strength. "And for who? Because I don't want or need someone else in my life making decisions for me."

He raised his eyebrows, but I did catch a glimmer of guilt mixed with his surprise. "That's not what I'm trying to do. But why can't you see this from my point of view?"

I took a slow breath to settle my frustration. Once I'd quietly released the air, I said, "I do understand it'll be hard for you to watch all of us graduate. Especially since...well, you know."

His jaw tightened.

"But there are these big things called social media," I continued, trying not to sound desperate. "And FaceTime. And school breaks." I paused, then added, "Staying in touch with Liam won't be easy, but you know Maddie is going to San Francisco State. And, yeah, everyone else applied to schools south of here. And me—" My path didn't seem quite so clear anymore.

The corner of his mouth lifted, but with a sad smile. "There you go again. Looking at everything the way *you* do."

I frowned. "It's called being positive. *You* should try it."

"And *you* are only thinking about right now," he shot back. "We see each other every day at school. Simple, right? Until you move to Berkeley. And start making friends and getting into the whole college thing and meeting...guys." He gave me an almost pleading look. "Then what? Are you really going to give up Friday and Saturday nights with your friends to hang out with me? Who will *still* be in high school." He shook his head. "Lexi, I can't ask or expect you to do that. And this is going make me sound like an asshole, but I also have to think about myself."

I closed my eyes and allowed his arguments to sink into my muddled brain.

Everything he'd said was completely valid, whether I ended

up at Berkeley or not. Well, except the meeting guys part. I'd meet them, of course, but I couldn't imagine being with just any boy. Not when I wanted this amazing boy, sitting in front of me, radiating defeat. Not after the connection we'd made over the odd combo of tap dancing to Gershwin and badass rock music. I'd never listen to any music the same way because of his lessons. Because of *him*. All of that had to count for something beyond special. More like extraordinary.

I opened my eyes to find him glaring at the floor. "Noah, I get all of your what ifs. But..." I began twirling a lock of hair around my right index finger. "What if I don't go to Berkeley? What if" —I shrugged— "I do choose dancing. And the city college."

He lifted his head, and our eyes snapped together. Magnets.

"I'm sure your parents would *love* that."

"And maybe I want to break *their* effing rules." Wow. Did that feel good to say, too.

He angled his head back at my defiant words. That I'd meant with every part of me.

I smiled. "So, in the spirit of badass rock music, 'Jump' with me?" I leaned toward him. "Noah, I don't know what will happen after graduation. For any of us. But I have this feeling *we* would be so awesome. Now and even *if* I went to Berkeley." Which was really beginning to feel like the biggest *if* ever at this moment in time.

He held my stare, and I caught so many emotions flashing through his eyes I knew I could stare into the rest of my teen life and beyond.

Shock. Excitement. Hesitation. And way too much fear.

Tears struck my eyes, and I lowered my head. Because I knew I'd lost.

"Lexi, you deserve to go to a school like Berkeley," he murmured. "And live *your* life."

I pressed my lips together and slowly shook my head while clearing my eyes. It was also past time for me to get out of here, so I stood. I would not let my dam burst in front of him.

He pushed his chair back and came to his feet. "I think we're pretty awesome as friends."

Hysterical laughter again rippled out of me, and his shoulders fell forward.

Yes. Friends. But if that's really all the coward wanted, it would now come with *rules*.

"Sounds. Great," I ground out, sounding an awful lot like my mom had earlier. "And since *you've* made this choice" —I narrowed my eyes— "stop flirting with me. It's confusing."

He opened his mouth, but stopped, then nodded. "Done."

Rage intertwined with rejection caused me to unleash my death glare.

How could he be such a coward? Give up so easily? Just like my parents had *years* ago.

"No more rock music lessons, either!" I snapped.

His eyes widened and he stepped toward me. But I went for his door.

"Lexi, the lessons are harmless fun."

I spun toward him. "No. They're more than that." I swallowed a wave of misery trying to make an appearance. "At least, they were for me." I paused, searching for the right words, then said, "The lessons were like...you letting me get to know *you*." I flung my right hand in his direction. "Letting me past that wall of yours you can't—won't—break down. And I'm done."

He shoved his hands into his hoodie's pocket and glowered at his feet.

"I loved Pink Floyd, by the way." I raised my chin. "So thank you, Noah Luis Sanchez, for showing me badass rock music that did get inside of me and will Never. Leave." I turned and fled his room.

Seconds later, I burst from the building and headed left. Toward home. But my steps came to a gradual stop at the thought of the misery waiting for me there.

No. I just couldn't deal with that house. Or watching my dad officially move out.

Between that reality, and Noah actually rejecting me, I struggled to suck air into my lungs. I could call my aunt, but I wanted and needed the closest person I had to a best friend.

I swiftly went right. To distance myself from the cowardly Noah and his building. Once I stood directly across from school, I pulled off my backpack purse and dug inside for my phone. She'd probably be with *her* adoring boyfriend, but we'd figure something out.

Natalie, surprisingly, answered almost immediately with, "Hi. Feeling better?"

Yes. I'd been "sick." But I felt zero guilt saying, "No. Are you with Shane?"

"Not anymore. I'm at home. We had to call it an early night because he caught a bad cold." She sighed. "He's been working so hard. At school. On the musical. And on my car on the weekends. He's really hoping to finish it by my birthday."

"Then can we hang out at your place tonight? You can pick me up at school. I really need you." My voice broke on the words. Then I added, because I could no longer hold any of it inside of me, "My dad's moving out, and they're getting divorced. I broke up with Henry on Valentine's Day, because I *want* to be with Noah. And I just told Noah that, but he—" I squeaked the last two words. A second later, the tears I'd been fighting exploded from my eyes.

"I'll be there as fast as I can," Natalie replied, sounding like she was walking quickly.

"Thanks," I managed to say, and I hugged myself after we hung up.

So much for badass rock music and "jumping."

Despite what I'd told him, I wasn't certain I'd ever listen to that song again.

Chapter Twenty

Natalie handed me a fresh box of tissues. Once I'd released the dam I hadn't been able to stop the flow. She dropped beside me on the cushy, sectional couch in her living room. Her dog, Chloe, then jumped up and into her lap. Because her parents' place was the penthouse in a fancy building in Nob Hill, the room, on clear days, had an amazing view of the city and bay. And thank goodness her parents wouldn't be back from their trip until tomorrow.

"Okay. Who do you want to talk about first?" she asked in her blunt, Natalie way. "Your parents or Noah. Because we're not talking about Henry." She scratched Chloe's face. "He'll get over you dumping him on Valentine's Day and realize you two didn't belong together."

I gave her a hard stare.

"Alright," she hastily conceded, "*someday* he'll get over it and realize that. And I knew those eyes I caught you drawing looked familiar. I can't believe I didn't make the connection to Noah." She returned my hard stare. "The way you two were so smiley before Snowflake Formal? I knew you liked each other. He's also the one who *really* texted you the other morning?"

I nodded, sniffed, and wiped eyes. "I guess we can talk about him first." *Get it over with, so I'd* never *have to talk about him or his rejection again.*

I felt her razor-sharp eyes as she said, "I think you're amazing for doing what you did. Going over to his place and telling him how you feel? That took guts. I'm proud of you."

I tried to smile as I continued sniffling. Unfortunately, *my* courage had gotten me absolutely nowhere. Well, except sitting by my amazing friend while fighting through the sharp pain in my chest that kept bringing tears to my eyes.

"A huge part of me," she nearly growled, "wants to march up to Noah Sanchez on Monday morning and slap the *crap* out of him."

I choked on a laugh at that fantastic mental picture.

"But," she more calmly continued, "I have to be honest."

And a huge part of me was beginning to despise that word.

"I understand where he's coming from."

I sniffed, peeked at her, and found her expression had changed into sadness. And fear?

"None of us know what's going to happen after graduation." Her eyes dropped to her dog. "Shane and I applied to UCLA." She cracked a smile. "Just like Kassidy, J.R., and Heather. And you know that school got Nicolas for their soccer team."

Yes. Nicolas taking their offer had been *big* news right before winter break.

I managed a small grin. "If all of you get into UCLA, it'll be a mini P.A. reunion."

She huffed. "The big word there is *if*. But that's the only school Shane and I both applied to. And his first choice is UCLA, but" —she lifted her shoulders— "he could end up at Cal State Long Beach or Monterey Bay."

Because his path was marine biology, and he'd applied to the California schools with the best programs.

"It sounds like Meg and Owen will definitely be going to different schools." She bit her lower lip and looked at me, fear and sorrow consuming her eyes. "Lexi, I can't imagine not seeing Shane every day."

And he had to feel the same way about her.

"That has to be how *everyone* else is feeling right now, too." Her lower lip quivered. "I also can't even imagine what Maddie and Liam are feeling," she added under her breath. She adjusted Chloe to fully face me, then rapidly blinked away her tears. "Sorry. We're talking about you and Noah. My point is, I get it. No matter where all of us end up, he *has* to stay here for another year." She cringed. "Of course he probably feels like he'd be holding you back."

"And I get all of that," I whined. "Honestly. But he made the decision for me. And us. That's not fair, and I hate that he's assuming the worst will happen." I glanced at her. "*I* don't even know where I'm going to end up after graduation. I told him that, too."

She frowned. "But your parents are making you go to Berkeley."

I threw the tissue box, and it bounced off a table and ended right side up.

Natalie's eyes flitted to the box, to me, and back to the box. "So maybe now would be a good time to talk about your parents? And they know you're here, right?"

"I texted them before you picked me up." I'd also received nothing more than "Okay" responses. I crossed my arms and slumped into the couch cushions. "They're doing what they should've done *forever* ago. What more is there to say?"

She started to rub Chloe's ears. "The fact you're not sounding or acting like the Lexi Pfeiffer I've known since our *first* Anti-Love Club meeting, tells me all their nastiness and pressure on you has finally caught your attention. And you've had enough." She unleashed her wicked smile. "Which is so fucking awesome."

I laughed, which made her laugh.

Yes. That's exactly how I felt at this moment.

"Lexi, you're eighteen. Are they really going to disown you if you don't go to Berkeley?" She rolled her eyes. "And from what you've told me, and I've seen, they don't have a right to tell you what to do. Go to Berkeley and be like *them*?" She made a sour face. "That's total crap."

I rolled my head in her direction and sent her an affectionate smile.

She'd just said, but in her own, Natalie way, what Noah had earlier today.

You should rebel. Break the effing rules. Just like these badass rock guitarists did.

But my smile vanished at the irony of him giving me advice *he* couldn't follow. In fact, Noah Luis Sanchez was a phony coward. And I was stuck being around him at school during the day *and* for the musical rehearsals—my eyes widened. In the flurry of my anger and humiliation over his rejection, I'd completely spaced our extra Saturday rehearsals.

I released the second longest, whiniest moan of my teen life.

"What was *that* for?"

I squeezed my eyes shut. "I've been helping him on Saturdays?"

"Oh, shit," she muttered. "*That.*"

I opened my eyes. "Nat, what am I going to do? I don't think I can be around him like that anymore." At this particular moment, I didn't *want* to, either.

"Does he still need the extra help? From what I've heard from Shane and Liam, and everyone else, it sounds like he's been killing the tap dancing."

Yes. He had been "killing" the dancing in the "Slap That Bass" number. But we still had the *big*, "I Got Rhythm" number ahead of us. And I told her as much.

She reached out and grasped my hand. "Maybe he'll catch on faster now?"

"Maybe," I said on a sigh. *But probably not.* The "I Got Rhythm" number was also the longest dance number in the musical.

She squeezed my hand. "*This* Lexi sitting beside me will figure it out." Her wicked smile came back. "And I have a feeling she won't be super nice." She laughed. "Dress like you did that first day we rehearsed for the lip sync competition. And don't forget your whistle."

We laughed for several seconds, then I asked, "Become *Sergeant* Lexi?"

She continued to laugh and nodded. "Noah won't know what hit him." She paused, then said, "Just like *we* didn't that day."

Yes. I could do that. And it's not like Noah hadn't already seen bits of that Lexi Pfeiffer.

"I know your parents separating and saying they're getting a divorce wasn't a huge surprise," she softly stated. "But I'm here if you need me." She angled her head left to catch my eyes. "Lexi, you can't hold everything inside of you. *Trust me,*" she added. "Or you'll explode again like you did when you called me."

I returned her warm smile. "Thank you for..." I didn't even know where to begin.

"Do *not* thank me."

I pressed my lips together and mimed zipping them shut.

"Good. Now, what do you want to binge watch on Netflix? *Riverdale?*"

It *was* one of my favorite shows. But in the spirit of the Anti-Love Club that we'd lost April of last year, and being rejected by the boy I wanted to be all mine, I was in the mood for a certain movie. I sat up and said, "How about *John Tucker Must Die*?" Also known as the movie we'd watched as an early club activity. That felt like a million and one years ago.

She giggled. "I'm liking where your head is at right now. And if we can't get it on Netflix, I'll find it on Amazon." She nudged Chloe off her lap, scooted off the couch, and darted for their massive entertainment system and equally enormous T.V. straight ahead.

Chloe settled herself right against me, and I rubbed her head.

Natalie was right. *This* Lexi could handle her parents divorcing, and facing and dealing with Noah. And I would do it without any more phony, bright smiles. Just *honesty* from this point moving forward. I then mentally shoved *him* behind the "friend" door and turned the bolt.

* * *

I opened my locker and sighed. All around me kids were doing the same thing. Getting ready for yet another *wonderful* day of high school. Above the rattling of locker doors being opened or slammed shut, laughter and various conversations surrounded me.

"How was the party?"

"Cool. Until you know who showed up."

"Then I'm so glad we didn't go. Adam and I had my house all *to ourselves." Giggle.*

I rolled my eyes.

Blah, blah, blah...Shut. Up.

I frowned.

Not only had Noah's badass rock music gotten into my blood, he had, too. Because at some point the last few weeks, I'd started thinking and talking Just. Like—I quietly moaned.

How was I going to get him out of my blood? And head?

I opened my backpack, yanked out a notebook, and shoved it into my locker.

Stop listening to the rock music? It would probably help. But could I do something that drastic? It had turned into a bit of an addiction. And a connection into his musician's soul. Which meant I did need to stop. Start listening to alternative rock again. Or pop music. Yes. Music Noah hated. But not Shawn Mendes, because that would make me think of us dancing to—*no*.

I vigorously shook my head. Then, from the corner of my eye, I spotted Henry walking down the hallway with Isabel and Curtis. And their death glares caused me to freeze. Henry, on the other hand, didn't even bother glancing my way.

Yes. Just call me Lucifer. *Alexis Lucifer Pfeiffer*. It did have nice alliteration.

They walked by, and I released a breath I hadn't known I was holding inside of me. But I lost my breath at the sight of another boy heading Right. For me.

I faced my locker, and began straightening my books and notebooks.

What could he possibly want after demolishing a chance with me? A chance for us? Yes. He'd made perfectly valid points, and I'd owned that Saturday night with him and Natalie. But it didn't change the fact he was a Big. Fat—oh, my *goodness*.

Noah stopped close to my left side, but I remained focused on my idiotic task.

"Hey," he mumbled. "Can we talk?"

I started to give him my phony, bright smile, but smashed my lips together. I then withdrew a notebook and said, "We *kind've* have somewhere to be right now? Like first period?"

He sighed. "Fine. Then at lunch?" He cleared his throat. "Just you and me?"

I halted, blinked twice, and glanced at him.

He, of course, was giving me that stare of his, but with a touch of making me feel like we were the only ones in the hallway. Or on this planet, for that matter.

But I raised my chin and said, "I'm busy." I paused, then added with complete *honesty*, "I also don't want to talk to you." *Because you didn't have the courage to "Jump" with me.*

Hurt and guilt landed in his eyes, and his shoulders slumped.

I zipped my backpack close and shrugged into the straps.

"Okay," he muttered. "I deserved that. But I also had a feeling you'd say something like that. So this is for you." He held out a white piece of paper folded several times.

I stared at what had to be a note. Not knowing what else to do, I slowly withdrew it from his fingers.

"I hope you read it." He moved around me while I kept my eyes trained on his note.

What was this about? What more was there for him to say? *I'm sorry I'm a Big. Fat. Coward*—I shoved his note into my sweater pocket and closed my locker door.

I had more important things to focus on right now. Like getting to my first class.

Just getting through this *day* and rehearsal later.

Chapter Twenty-One

Maddie's pretty and powerful soprano voice filled the auditorium as she stood alone on the stage while singing "Someone to Watch Over Me."

Aunt Daphne and I sat several rows behind most of the cast in the house's center section.

Mrs. Chaplin had surprised everyone today when she announced she wanted to focus on rehearsing the smaller singing and dance numbers; no "Slap That Bass" today. She'd also told my aunt she didn't feel the cast was "quite ready for the 'I Got Rhythm' number."

Totally fine with me, too. Because I wasn't *quite* in the mood to deal with the chaos that would take over the stage from starting to rehearse that huge number. But I also didn't like having to sit here and listen to Maddie-Polly singing her heart out about wanting a super-special boy who would "watch over her." In fact, I wasn't in the mood for sappy Gershwin music at all.

Loud, alternative rock was calling my name for the first time since—*no.*

I dragged my eyes to my lap, sighed, and began to play with the hem of my shirt.

When would this song be over? But more *romantic* Gershwin would follow.

Yuck times ten.

My aunt leaned toward me. "I'd like to talk to you while I have the chance," she whispered. She stood and pointed to the back of the auditorium.

I mentally moaned. Because I knew what she wanted to talk about, and it was a topic I'd managed to keep far from my mind since Natalie dropped me off at my house Sunday afternoon.

I sluggishly lifted myself from the seat and followed her through the auditorium doors.

Once we were in the lobby, she faced me. And subjected me to a concerned frown.

"Sweetie, I'm worried about you," she stated. "Your text back to me on Sunday didn't sound at all like you." She tilted her head right. "And it's clear by your distance and mood today, what happened with your parents on Saturday is affecting you."

Among other things.

I crossed my arms. "Aunt Daphne, none of that was a surprise." Though I'd spent the rest of my Sunday afternoon and evening closed up in my bedroom, trying not to picture my dad's empty closet. While my mom, of course, was *working*. "I don't want to talk about this!" I snapped. "Especially right now."

With round eyes, she angled her head back.

I was sick of people looking so shocked by my snarky attitude, too. Where had being oh-so sweet and positive Lexi Pfeiffer gotten me? Nowhere. Just like stupid courage.

"The only thing that's changed in that *miserable* house," I continued, "is that I don't have to hear them fighting anymore. Not that they've actually been around *to* fight," I muttered under my breath. I lifted my chin. "It's better this way. For everyone." Yes, I'd quoted *him* almost exactly. But maybe, just maybe, he'd been right when he'd said that about *us*.

I went around her and said, "I'm going back inside."

"No. You're not."

I spun toward her and halted at the sight of her grave, still concerned expression.

"Lexi, you're angry," she calmly said. "And you have every right to be, considering what you've had to experience in that house. Including their selfishness and stupidity," she muttered. "Because you're right. The decisions they made and announced Saturday weren't surprising, and should've happened a lot sooner." She stepped toward me. "They should've made that choice sooner for *you*, first and foremost."

Moisture, once again, filled my eyes. From her kind, affectionate, loving words. And guilt from snapping at her for no reason. She was the last person on this planet who deserved the nastiness I couldn't seem to contain. Then again, I wasn't trying very hard, either.

"I want you to go home."

I froze, blinked twice, then my mouth fell open. "I'm sorry I snapped at you, but—"

"Go home and allow yourself to feel whatever it is you need to feel right now."

I clenched my teeth. "That's *not* what I want to do."

"But it's what you and this musical need." Her mouth formed a firm line. "I—we—need my niece. The one who loves dancing, is full of positivity and encouragement, and wants to be here." She released a sad sigh. "I've been watching you since rehearsal began and you're radiating antagonism. And your friends—the cast—is picking up on it."

Her words pricked every part of me. As if I'd fallen into a

bed of needles. But I shrugged. "I'm having a bad day. And why is *everyone* on this planet allowed to have a bad day but me?"

She paused, then said, "Please go home. Call Natalie. Talk to her. Or call Henry—"

"We're not together anymore."

She frowned. "When did that happen?"

"It doesn't matter." I stepped backward. "Guess I'll go get my backpack now."

"Lexi, you're not being punished."

"Well, it feels like it." I smirked. "When am I *allowed* to come back?"

She narrowed her eyes. "When you're my niece again."

The hurt and sadness in her words shrouded me as she walked back into the auditorium.

I took a shaky breath to control yet another powerful wave of misery making my shoulders wilt from the pressure.

"Breathe (In the Air)."

Yes. I could do that. I'd breathe when I darted back inside to get my backpack. I'd breathe as I forced myself to walk to my dark, silent, broken home. I'd breathe when I got there and as I headed up to my room. To my sanctuary where I could count on Coda to greet me.

I could follow the wise words of Pink Floyd without shedding a tear over my rotten life.

* * *

I leaned toward Coda's cage and said, "I *hate* Noah."

"Noah's so stupid."

"Yes," I replied around my triumphant smile. "But I also *hate* Noah."

Coda stared me.

"You can say it. Really. I *hate* Noah."

He shook his head.

"Then let's try, Noah's a big, *fat* coward." *And stupid.*

He tapped his toy bell with his beak.

"Coda," I whined. "Come on. I *hate* Noah."

"*Noah's so stupid.*" And he tapped his bell once more.

I moaned. "Fine. Be that way. But I do hope you remember *all* of this." I gave him my back, marched toward my bed, and threw myself down.

I glared at the ceiling, and my phone buzzed. I picked it up and read the screen.

Natalie had written, *Are you okay? Shane just texted you left rehearsal. Everyone's confused and worried. Including Noah.*

I sighed and typed, *My aunt sent me home because of my bad attitude. Not sure when I'll be back to work on the musical.* I then hit send and somehow stopped myself from hurling my phone across the room. Unlike the tissue box, it wouldn't survive that kind of treatment.

I frowned.

What now? No more Noah. No more musical. No more rock music lessons. No rock music at all, if I could help it. Mom was hiding at work. Dad was officially gone, so no more fighting. Which was a good thing. But the stillness of this broken house seemed more intense than their fighting. I'd also failed miserably at teaching my parrot to say nasty things about a boy I didn't actually hate. But it had felt somewhat liberating saying those things.

I'm out with my parents, but I can call you when I get home.

I cracked a smile. I loved Natalie's support. At the same time, I didn't feel like talking. I wasn't even certain what I'd say that she hadn't already heard. So I texted, *I love you for saying that. But let's talk later?* I added the pink hearts emoji and tapped send.

Her first message had said, *Everyone's confused and worried. Including Noah.*

I reached into my sweater pocket and withdrew his note. That I still hadn't read. I'd left it in my pocket all day; it's weight feeling equal to my phone.

I stared at the folded piece of paper, again wondering what he could have possibly written. It couldn't be another lesson. I'd made my feelings clear on that topic. Curiosity had caused me to *almost* open it twice today. But humiliation and rejection had swooped in, pummeled curiosity, and I'd shoved the note back into my pocket.

Okay. Call if you need me.

I dropped the note to text, *I promise I will.*

Actually, what I really wanted at this moment was to shut out the world.

I turned off my phone and dropped it on the floor. But now I couldn't use it as an escape, on top of everything else I'd recently lost. Which was probably a good thing, since that's where my collection of badass rock music existed. Song after amazing song. So many I'd lost count. Songs he'd specifically led me to, because he *did* want to be with me. Or did he?

I rolled onto my side and hugged the pillow.

What kind of boy pushes away a girl who wants to be with him? A girl who was willing to "Jump" because that's what people did in life. And love. People who want to truly live take chances. They don't hide behind walls and...miserable marriages.

I tightened my arms around the pillow.

Aunt Daphne, who'd rightfully sent me home, thought I was angry about them separating and divorcing. But what was truly upsetting me was the fact they'd settled for misery for so long and kept me in the middle of it. No one deserved to be that unhappy. Especially when it came to family and love. Their decisions *were* best for everyone. And maybe, just maybe, they'd find happiness again. Like they'd been years ago, before hatred had appeared and settled in for a long stay. And Noah—I shook my head.

I did understand his fears, but there were never any guarantees in life. That's why it was called taking changes. *Jumping*. And what about him meeting another *girl*?

I narrowed my eyes.

He'd conveniently not brought up that very real possibility. He wore tall, dark, mysterious, *hot* musician extremely well. In fact, I couldn't believe all the single girls at P.A. weren't throwing themselves at him on a daily basis. I guess he could be considered a *little* intimidating. But I'd seen numerous glimpses of the Noah *not* hiding behind his wall.

He loved all of his friends and was fiercely loyal. He loved and respected his family; his parents' tough jobs. I'm sure he even loved Beelzebub and Lucifer, though he'd never admit it. He was also funny, in a dry sort of way. Charming, too. When he wanted to be. And so ridiculously hot when he talked about guitar playing and badass rock music.

I squeezed my eyes shut.

And, most importantly, the hardest worker I'd ever met. Not just because he had to; he'd long ago made that choice. So why did he hide behind his wall? It didn't make any sense, since he *was* amazing. And I just knew we would have been— oh, my *goodness*.

I needed to stop. Focus on something else, like homework. Specifically my research paper that I still hadn't started. But Mr. Washburn had approved my topic change.

I opened my eyes and sat up.

No more sketching *him* while listening to rock music, either. It was time to lose myself in my new research topic. A topic I wanted to learn more about.

Chapter Twenty-Two

My door opened, and I jumped.

"Sorry," Mom said. "What are you still doing up? It's almost 11:00." She then made it a point to look directly at Coda's cage I had long since covered. To no doubt make sure she didn't have to see or hear him.

I slid my eyes to my computer's clock, and *wow*. I'd been so successful at getting lost in my research paper, the time hadn't once registered.

"I'm working on my paper. For Mr. Washburn's class?" In that moment, the late hour fully hit, and I faced her with my own frown. "Where have you been?"

She narrowed her eyes at my tone that had sounded more than a little accusatory. "With Daphne. We met up for dinner. Which reminds me," she continued, glancing at my desk, then bed, "where's your phone? I texted you a couple times. And called twice, but it went right to your voicemail."

Yes. Right. My phone.

"I turned it off earlier. It's over there by my bed." I thumbed behind me. "I wanted to concentrate on my paper." *Not a complete lie.*

She opened the door a bit more. "Since you're still up, we can talk about what happened between you and your aunt."

I somehow stopped myself from rolling my eyes.

Of course Aunt Daphne had felt it necessary to call my mom about my bad attitude and asking—more like telling—me to go home. And to not come back until I "was her niece again." But I deserved it. Especially after my snottiness she *hadn't* deserved.

"Alexis, you're overwhelmed right now," Mom stated. "Daphne understands your dad and I must have caught you by surprise on Saturday."

I pressed my lips together and focused on my computer screen.

"He and I have agreed to make everything as seamless as possible, so it doesn't affect you *and* school."

Because, no matter what, school comes first, Alexis Evelyn Pfeiffer.

"But your grades have already slipped since you took on helping with that musical."

I whipped my head in her direction. "My grades are *fine*." I crossed my arms. "I just stopped doing the extra credit." And some homework here and there. Because I'd been way more interested in listening to rock music while working on my sketch of *him*.

She sighed. "Why would you do that? You've always done the extra credit. Until you started working—"

"I have A's in all of my *honors* classes!" I snapped. "I don't need the extra credit."

She straightened and punished me with her hard, "mom" stare. "If this is how you were talking to your aunt earlier, then it's good she sent you home."

I gritted my teeth and looked away.

"Which leads me to, I told her I felt it would be best if you didn't return to the show."

I glared at my lap as I began trembling from White. Hot. Rage. My face began to burn, followed by ringing in my ears. I couldn't remember a time I'd ever been this angry with anyone in my life. Even the anger and hurt from Noah's rejection hadn't come close to what I felt for my mom at this particular moment in time.

"I know if your dad were standing here, he'd agree with me."

But he wasn't. And why should I care about what *either* of you think or want?

"School has and always will come first, Alexis."

I smirked.

"I want to see those grades go back up to where they were a month ago. And though I think it's very encouraging that you're still working on your paper at this hour, you need to go to bed. I don't want you missing anymore school." She stepped into the hallway and soundly closed the door behind her.

I pictured myself leaning toward Coda's cage and saying, "I *hate* my mother." Or more accurately, "I *hate* my parents."

What did they want from me? Blood, sweat, and tears in my schoolwork, served to them on a shiny platter of perfection with a side of extra credit?

I lifted my eyes to my paper, filling the computer screen. A huge, important assignment that would probably be close to perfect by the time I turned it in, because I'd connected so strongly with the topic. Which made me think of Noah and the fact focusing so hard on my paper had caused the hurt from his rejection to ease into empathy.

Maybe it was time for me to read his note? Curiosity was making a powerful comeback. Especially after spending all this time "with him" via my research topic.

I pushed back my desk chair and stood.

Within seconds, and with shaky fingers, I unfolded his note. That he'd typed.

Dear Lexi,

I went after you. It took me about a minute after you left my room for me to realize I was being the <u>dumbest</u> asshole. Ever. I put my shoes on as fast as I could, and I thought for sure I'd catch up with you. But you must've developed super-human running skills, because you were nowhere in sight.

After you read this, please text or call me? Because I really want to "Jump" with you.

Noah

I froze, blinked twice, then re-read his note—three times—and my mouth inched open.

He'd *gone after me?* Really? And I'd missed him coming after me?

My brain rewound to that moment when I'd burst from his building. I'd gone left, stopped, decided to call Natalie, then I'd—oh, my *goodness*. He hadn't caught or seen me because I went right. Toward school. Because I hadn't wanted to go home. But he wouldn't have seen me at the school, since I'd waited for Natalie *across* the street. She'd been coming from Nob Hill, so I'd decided to wait there so she wouldn't have to deal with turning around to pick me up right in front of the school. And now known as a *huge* mistake.

The amazing boy I wanted, and who wanted me, had actually come after me.

I cringed as yet another memory filled my head. *This* was obviously what he'd wanted to talk to me about this morning. And I, lost in my hurt and rejection, had blown him off.

I released a quiet moan and practically dove for where I'd dropped my phone.

Once it was on, I went right to our texting thread I hadn't deleted.

Maybe, just maybe, he was still up? Because of the late hour, I didn't feel comfortable calling him; sending him a message would have to do for now.

I paused to think about what to type as different emotions whirled through me.

A little guilt for not giving him a chance, mixed with shock at the fact he'd *gone after me*, mixed with excitement that he was willing to take a chance; he was willing to "Jump."

I took a quick breath and tapped out, *Meet me in the library at lunch tomorrow?*

Everything I needed and wanted to say to him, and probably vice versa, would have to wait until we were face-to-face. Or side-by-side? An even better thought.

My phone buzzed with his response, and I smiled.

Done. I'll see you then. He'd even added two smiling emojis.

I pressed my phone to my chest and shivered. From anticipation and excitement.

My mom had told me to go to bed, but adrenaline pulsed inside of me, and the last thing I wanted to do was sleep. Nope. Not this *good girl*. And did that girl even exist anymore?

I went back to my desk, reached right, and shut off my desk lamp. The computer screen gave off more than enough light for me to see the keyboard.

Smiling like Lucifer the cat in *Cinderella*, I sat and continued *working*.

* * *

"Hi."

I managed to smile at Noah through my full-body yawn that had distracted me from keeping an eye out for him.

He gave me his lopsided grin that was a tad blurry due to my tired eyes.

"It's nice to see you, too," he teased as he set his lunch bag on the table.

"Sorry," I murmured while he sat in the chair across from me. "Not the way I'd planned to say hello. But I was up until almost 2:00, working on my research paper for Washburn's class." I lifted my shoulders. "I didn't feel like going to bed after I...read your note. And texted you." The adrenaline rush had lasted until I'd written half my paper that would be a little over ten pages when I finished; the curse of taking honors classes.

He slowly nodded. "That would explain why you texted me so late." Concern consumed his eyes and face. "You look wiped out." He hesitated, then added, "Thanks for reading my note." He ran a hand through his hair. "By the time I got home from rehearsal, I'd convinced myself you were *never* going to read it. Or had tossed it into the garbage."

"No," I slowly said, "but I'll be honest. I wasn't sure I was going to read it, either." I tried on a soft smile. "It was perfect, too. Thank you."

Our eyes locked.

"I missed you yesterday," he quietly continued. "And *everyone* missed you at rehearsal."

I mentally wrapped myself up in his words and hugged them to me.

His face transitioned into confusion. "What happened? I wanted to text you after you vanished, but" —he cleared his throat— "didn't want to push. So I asked your aunt what happened to you." Panic joined his confusion. "All she said was that you weren't feeling like yourself, went home, and *wasn't sure* when you'd be back to work on the show."

Yes. That sounded about right. And I still had to figure all that out. Somehow.

"This is going to make me sound like a selfish asshole—which is nothing new, I know—but I can't do this musical without you." We stared at one another. "Your aunt's a great teacher. Really. But she isn't *you*. And I'm not the only one who feels that way." He leaned forward. "Will you *please* tell me what happened yesterday at rehearsal?"

I tightly folded my hands and rested them on my lap.

All he wanted, per his usual, was the truth. And there was now absolutely no reason for me to shut him out. "Okay," I said on a breath. "My aunt, and rightfully, sent me home yesterday, because of my...pretty bad attitude. Which I'm sure you and everyone else noticed."

Sadness filled his dark, penetrating eyes. "Because of me."

I shrugged. "Yes. But also no." I paused, then added, "My aunt was worried about me, since...my parents told me on Saturday that my dad was moving out. And that they're getting a divorce." Now he knew everything, and my shoulders —my soul—seemed so much lighter.

His eyes became round as his mouth formed an oh.

Silence, outside of some nearby whispering, settled between us.

Shaking his head, he sat back in his chair. "So *that's* the reason you came to my place. And why you were acting...well, not like you." He huffed. "I really am an asshole."

He appeared and sounded so guilty, I had to continue being honest. "Actually, I made the decision to go to your place about *that* before they told me." His eyes wandered back to mine. "They caught me as I was leaving."

We held our stare.

The emotions swirling through his eyes mesmerized me.

Shock. Concern. Sadness. And not just a little affection.

My heart hammered my chest, forcing me to take a shaky breath.

"I'm thinking," he said, still holding our stare, "when you came over, you probably should've started with what had happened with your parents." He frowned. "You were kind've scaring me. The way you were laughing? And talking about that cat from *Cinderella*?"

I fought a smile at the fact I'd definitely sounded insane.

His frown deepened. "Lexi, I really wish you would've told me."

I sighed. "That's not why I was there." He unleashed his trying-to-read-my-soul stare, which made me ask, "Why didn't you call? After you couldn't find me?"

He raised his eyebrows, clearly *his* version of the are-you-kidding-me look.

My face burned as I murmured, "Dumb question. And the reason you couldn't find me is that I didn't want to go home. So Natalie came and picked me up *across* the street from school."

He nodded once. "Right. I get it."

Silence again descended, which was strange, considering what he'd written in his note. Also known as why he was sitting across from me.

Timing hadn't worked for us Saturday night. But what if it had?

"Here's a better question. What if you had caught me?" I started twirling a lock of hair around my finger. "What were you going to say?"

His face turned that spectacular, yet *kind of* adorable shade of tomato red. "I was going to apologize for being the *dumbest* asshole ever. Then I was going to ask you to go on a date. For that night," he swiftly added.

My shoulders fell.

Oh, my *goodness*.

"And if I'd stopped listening to my head while you were asking me to *'Jump'* with you, we would've gone out, and I know you would've told me what happened with your parents."

I suppressed a moan as I leaned forward. "I don't want to talk about that or them. *Please*?" I wanted to talk about much happier things. Like us. And the date he'd had on his mind.

"Lexi, no matter what you say," he softly persisted, "you have to be in some sort've shock about your parents. I hate to say this, too, but it sounds like your aunt sent you home yesterday for good reasons." He released a long, slow sigh. "But you win." He gave me an affectionate smile. "When you're ready to talk about all of that, I promise I'm a good listener."

There he was; the Noah Luis Sanchez who *could* step out from behind his wall. The same Noah who'd chased after me. And danced with me to a cutesy Shawn Mendes song. And worked so hard at everything, including being Pete, the tap dancing cowboy from Deadrock, Nevada. And made guitar playing look so easy. And let me get close to him through badass rock music.

I could only hope the Noah sitting across from me would stay outside his wall. With me.

"Thank you," I finally replied.

The corner of his mouth lifted into his *pretty* adorable shy smile. "So, Alexis Evelyn Pfeiffer, will you go out with me this Saturday night? We can do anything you want."

Every part of me began tingling as I smothered a series of giggles. At the same time, a part of me couldn't believe this was *finally* happening.

"Yes, Noah Luis Sanchez," I said around my goofy smile I couldn't stop. "I would love to go out with you Saturday night."

We burst into ridiculous laughter, and were quickly shushed by a girl sitting a table away.

He opened his lunch bag and said, "Tell me about your paper. What's your topic?"

My breath became lodged in my throat at his question. Then I felt my face become that spectacular shade of tomato red.

He glanced at me and grinned. "Whoa. What are you writing about over there?"

If I hadn't been so embarrassed, I probably would've turned into a puddle at the way he lowered his voice and asked his question.

"Lexi?"

"You." I flinched. "Well, sort've you." I sighed. "I'm writing about dyslexia."

His eyes became round.

"I wanted to know more about it, so I chose it as my topic." He didn't need to know I'd originally had a completely different topic chosen.

His surprise gradually eased into something resembling awe. And affection.

"That's really cool." He smiled. "Sounds like you could teach me a few things."

I huffed. "I doubt it. And you're not mad?" He was extremely private.

"No. I'm...flattered." He focused on his lunch bag. "And I'm being serious. What have you learned?"

I hesitated, but his interest seemed so genuine, I launched into what I'd discovered. While savoring the fact he was right *here*; right where I wanted and needed him.

Chapter Twenty-Three

I *think we should skip rehearsal today and go right to our date.*

Laughter bubbled out of me as my dad parallel parked his car.

I did *love* that idea, but I typed, *Tempting. But be at the studio at 11. Don't be late.*

We'd decided Nicolas and I would keep up the extra rehearsals, even though my future with helping on the musical was still unclear. And not because Aunt Daphne wouldn't want me to come back. But there was a chance she'd resist due to my mom's interference. My aunt could definitely be a rebel, but when it came to this situation, she might stay loyal to her older sister out of respect and as a way to keep the peace.

I've never been late to your classes, Miss Pfeiffer.

Grinning like a giddy moron, I shook my head.

No. If anything, he'd been early.

Very true, Mr. Sanchez. I'll see you soon! And I added the smiling emoji.

Dad turned off the car. "Alexis, we're here. Please put your phone away."

A tiny sigh escaped, but I closed out of text messaging and shoved my phone in my hoodie's front pocket.

Time for that quality Dad and daughter breakfast he'd forced me into last night during our tense, but quick, call. Funny that *now* he wanted to actually spend time with me.

Several minutes later we were at a table by the window in the cozy cafe in the heart of Pacific Heights, and had already placed our orders. The place was buzzing with the Saturday morning breakfast busyness; the air saturated and thick with cooking bacon and brewing coffee.

The silence between us was louder than the chatter going on around us. At the back of the cafe, a little kid's fussiness rose above the boisterous conversations.

Yes. I feel your pain.

I started spinning my full water glass, then concentrated on the condensation forming on the outside. This Dad and daughter time ranking up there with watching paint dry. Or watching condensation slide down a glass of ice water.

"How's school?" Dad finally asked.

"Fine."

"Your grades have slipped."

I subtly rolled my eyes.

"But it sounds like your mom's on top of it. I agree with what she told your aunt, too."

Of course he did, because—

"School comes first, Alexis."

I smirked. At the same time, I wanted to release a round of hysterical laughter. Couldn't they come up with anything original? Or better? Something like, *School's important, and we only want you to be successful. And happy. Because we love you.*

In fact, I couldn't remember the last time they'd said those three little words to me.

"Were you texting Henry just now?"

I sighed. "No. We broke up."

I wasn't certain if I'd ever hear them say it again, either. Their crummy jobs and hatred for each other seemed to have hardened their hearts. And souls.

"I'm sorry to hear that." Dad picked up his water glass and took a drink. "He seemed like a good, solid kid. What happened?"

I sat back. "He's into Marvel and superheroes, and I *hate* all of that."

Marvel versus DC Comics? I. Don't. Care. And thank you, Noah, for articulating that so perfectly. I then fought a smile at the memory.

Dad nodded once. "Okay. Then who were you texting? Must be someone you really like."

Oh, you have no idea. I wasn't certain I wanted to talk about Noah with my dad, but I guess it was better than sitting across from him in excruciating silence.

I peered at him. "His name's Noah. The boy I've been helping Saturday mornings?"

"Sounds familiar." He set his glass down. "Where's he going to college next year?"

I paused, debating how far I should really go with this. Then again, if Noah and I ended up being totally awesome as a couple—and I had a feeling that's exactly what *would* happen —my parents would want to meet him. Though clearly not at the same time.

"Actually," I slowly began, "he's a junior." But I would never give up his confidence and trust by saying anything more than that. It was also none of my dad's business.

"Oh." He frowned. "I don't think it's a good idea for you to get involved with a boy who's a year behind you. Your future is in Berkeley."

I swallowed a growl before I said, "Noah's an amazing boy. He's smart and the hardest worker I've ever met in my life. He's also a complete gentleman. And an Awesome. Guitar player." I crossed my arms. "I don't care that he's a year behind me. He's worth it."

Dad's face tightened with irritation and frustration. "A guitar player. And he probably wants to be a rock star when he grows up. *If* he grows up," he harshly added.

Hot fury raged through me so swiftly my vision blurred for several seconds. But then I leaned forward and snapped, "Dad, you don't even know him! And you're judging him based on the fact he's a musician?" I didn't know what Noah had planned for his future. He didn't seem to know, either. But if he did want to be a "rock star," that was *his* dream. That no one, especially my snobby, uptight dad, could take away from him.

Dad exhaled though his teeth. "Alexis, you're a beautiful, *smart* young woman who's going to meet so many kids at Berkeley, including boys, who are on the same path as you." He sighed. "The last thing a dad wants his college-bound daughter to do is get involved with some boy who's a musician and is a year younger than her." He stared at me. "You're better than that."

His harsh, blunt words, that reminded me of what Noah had initially said to me Saturday, fueled my rage. I began to tremble; the same trembling I'd experienced when my mom had declared I wasn't to go back to the musical. And all I wanted was to run from here. As if I had developed super-human running skills. I knew exactly where I'd run, too.

When was the last time I'd put on my pointe shoes and danced my effing heart out?

"We need to talk about something else," he said, leaning back as the waitress delivered his coffee. Once she left, he tried to smile. "I have some good news."

I narrowed my eyes.

And I. Don't. Care. I also now had every intention of taking Noah up on his suggestion of cancelling the rehearsal and starting our date early. I just needed a minute to text him and Nicolas the change of plans. And fit in giving myself some quality alone time with my pointe shoes.

"I was offered a partnership at another law firm yesterday afternoon."

I continued staring at him, while imagining slipping on my pink, satin—

"But the firm's in Chicago."

I halted, then blinked twice.

"I went to law school with one of the senior partners, and he's been after me for a while," he easily continued. "The timing was never right. But now that your mom and I have decided it would be best for us to move on, and with you grad-uating soon, I took the offer."

I squinted at him as my head began to buzz. I didn't particularly like my dad right now, but had he just announced *he's moving to Chicago*?

"Your mom and I have discussed it, too, and she's being supportive."

My mouth opened and I said, "You're moving to Chica-go." Also known as more than halfway across the country. From me. "When?"

He watched me closely for several seconds before saying, "Within the next couple weeks. Because they want me out there so quickly, they're paying for the entire relocation."

In that moment, I realized my dad, who I'd adored when I'd been a silly little daddy's girl, *was* a coward. And selfish. Running off to Chicago, as their divorce barely began, to forget the misery of San Francisco and start over. Another, yet permanent form of escape. While my mom and I—mostly me —were left in that horrible, shattered house.

"I know this is a surprise."

I barely heard his voice while the buzzing in my head amplified. Like I'd put my head in a beehive.

"But I will be back for your graduation."

I swallowed the bile that had risen from my stomach and into my throat. Which meant it was past time for me to leave. And at this precise moment, I didn't care if I *ever* saw him again.

How could he be so incredibly insensitive and selfish? He couldn't even wait until the ink dried on their divorce papers? Or, better yet, wait until I *did* graduate and officially started my own life. Whatever that ended up being.

"I was really hoping," he added with too much excitement, "that after your graduation, you'd come back to Chicago with me for a couple weeks? I plan on getting into an apartment or condo with at least two bedrooms and baths—"

"No," I ground out. "I can't and won't do that."

His eyes widened.

Quivering, I stood and grabbed my backpack purse.

His mouth hardened and he leaned forward. "Alexis, *sit down.*"

I unleashed my death glare. "Like I heard you *yell* at Mom not too long ago, I'm eighteen. I have my own life here in San Francisco." I shrugged into my purse's straps. "I'm not about to lose two weeks of my summer—time with my friends who *love* me—to go to Chicago and be All. Alone." I smirked. "Because you'll be *working.* Like you always do."

He held my hard stare as he sat back. But I saw nothing in his eyes or on his face. It had transformed into a blank mask with deep wrinkles around his mouth and etched into his forehead. That's what misery had done to him and my mom, who looked no better than he did.

No. That would never be me.

"I have somewhere more important to be." I then turned and, with my head held high, I stalked out of the restaurant.

I veered in the direction of my number-one sanctuary,

anger and disappointment in each heavy footstep. That's when I remembered I needed to text Noah. And Nicolas.

I removed my phone from my hoodie's pocket, and my steps wavered when I realized I'd missed a text from Noah.

Good luck with your dad?

Hysterical laughter rippled from me.

I texted Nicolas, *Change of plans. No rehearsal today. I'll see you later.*

For Noah, I wrote, *We are skipping rehearsal. I texted Nicolas. But meet me at the studio in a couple of hours?*

All I wanted at this moment was to lose myself in the one thing I loved most in my life; the one thing my parents could *never* take away from me, no matter how hard they tried.

I raised my chin and continued heading right for the studio.

Chapter Twenty-Four

I ignored the burning in my legs as I completed yet another grand jeté leap, then landed perfectly, paused, and finished with a triple pirouette. The high-energy, pop song continued to blare from my bluetooth speaker while I sucked air into my lungs.

I couldn't remember the last time I'd danced like this. Pushed myself to the point sweat dripped off of me. My body wasn't used to hours of *real* ballet. The kind of ballet that went far beyond warming up. The ballet that was in my blood. But I'd needed to feel the satisfaction of working off the adrenaline from so many sickening emotions and replacing it with something positive. Like endorphins.

I relaxed my posture and swiped my damp forehead.

And I did feel somewhat better. But the endorphin high wouldn't last forever. Anger and resentment and disappointment with my dad *and* mom would return. So would the dread when I thought about having to go back to that horrible house. And my parents' expectations of me. Their *good girl*. Who didn't want to go to UC Berkeley. In fact, I'd *never* cared about going to that school. All I'd ever wanted to do was dance. The kind of all-in dancing I'd been doing since I'd changed into my pink tights, leotard, a black ballet skirt, and my pink pointe shoes. But my parents had stopped my dancing the best they could before my freshman year.

Because they wanted me to go to oh-so wonderful UC Berkeley. Just. Like. Them.

I tightened my hands into fists as rage burned inside of me. Rage so strong my vision blurred from hot tears.

My endorphin high hadn't lasted very long.

I again filled my lungs with air to diffuse the anger and resentment.

"Lexi?"

I turned at the sound of Noah saying my name above the loud music.

He went right for my phone, then silence filled the studio.

I squinted at him through my hazy eyes as my dark emotions eased into relief at the sight of him. "Hi. It's been two hours?" I released a humorless laugh. "It feels like I just got here."

He walked toward me, his face tight with concern. "It's actually almost one. And you texted me around ten."

My eyes widened. "Oh. Wow. Really?" I shook my head.

"Yeah. I can show you the time if you want." He reached for his back jeans pocket, but I grasped his hand.

"No. It's fine." His sharp features began to swirl together as the hot moisture returned with a vengeance. "I'm just glad you're here." And though I'd needed to lose myself in my dancing, which I'd successfully done, every part of me meant those five little words.

"Lexi, what happened with your dad?"

His simple, softly spoken question was all it took for my dam to shatter.

He pulled me into his arms and allowed me to free my emotions into his warm chest. I then sobbed, sniffed, and hiccuped through telling him my cowardly dad's announcement.

Moving to Chicago with barely a backward glance. Moving over halfway across the country where another city waited. With his new life. Far away from me. His only child and former daddy's girl.

Noah gently lowered us to the studio's floor, and I ended up curled in his lap. But now sobbing into his shoulder as I released all the yuck I'd been holding inside for a long time.

"I *hate* that house," I eventually managed to say, then hiccuped. "I *hate* her. And I *really hate* him. He couldn't... wait...a few more months?" I loudly sniffed twice, and Noah tightened his arms around me. "And he...actually said...he wanted me to go back to *Chicago* with him...for two weeks. After graduation." I growled. "Can you...believe that?"

Noah rested his chin on my head. "It's probably his way of trying to include you in his new life."

"Well, I don't want any part of it," I muttered, followed by a noisy sniff. "Especially since...he wasn't happy when I told him...about you." The memory of his ugly judgment reignited fury as I swiped my wet nose.

Noah leaned back to look at me and frowned. "What did you say about me?"

"The *truth*," I declared. I then repeated almost exactly what I'd said about him to my dad.

"Whoa." His face turned that super adorable tomato red. "You made me sound kind've perfect. And I'm far from it."

"I'm not...perfect, either." *And proud of that fact.*

"Nope. But you're pretty close." He paused, then said, "Which is why your dad wouldn't like the idea of you going out with me."

I frowned. "What are you talking about?"

"Hot guitar players like myself," he playfully said, "do have the rep of being bad boys."

I stared at him. "You're *not* a bad boy."

"Just a hot guitar player?"

I rolled my eyes.

Noah Luis Sanchez didn't miss a thing. It wasn't fair. But I sank myself into the fact he was doing the perfect job of lightening the mood. Being there for me the best way possible.

"And who says I'm *not* a bad boy?" Challenge and excitement flashed through his smoldering eyes. "I promise I'll keep taking you places you've never been, Miss Pfeiffer."

I froze, blinked twice, then my head started to hum. I also felt the sudden urge to vigorously fan my face—my entire body—with both hands.

He shot me his devil-worthy grin. "The rock music lessons were only the beginning."

Something about his oh-so yummy, confident words, that grin, and the way he was looking at me made me fully shove aside Alexis Evelyn Pfeiffer, *good girl*, and embrace Lexi. Also known as his Miss Pfeiffer. "Okay," I challenged. "Prove it."

His smile grew. "And it's on. Again."

I, and very reluctantly, started to pull myself out of his lap, but he stopped me.

"Feel like getting the hell out of this city?"

I raised my chin. "Absolutely." And every part of me meant that, too.

We came to our feet.

"I need to call my sister or parents. To borrow a car." His eyes drifted down and up me. "I have to be *honest*. I really like what you're wearing," he admitted with his lopsided grin. "But you'll probably want to change?"

Even though I felt like a sweaty, sticky, bundle of ick, I still shivered at his compliment. And, *wow*. Once Noah let down that wall of his, he was almost unrecognizable. But in a trusting, relaxed, this-is-me, take-it-or-leave-it, incredibly irresistible way.

"Yeah. I'll be right back." I felt his eyes as I strolled out of the studio.

I'd text my mom and tell her I was spending the day with my new boyfriend, Noah. And I grinned at how superbly awesome that sounded in my head.

By now my dad must've called her about what happened at the restaurant.

Alexis Evelyn Pfeiffer, good girls *don't make scenes in public.*

But I was Lexi—or Miss Pfeiffer—who no longer knew the meaning of *good girl.*

I pulled my hair from its tight knot, shook out the long, thick locks, then rolled the passenger-side window down about half-way. And I deeply breathed in the salty sea air.

Weather wise, it wasn't exactly the best day to be on a road trip. The clouds were gray with endless moisture and the temperature hadn't quite reached sixty degrees. But the overcast weather would not ruin our spontaneous trip. I also didn't care one bit I only knew we were headed north. I saw this as getting farther and farther away from the city. My—our—escape.

I slipped off my Vans, brought my legs to my chest, and hugged my knees.

My eyes wandered to Noah, focused on the road, and a soft smile tugged the corners of my mouth. "This was a good idea. Thanks." A thought occurred to me, and I added, "Thanks for giving me so much time at the studio, too."

He shook his head. "Don't thank me for that. It was obvious something big had happened with your dad and you wanted to be alone. I get it." He flashed his lopsided grin. "And don't thank me until the end of the day for the road trip.

Because you don't know what I have planned, Miss Pfeiffer."
He released a low, playful growl.

I giggled. "You don't scare me, Mr. Sanchez."

At that moment, something warm flickered deep within me, then peace and safety shrouded me. *So this is what I'd been missing with Henry and Cam.* What all my girlfriends felt when they were with their boyfriends. And it occurred to me I was already referring to Noah as my boyfriend when I still didn't know nearly enough about him. Since he seemed to have fully walked out from behind his wall, I said, "Can I ask you a personal question?" *Many, in fact.*

"Yeah." He eyed me for a second. "But let's take turns asking each other questions?"

I smiled. "That's fair."

"Cool. Ask away."

I hesitated, then said, "Is your family...religious? I mean, you're *Noah*. Your sister's *Eden*. And you said your mom named her dogs after saints."

He shrugged. "Yes and no. It's mostly my mom now." He rested his head against the headrest. "She and my dad come from big, Catholic families. But my dad kind've pulled away from it a long time ago. I think because of all the *rotten* he's seen in his job," he muttered. "And a few years ago they gave my sister and I a choice, but we've pulled away."

I nodded.

He said, "Okay. Your turn. When did you know your parents weren't going to make it? On Tuesday when we were talking, it seemed like you weren't surprised by the divorce."

"I wasn't." I focused on my toes, inside pink ankle socks. "And I'm not sure. Their *misery* had been building for a long time. But it got really bad my junior year. So maybe then?"

He frowned. "Lexi, I'm sorry. And I kind've get it, because of my dad's job." He sighed. "It's been tough on my family. Especially my mom."

I looked at him, and his *honest* statements made me say, "You don't seem to like his job. Is that why?"

He cringed, then said, "It's not that I don't like it. I'm actually proud of what he does." He paused, and it seemed he was searching for the right words. "My dad started out as a cop in Washington D.C." His eyes briefly found mine. "That's where I'm from. My dad was transferred to the FBI's San Francisco field office."

I smiled, mentally hugging all of this incredible info to my heart and soul.

"When he made detective," he continued, "he decided to pursue *his* dream of joining the FBI. And they wanted him, too." He cracked a smile. "One of the reasons he's so good at his job and undercover work, is that he's fluent in a few languages. The big one being Spanish."

My mouth inched open.

Wow. And I suddenly felt like I was in a T.V. show or movie.

"Ironic, right?" he said with a trace of bitterness. "My dad, the big-time FBI agent who fluently speaks, reads, and writes *three* languages, has a son with dyslexia."

I squeezed my eyes shut as his bitter tone sliced me in half.

Oh, my *goodness*. This also seemed to further explain his carefully guarded Noah Sanchez puzzle pieces. Clearly he saw dyslexia as a huge, embarrassing defect. But from all the research I'd done, he was beyond beating the odds of having a successful future. In fact, him constantly working so hard made his odds of success greater than *a lot* of kids we went to school with who didn't have any learning challenges.

I opened my eyes, reached across the console, and placed my hand over his right one, which gripped the steering wheel. "Your family—your dad—is proud of you. How could they *not* be?"

He tried to smile. "I know that. Really. It's my hang up."

He shook his head. "Anyway, unlike on most T.V. shows and movies, undercover assignments can last for months."

And had to be super scary work. But I kept that thought to myself.

His face darkened. "And during his first, *deep* undercover assignment, my sister and I weren't sure our parents would make it. So I guess what I'm trying to say, is that I kind've get what you're going through."

I frowned. "But they *did* make it."

He huffed. "Yeah. They worked hard at it, though. It didn't happen overnight."

They'd also clearly still loved and respected each other through their dark times, and those two things my parents had lost years ago.

I pushed that thought—them—to the back of my mind. "What are your parents' names?"

He grinned. "I believe it's my turn?"

I rolled my eyes. "Fine. What do you want to know?"

He paused, then asked, "What are *your* parents' names?"

I smiled. "Cheater. Jeff and Denise. Your turn."

"Trey and Veronica. My mom was named after a saint, by the way."

"Ahh," I said around my growing grin, "she sort've continued a tradition with you and your sister. And her dogs," I swiftly added.

"Yep." He relaxed into the driver's seat, obviously relieved we were done talking about his dad's job and the impact of his work on his family's life. "What is it about ballet that you love so much?" He cleared his throat. "I can't *believe* you can dance like that. From what I've seen, you're perfect, too."

My face warmed at how impressed he sounded. "Thanks. And I love it because of the physical and mental stamina it requires." I stared at the console. "When I'm doing ballet, it's impossible to think of anything but the movement. So I get lost." I slid my eyes toward him, and he gave me a soft smile. "Like the way you must get lost in your guitar playing and rock music?"

He laughed. "Sounds like it. I guess we have that in common, too."

"Yeah," I murmured, while sinking myself into the fact he'd also noticed we had more in common than the tap dancing to Gershwin and badass rock music. That thought made me smile and I playfully asked, "When are we going to start up the lessons again, Mr. Sanchez?"

He unleashed his devil-worthy grin.

My insides hummed from the excitement only he ignited.

"You're going through withdrawal, aren't you?"

I lifted my shoulders. "Maybe." But another fact hit me, and I asked, "Noah, when will I get to see and hear you play? For *real*?" Seriously. Why did I have to keep asking that when he loved playing guitar as much as he did?

He glanced my way for a second. "Very soon, Miss Pfeiffer. I *promise*."

I narrowed my eyes. "Fine. But I'm going to remember you said that."

"I know," he mumbled around a quick laugh. "So, what did you *love* about Pink Floyd?"

I straightened. "Oh. Yeah." I guess I had thrown that statement at him last Saturday before I fled his room and building. "I love how different their sound is. Compared to the other bands in your lessons?" I focused on him, and he nodded. "Their music is kind've soothing. Dreamy. But totally cool in their own, rock music way. If that makes any sense?"

He nodded. "Yep. They're my go-to band when I'm doing my homework. Their music helps me concentrate. Especially when I'm reading or writing."

I smiled at having yet another piece of info about him.

He picked up his phone he'd placed in the cup holder and

handed it to me. "Let's call this Lesson Five. Joe Perry from Aerosmith."

I giggled and snatched his phone. "Yay! And that band sounds familiar, too."

He pointed at his phone. "After you plug it in, find the song 'Sweet Emotion'."

"Cool song title. And don't tell me. Totally. Badass. Guitar playing?"

He laughed. "Yeah. But it's also a fucking *badass* song. It's from *Toys in the Attic*. Which we'll listen to after we blast 'Sweet Emotion'." He grinned. "It's that kind've song."

Anticipation and exhilaration shot through me while I did what he asked.

As the song's surprisingly quiet beginning filtered through the speakers, Noah reached for the volume nob and Cranked. It. Up.

Chapter Twenty-Five

"Noah, what are you doing?" I frantically whispered as fear slithered through me.

"Give me a sec. And let me know if anyone sees us."

I quietly moaned, then kept my wide eyes trained on our quiet surroundings. "You know," I mumbled, "when I told you to prove you're a bad boy, I didn't think that would include breaking and entering into a deserted house on Stinson Beach."

"Found it!" he proudly announced.

I turned to find him grinning as he held out a key.

"And breaking and entering?" He cringed. "Bad boy doesn't mean *criminal*. My dad's also an FBI agent?" He huffed. "He'd be the one to throw my ass behind bars if I was caught breaking and entering into a soup can, much less a house."

I sighed. "Fine. You're right. So who's house is this?"

"It belongs to Owen Garrett's family." He swiftly unlocked the door, stepped inside, and went right to the alarm system's box. "Owen couldn't remember exactly where he'd put the key when he left last Saturday with Meg."

I froze, then blinked twice.

That had probably been more info than I needed.

"But he did text me the alarm code," he said, pushing a series of buttons.

The system beeped twice, and Noah released a quick breath.

My eyes drifted over the pretty impressive, two-story *beach* house. "I didn't know you were such good friends with him." Owen qualified as a jock, like his long-time girlfriend Meg, but they sat at our table, being best friends with J.R. and Kassidy.

He shrugged. "We became good friends through J.R. while J.R. and I were in *Romeo and Juliet*. I've been here a couple times with the guys." He smiled and held out his left hand. "Are you brave enough to enter, Miss Pfeiffer?" he asked in his totally *hot*, lowered voice.

I fought a smile as I shook my head.

Oh, my *goodness*. Maybe he really was a bad boy. But that sure didn't stop me from taking his hand and savoring the warmth of his fingers. "Actually," I playfully threw at him, "taking me to an empty house right on Stinson Beach is feeling more *romantic* than bad boy."

He slowly nodded. "I see your point." He fell silent, seeming lost in thought, then pulled me toward him.

Before I knew what was happening, he had me over his shoulder, as if I weighed no more than a pillow, and was closing the door with his free hand. And locking it.

"Noah," I said around my breathless giggles, "this isn't funny."

"This from the girl who's laughing pretty hard."

He strode straight ahead, and I tried to lift my head enough to see our surroundings. But my hair draped my face.

"Where are you going?"

"Just back outside for some fresh air," he answered. With *way* too much innocence.

He opened what sounded like a patio door, then he was striding across the sand.

The ocean waves pounding into each other became closer, and my eyes widened.

He wouldn't dare.

"Noah Luis Sanchez, don't you even think about it."

"Too late."

I squealed right as he stepped into the wet shoreline.

"Your shoes and jeans will get soaked. And what if someone sees you? Us?"

He halted and whipped right, which made my head swing. "No one in sight." He whipped left, and my head swung again, but his time I laughed. "I see someone way down the beach with their dog. So there's *no one* to save you." He eased forward and slightly loosened his grip.

"Dropping me into the Pacific Ocean *doesn't* make you a bad boy," I loudly declared. "It would make you a complete jerk."

He straightened and effortlessly adjusted me until I was cradled in his arms. Though he still hadn't moved from the shoreline; the waves pushing closer to his shoes.

He gave me that stare of his. "Alexis Evelyn Pfeiffer, you have to know I'd *never* do something like that."

I buried my face into his even yummier smelling shoulder covered by a snuggly, black, fleece sweatshirt. "Well, you are a pretty good actor." And him saying my full name made me ask, "Can you do something for me?"

He rested his head on mine. "Anything."

"Can you not call me my full name anymore?"

His body tightened before he raised his head and leaned back, which forced me to look up and into his confusion.

"Yeah. Sure. But you don't like your name?" He cleared

his throat. "It's really pretty. And fits you. That's why I call you that so much."

I gave him a soft smile right as another wave pounded the shore and—he took several steps backward; the water just missing the toes of his black Nikes.

"I do like my name," I admitted, avoiding his eyes. "But my parents are the only ones in my life who call me Alexis. And my mom's the only one who calls me by full name."

He nodded. "Okay. I get it. Done."

"*But* I'm way okay with you calling me Miss Pfeiffer." And there came his delectable, lopsided grin.

"I can do that."

I again snuggled his shoulder.

"So are you hungry? Have you even eaten today?"

"I ate a protein bar before my ballet workout. But I'm not hungry." Which really meant I didn't want *this* to end.

"Alright. I'll ask again later. In the meantime" —he turned and headed back toward the house— "I have an idea."

I smiled into his shoulder, then shivered. And not from the cool, ocean air.

He stopped walking when we were a few feet from the patio of the Garretts' beach house, and lowered me until my shoes touched the sand.

Our eyes locked.

"It seems like you're feeling better," he quietly said.

I gave him a soft smile. "*Much* better." Because of dancing earlier. All this. And him.

He returned my smile, and we stared at one another. The busy ocean now sounded miles and miles away as I stepped toward him.

He lifted his left hand, brushed wisps of my hair aside, and gently cupped my face.

I went up on my tiptoes and angled my head up. He lowered his. Then our mouths fused. And only seconds into our first kiss, I realized exactly what else I'd been missing. But instead of tingles, goosebumps covered my skin beneath my jeans and sweatshirt. Followed by a mist that surrounded us and blocked out everything. But him and me.

I gripped his soft sweatshirt with both hands and pulled him even closer.

We, oh-so gradually, brought our kiss to an end.

I slowly opened my eyes to find him giving me his devil-worthy grin. Between that and wanting to know if our second kiss would be as scrumptious as the first, I asked, "Can we try that again?" Before he could reply, I pulled him down and our mouths fused once more.

I sank myself into the goosebumps. The mist. *Him*. Then we ended kiss number two.

He swallowed and shook his head.

"And one more time just to be sure?"

He peered at me. "Sure about—"

I silenced him with kiss number three. Which lasted until we had to come up for air. Also known as our Best. Kiss. Yet.

Breathless, he pressed his forehead to mine. "Do I need to prepare for a round four?"

Giggles rippled out of me.

He lowered himself to the sand, brought me down beside him, and I nestled into his warm, cozy arm. I then released the first girliest, lovesick sigh of my teen life.

Lovesick.

How could I not feel that way for him? I felt pretty confident his feelings for me were the same. After everything he'd said and done? Especially today.

I rested my head on his shoulder. Right where it belonged.

"So the *real* reason I brought us over here," he said, followed by a quick laugh, "is to do something I haven't done since I was a little kid." He proceeded to lie backward, bringing me with him, and wiggled into the cool sand.

I copied his actions, and his warm hand found mine.

"If you stay still long enough, you can feel the ocean hitting the shore."

We fell silent, and I breathed the last couple of hours with him into my lungs. My heart. My bloodstream. The day's lousy beginning with my dad becoming almost a bad dream.

"Can you feel the ocean?" he asked.

I rolled my head left. "I feel *everything* right now."

He rolled his head right. "Yeah. I know what you mean."

I squinted at him. "What made you change your mind? To come after me?"

He pierced me with his stare. "You. Your guts. Everything you said to me. Which was *true*." He rolled his head forward. "Moving here was hard for me. I left my best friends, who I'd known for years. I also had to leave the best tutor I'd ever had *and* my guitar teacher. Who I'd known since I was twelve."

I scooted so close to him our sides touched. "I'd never thought of that." I flinched at how nasty I'd sounded while trying to flee his bedroom. "I'm sorry about what I said."

"Don't be. You were being *honest*." He placed his left arm under his head. "It wasn't easy, but I needed to hear all of that. Hiding behind a wall?"

I nodded.

"I guess I did that mostly because of my dad's job."

Just like I'd suspected. But I stayed silent.

"I mean, he could be transferred to another field office somewhere in this country," he mumbled. "Then I'd have to start over again. And I know my sister would stay if that happened. She loves living here. She has school, a job, a lot of friends, and a boyfriend."

I eyed him. "You don't like living here? Noah, you have a lot of friends. *And* me."

"I don't hate it." He grinned. "Living here is actually

getting better and better by the second. So, I hope he doesn't get transferred. Or *I'll* rebel."

I laughed.

"It just really sucks that most of my closest friends here are seniors." He shook his head. "Didn't think that one through last year."

I hugged his arm. "You'd still be good friends with *all* of them."

"Yeah," he said on a breath. "Definitely. And no more walls. With any one. I promise."

I sighed.

Just what I'd wanted and needed to hear.

"It didn't hurt that you referenced one of my favorite Van Halen songs last Saturday."

I grinned. "You liked that, huh?"

"You knew exactly what you were doing." He laughed. "Like I said. Close to perfect."

No. Not even close to perfect. Totally fine with me, too.

I asked, "How about we agree we're amazingly *imperfect*?"

He squeezed my hand. "I like the sound of that."

"And we'll seal our deal with a long kiss—or two or way more—later?"

"Oh, *hell* yeah."

We shared a round of giddy laughter. Then I released the second girliest, lovesick sigh of my teen life.

Chapter Twenty-Six

"Lexi, wake up."

Warm fingers gently squeezed my arm.

I moaned and buried myself deeper into—my eyes fluttered open.

Where was I?

"We fell asleep."

I blinked the fog from my vision to find Noah sitting beside me, but leaning forward as he rubbed his eyes. That's when it clicked.

Stinson Beach. The Garretts' big, empty beach house. We'd been stretched out on the sand, feeling *everything*, then the sky had started to spit rain. So we'd gone into the house and...I glanced at myself under a thick, fuzzy blanket Noah had found. We'd curled up on this couch that had a view of the ocean and became lost in each other. All the talking. Sharing. Kissing.

My eyes widened.

So much yummy kissing.

Noah started to pat the couch, then lifted and looked under the blanket.

"What are you looking for?" I hoarsely asked, and I cleared my throat.

"My phone," he muttered. His eyes lit up when he found it between the couch cushions. "It must have fallen out of my pocket at some point last night."

I pressed my lips together when the memories of *so much yummy kissing* filled my brain.

He went into his phone. "My parents and sister have been trying to get a hold of me."

I froze, then blinked twice.

Oh, my *goodness*.

I sat up and asked, "What time is it?" Because it was still dark outside.

"Almost six in the morning."

My mouth inched open. "Oh, *crap*."

"More like oh, *fuck*." He groaned. "If we're lucky, my dad *doesn't* have half the field office out looking for us." He threw off the blanket. "I have to call him. Now." He stood and focused on me. "Where's your phone?"

I frowned. Because that was a really good question.

Noah continued staring at me as I struggled to remember the last time I'd used it.

"Um..." I shook my head. "I think the last time I was on it was at the studio. When I texted my mom before we left." Yes. That memory was replacing all the awesomeness from last night. "Then I...put it in my backpack purse." More like put it on silent and shoved it to the bottom. *Out of sight, out of mind.* I huffed. That had worked incredibly well yesterday. "But I left my purse in the car."

He reached into his jeans pocket, withdrew the key, and handed it to me. "Lexi, just blame it on me." He smirked. "It sounds like your dad's already made up his mind about me, anyway. And I'm sure your mom will feel the same way after this," he added under his breath.

I threw off the blanket, stood, and shook my head. "I'm not going to do that. Especially since I *wanted* to go with you yesterday. And I have absolutely *No. Regrets.*" I lifted my chin. "I don't care what they say or how angry they are right now."

He cracked a smile. "Well, I do. I mean, I don't care what they think of me." He frowned. "But there's a real chance *we* may be grounded from life after this." He paused, then said, "And I don't have any regrets, either."

I smiled and mentally hugged his words to me. "Noah, we fell asleep. It was an accident."

He stepped backward. "And I know I'll be playing that card in less than a minute." He held up his phone. "Go call your mom. I'll meet you at the car." He swiftly headed to the patio door, stepped outside, and closed it behind him.

I released a long, frustrated sigh, then turned and dragged myself to the front door.

Yes. I needed to be a good daughter and call home. So she —they—knew I was safe. But I also knew exactly how that call would go.

Alexis Evelyn Pfeiffer, good girls *don't run off with boys and end up falling asleep with them on a couch in a big beach house.*

I ripped the door open and slammed it behind me.

Within a minute, I held my phone. And released the third longest, whiniest moan of my teen life at seeing so much green. From missed texts and calls. I even had three voicemails.

Some of the texts were from Natalie. And Heather and Maddie and Kassidy. All of them wanting to know how the "big date" went with Noah. That's when I remembered we'd planned to simply meet up and see where the night took us. Until my dad had dropped his "good news" on me yesterday morning. Then the day had taken a completely different turn. Awful to amazing. But I could relive my extraordinary day and night with Noah later.

Now I needed to focus on damage control. The other texts, the missed calls, and three voicemails were from my mom, dad, *and* aunt.

I shook my head at them dragging her into this. Probably because she knew Noah. I then breathed in the thick, salty air, hesitated for several seconds, and chose my mom's name.

"Alexis Evelyn Pfeiffer, where the *hell* are you? It's 6:00 in the morning. Me, your dad, and aunt have been trying to reach you *all* night."

I gritted my teeth before I said, "I know what time is. And I'm fine, by the way."

"Don't you dare use that tone, young lady. You're already in enough trouble. Where are you? And are you with that *boy*, Noah?"

I narrowed my eyes at the way she'd said those last few words. Making it sound like Noah really was some *criminal*. "Yes. And we're at a house in Stinson Beach. That's where we were *all* night." I smirked, since I didn't care one bit what she was assuming at this moment.

A long silence fell, and my smirk grew.

"You tell that boy to bring you home right now. Do you understand me?"

I gripped my phone as I trembled from White. Hot. Fury.

"At this time of day," she quietly continued, "you should be home within the hour."

Silence, then the call ended. Which meant she'd hung up on me.

A humorless laugh escaped.

I wanted to believe my parents had spent the night trying to reach me out of genuine concern. And maybe, just maybe, they had been worried. Even a little scared. But would it have killed her to say that? Especially since I'd *never* done anything like this before.

You scared us, Alexis. But we're relieved you're safe. And love you. Now come home.

I didn't know Noah's parents outside of the minute or two I'd been around them over a week ago and what he'd told me. But I had a strong feeling, and despite his dad's job, that's probably what he'd heard from them. After they'd torn into him.

I shoved my phone back into my backpack purse. Then Noah walking swiftly toward the car caught my attention. He wore a mask of shock, fear, and a hint of relief.

He stopped at the driver's side and pierced me with his stare. "Your parents are pissed."

I shrugged. "Yeah. And I. Don't. Care." Every cell in my body meant those words, too. "How'd you do?"

His face relaxed a fraction. "Well, my dad didn't go all FBI agent on us. Which is good," he swiftly added. "And I was able to calm him and my mom down. But I'm pretty sure life as I know it will be over for a while."

I nodded. "Same here." Or would it?

He, surprisingly, gave me his irresistible, lopsided grin. "No regrets."

A smile tugged the corners of my mouth. "*Never.*"

"Excellent. Answer." He opened his door. "Now we have to haul ass back to the city."

More like back to reality.

We settled into our seats, buckled ourselves in, and he started the car.

I eyed his phone, back in the cup holder, and said, "I think we need some 'Sweet Emotion'. Don't you?" We'd actually blasted it a second time, while listening to *Toys in the Attic*. Also known as yet another series of badass rock songs I'd be adding to my collection. And the first one I'd be getting was "Sweet Emotion."

As we drove away from the house, he said, "I *love* that you love that song. But I'm thinking we really need some Tom Petty & The Heartbreakers."

I smiled. "Would he—they—happen to be Lesson Six?" Getting lost in another rock music lesson with him sounded so incredibly perfect.

"Actually, no."

I pushed out my lower lip.

"I mean, Tom Petty was an awesome guitarist." He smiled. "I like to think of him as being in a class all his own." He nodded at his phone. "You'll see what I mean after we play some of his songs. Two in particular." He lifted his shoulders. "No lesson. Only listening."

I slowly nodded. "Okay. So what am I choosing?"

He told me, and like yesterday on our way to Stinson Beach, I quickly plugged in his phone and chose the song. Mellow guitar playing filtered into the car, and Noah turned it up, but not to cranked.

I settled into my seat and stared out at the ocean flying by us.

Flying.

The song he'd told me to play was titled "Learning to Fly." And as the song played, I concentrated on the lyrics. The pretty...*intuitive* lyrics. Especially the chorus.

I smiled, laughed softly, and eyed him, focused on the road. "How do *you* do that?"

He raised his eyebrows. "What do you mean?"

I rolled onto my left side to fully face him. "Know the right songs to play?" I grinned and shook my head. "Almost all of the songs in your lessons were that way, too."

He shrugged. "Music. It's my thing."

"It's more than that," I countered. "It's a part of you. A *big* part."

His face turned that super cute tomato red. "Yeah. But not *all* music."

I giggled. "Right. No Gershwin or Shawn Mendes for the hot, guitar playing *bad* boy."

He burst into laughter.

I released the third girliest, lovesick sigh of my teen life at the sound.

"I'll tell you a secret," he said in his lowered voice. "Gershwin's not *that* bad."

My smile doubled in size. "No. But he's no Tom Petty." I paused to listen to the perfect chorus. "I think I have a new favorite song."

"Well, if you like this song, you'll *love* the next one I want you to play."

"But can we listen to this again first?" I asked, reaching for his phone. In fact, I wanted to listen to it until I could feel the lyrics in my bloodstream. I had a feeling he'd be okay with that.

"*Hell* yeah."

I hit the back arrows, there was a pause, and the mellow guitar playing started once more. My eyes drifted close, and I lost myself in another awesome guitarist, band, and song Noah Luis Sanchez had led me to, and at the perfect time.

* * *

My heart pounded my chest as Noah pulled up in front of my house. A shattered place I now despised. Love didn't wait for me inside those walls. Well, unless my aunt happened to be in there, which wouldn't surprise me. And I couldn't forget about Coda, my spirit animal.

"Lexi, it'll be okay."

I burst into hysterical laughter. "No, it won't," I managed to say.

He frowned. "It freaks me out when you laugh like that."

I pulled on a straight face and peeked at him, giving me

that stare of his. "Sorry." I sent him a tiny grin. "You definitely proved that you're a *bad* boy."

He sighed. "You needed a break, and I wanted us to be alone. For longer than thirty minutes." He cringed. "My *bad* boy plan never included keeping you—us—out all night." He reached across the console and grasped my hand. "It's not too late. You can still blame me."

I faced him. "My hero." I squeezed his hand. "But that'll *never* happen."

He nodded, and we stared at one another. Like we had on the beach, moments before our unforgettable first kiss. Followed by our even better second kiss and mind-melting third kiss.

I mentally moaned at the thought of leaving him and going into that awful place where my mom waited. And my dad. His car was in the short driveway. Really surprising he hadn't escaped my unplanned rebellion by *working*. Or getting ready to move his life to Chicago.

I gripped Noah's hand.

He responded by pulling me toward him, and we met at the console. Where we shared yet another long, head-spinning kiss. As if we'd never see each other again.

When we broke apart for air, he said, "I have to tell you something, because I don't think we'll talk again until tomorrow at school."

Yes. Tomorrow was Monday. But it felt like an eternity had happened since Friday. An eternity filled with a spontaneous road trip, rock music, a quiet beach, an ever quieter beach house, a warm blanket, talking, kissing, and all with *him*. The boy I absolutely loved.

"Lexi, yesterday was the best fucking day of my life."

We laughed, then I sighed.

"Believe me when I say Me. Too." And I couldn't help but think that was his way of saying how he felt about me. *Perfect.*

We kissed again, and I grudgingly opened my door.

"If we," he firmly said, "by some miracle don't get our phones taken away from us—"

"I promise I'll call you," I assured him.

"Same."

I shot him a tight smile that he returned, and I slid from the car.

As I headed toward my house, I felt his eyes. I knew he wouldn't drive away until I disappeared behind the front door. So I needed to make this quick. He had his own family drama waiting for him at his place. That was actually a *home*.

I squared my shoulders and the lyrics from the second Tom Petty & The Heartbreakers song we'd played twice, and on the loud side, landed in my surprisingly clear head.

"I Won't Back Down."

I smiled at the fact my boyfriend—the hot guitar player —was gifted when it came to music. The thought powered my strength, and I opened the front door.

Chapter Twenty-Seven

I eyed the staircase.

Maybe I could dart up to my room before—

"Alexis, get in here."

I sighed at the sound of my dad's angry command from the living room.

Wishful. Thinking. But how nice of him to pause his big, awesome move to Chicago to be an actual dad for this brief moment in time.

I forced myself to head left and stopped on the threshold of the living room and foyer. My eyes immediately landed on Dad, standing near the fireplace. He had his arms crossed; his face set in unhappiness. Which was nothing new. My eyes then went to my mom and—of course—Aunt Daphne, sitting together on the loveseat. Mom's expression matched my dad's. Again, nothing new there. But Aunt Daphne's eyes were wide with relief and something else I couldn't interpret. Still, at least someone in this room seemed happy and relieved to see me.

"Your mom and I have been talking," Dad stated, "and

we're not going to discuss the how and why you ended up in Stinson Beach all day and night with that kid."

I narrowed my eyes. "His name is Noah and stop talking about him as if he's worthless. All we did was fall asleep." *For the most part.* "It was an accident." I glanced at Aunt Daphne who gave me a ghost of a smile and tiny nod. At least she had my back *and* Noah's, who didn't deserve the disdain dripping from my dad's words.

Just blame me. Your dad's already made up his mind about me.

Yes. Very true. But I wasn't in a million years going to "back down."

"And I can promise you *Noah*," I added, "is in huge trouble with his parents right now, because his dad is an FBI agent." And boy was that super strange to say out loud. But based on their wide eyes—even Aunt Daphne's—I'd finally caught their attention. "His dad is also fluent in three languages. And his mom, who's fluent in Spanish, is a trauma nurse." I smirked. "They have *heroic* jobs."

Aunt Daphne nodded while fighting a smile. My snotty parents, of course, had lost their shock and gone back to unimpressed. And irritation.

"All that matters," Dad quietly continued, "is that you're home. But you're grounded. Indefinitely."

I froze, then blinked twice.

Mom stood and punished me with her unhappy stare. "No friends. No dancing. No more helping your aunt with anything dance related. Only school until you get focused again and bring up those grades."

I briefly eyed my aunt and caught her cringe before she looked away.

Dad stepped forward. "I don't care what that kid's parents do for a living. It's clear he's a bad influence on you. And we can't control the fact you'll see him at school, but once you're no longer grounded, you're not to see him. Your mom and I have also agreed on that. Do you understand, Alexis? This nonsense ends now."

A combo of strength, loyalty, love, and inspiring song lyrics caused me to cross my arms and lift my chin. "I'm eighteen. You can't ground me. Or tell me who I can spend time with." *Or love, for that matter.*

Aunt Daphne's head shot up at my defiant tone and words. And there came that ghost of a smile. Because everything I'd just said to my parents was the truth.

My parents' eyes and mouths hardened.

"Alexis Evelyn Pfeiffer," Mom ground out, "I don't know *what* has gotten into you lately. Yes, you're eighteen. But you're still in high school and live at home. Where there are rules you are expected to follow."

I released a round of hysterical laughter, which made all of their eyes become round. "*Home?*" I managed to say. "This house isn't a home. And it hasn't been for" —I frowned— "I can't even remember, it's been miserable for so long." I leaned forward. "Because of you two. And all of your hate for each other." I laughed again. "And the way you two hide behind your miserable jobs? *Working?*" I straightened. "I've been on my own in this horrible house for weeks." I paused, then added, "Actually, more like months."

Aunt Daphne nodded once, as if punctuating my truths with an exclamation point.

Dad faced my mom. "I told you she'd been spending way too much time alone."

She glared at him. "And you just officially moved out a week ago. So don't look at me like that. I'm *not* her only parent."

My aunt's eyes rolled upward. Between her support and watching my parents give each other their oh-so familiar death glares, I remembered my aunt's offer from that night she'd dropped me off, after we'd gone to get a Valentine's Day gift for Henry. And, *wow*. Did that feel like a million moons ago.

Dad sighed. "Alexis, go to your room. Obviously your mom and I need to talk about making some *big* changes in this house before I move to—"

"No!" I nearly shouted. "I'm not going to listen to you two anymore. Especially you," I threw at my dad. "You're on your way to a new life more than *halfway* across the country."

He took a deep breath, then said, "Go to your room. Now."

I groaned. "You're not listening to me. I *hate* this house!" I looked at my aunt, her face full of genuine love and compassion, and back at my parents, giving me their death glares. "I'm eighteen. And I'm ready to get out of this rotten place and start a *new* life." I focused on Aunt Daphne. "You said I could stay with you on nights I couldn't stand it anymore."

My parents turned their death glares on her as she stood, her eyes never leaving me.

"What if it was more than a night? Or two or three?" *More like indefinitely.*

"Daphne, what is she talking about?" Mom snapped.

"And what the hell have you done *now*?" Dad barked at her.

"Don't talk to her like that." I pointed at my aunt. "She's the only person in this room who's been there for me, since you two fell into so much hate you *kind've* forgot about me." She also knew Lexi Pfeiffer. The positive, encouraging girl who loved to dance and teach dance. Which I guess *did* make me a good girl. Just not my parents' definition of that phrase.

Mom released an exasperated sigh. "Alexis, don't be dramatic and go to your room. Obviously your dad and I need to talk to your—"

"Aunt Daphne?" I faced her. "*Please*?"

Her eyes slid to my outraged dad, then my baffled, outraged mom.

I began to shake while she stayed silent, considering my plea, her offer, and what my parents' reactions would be if she opened her *home* to me. Indefinitely.

Dad shook his head. "Alexis, we're not going to tell you again. Go to your—"

"Lexi, go pack as much as you can. And don't forget Coda and all of his stuff."

Tears consumed my eyes at not only her decision, but also the defiance in *her* voice.

"This is ridiculous," Dad muttered. "Denise, will you do something about your *sister*?"

Aunt Daphne faced him. "I've never liked you, either." His jaw tightened, and she smiled at him, then turned toward my mom. "Denise, I've been telling you for months this" — she threw her hands out— "would happen. But you don't listen to me any more than you listen to your daughter, who's telling *both* of you she's had enough of *your* nonsense. And so have I." She shot me an affectionate, proud smile. "I don't blame her one bit." She huffed. "I just can't believe none of this happened sooner."

I blinked my eyes clear and mouthed, "*Thank you.*"
She nodded.
Dad turned, yanked his jacket off the back of the lounger, stalked past me without a glance, ripped open the front door, and slammed it behind him. With so much force the pictures on the walls rattled. And it hit me there was a good chance that would be my last memory of my father for an *extremely* long time.

"Well," Mom said to my aunt, "thank you for making this situation even worse."

Aunt Daphne sighed. "Denise, someone needs to think about Lexi—"

"No," Mom ground out. "You crossed a line. And we're finished here." Mom gave my aunt her back and stiffly followed the same path as Dad. Also without a glance in my direction. But she went upstairs. Seconds later, she slammed what had to be her bedroom door.

Aunt Daphne's shoulders fell forward and she eyed me. "This is going to be *very* ugly for a while. Lexi, are you absolutely sure this is what you want to do?"

I leaned forward. "I've never been more sure of anything in My. Life." *That and my feelings for Noah.* "Are *you* going to be okay?" She had just possibly lost her big sister, because of being so incredibly loyal to me.

Her face relaxed as she headed for me. "Your mom and I have always had a bit of a love-hate relationship." She frowned. "That only got worse after she met and married your dad."

A giggle escaped when I remembered what she'd said to him, followed by her defiant smile. But my inappropriate laugh was most likely due to my adrenaline starting to wear off.

"I came over here last night by choice. As a way to try and save you *and* Noah." She shook her head. "Your parents were so angry, and too much of it was directed at him."

I rolled my eyes and muttered, "Because I made the mistake of telling Dad he's a musician and a year behind me in school. But you know he's eighteen." I'd kept that from my dad, though, as a way to protect Noah. Clearly, I'd done a lousy job of it, too.

"I know," she replied. "And your dad made his displeasure with all of that quite clear last night. Your mom, being too much like your dad, joined his blame-Noah bandwagon." She stared at me. "I tried to tell them—since I do know Noah— that he's always been nothing but a sweet, respectful, hard-working boy during rehearsals." She released a quick laugh. "And has said some pretty funny things. I also told them he really cares about you." Her smile slipped. "But they wouldn't listen to me. Which was why I stayed here all night, even though your dad never wanted me here to begin with. I knew you and Noah would need me."

I threw my arms around her and squeezed as hard as I could. "I love you, Aunt Daphne."

She hugged me back as hard. "I love you, too, Sweetie." She loosened her grip enough to lean back. "Now, go upstairs and pack. Bring whatever you'll need to make that spare room of mine yours, okay?"

Tears again filled my eyes while I nodded.

Noah had saved me yesterday, and my aunt had saved me today.

For the first time in forever, the sense of being loved and protected exploded within me, then came the gooey warmth.

A few tears slid from my eyes before I could stop them.

She placed her hands on my face. "We'll figure the rest out as we go, and you'll be fine."

I smiled, and she kissed my forehead.

"I'm going to run back to my place and get that room ready for longer than a night's stay." She stepped backward. "Call me when you want me to come back."

"I will." She started to walk around me, but I stopped her with, "Can I call Noah to help?" I cringed. "If he's not grounded for life by now."

She smiled. "Of course." She paused, then said, "And, no, you're not grounded."

Yes. I'd kind of forgotten about that and my defiant reaction in the last few minutes.

"But," she slowly continued, "I think it would be a good idea if you and Noah figure out some way to keep better track of the time when you're together?"

Heat consumed my face as I pressed my lips together and nodded.

Her smile grew and she *quietly* left the house. This horrible place I'd never have to walk into again. If that was my choice.

My eyes drifted up and toward my mother's bedroom.

I probably should have felt guilt or sadness or regret for my behavior and choices. But all I could find was immense relief. And excitement. Maybe I was in shock and denial about everything that had just happened, and the guilt, sadness, and regret would come later. Maybe at some point I'd start to miss my mother. My parents. Or more like miss what we'd been as a family, years ago when they'd loved each other and made it clear they loved me. Their only child and daughter. But at this moment in time, I wanted and needed what they and this house couldn't give me. Not anymore. And didn't I deserve to be happy? Be with my aunt and Noah and my friends who made me smile and laugh? And Coda. I couldn't forget about my spirit animal.

I also deserved these last few months of high school to be amazing and unforgettable. That meant going back to work on the musical and being a dance teacher. Which I did love. I really loved helping my dearest friends master tap dancing to Gershwin. Especially Noah, my hot, guitar playing boyfriend who really wasn't a *bad* boy, even when I remembered all the yummy kissing. And that devil-worthy grin of his.

I glared at where my mother now hid. It wouldn't surprise me if she was up there getting ready to go hide at work. At that thought, I headed up to my room so *I* could start preparing for the life I wanted, far away from hate and misery.

Chapter Twenty-Eight

I opened what was soon to be my former front door and there he stood, looking oh-so perfect while wearing his irresistible, lopsided grin. And thank *goodness* my mom had stayed true to herself by escaping to her job. At least, that's where I had to assume she'd gone not too long after Aunt Daphne had left, and I'd shut and locked myself inside my room.

"So there's something I really need to tell you," Noah said.

"Me first." I grabbed his left hand, tugged him toward me, brought his head down to mine, and kissed him. As if we hadn't spent *a lot* of last night doing just that.

I deeply breathed his fresh, right-out-of-the-shower yumminess into every part of me.

We leisurely broke apart.

He swallowed, slowly nodded, then backed out of the house. And closed the door.

I squinted.

What the heck had just happened?

The doorbell exploded above my head, and I slowly

opened the door a second time. But now he leaned against the frame and wore his devil-worthy grin.

"Hi," he said in his tummy-tingling, lowered voice. "I'm here to see my *hot* dance teacher, Miss Pfeiffer."

Fighting a smile, I repeated how I'd greeted him the first time. Only this kiss lasted several seconds longer.

We again leisurely broke apart.

"And one more time just to be sure," he said, taking a step backward.

"*Noah*," I said around my giggles I could no longer hold inside.

He crossed his arms in pretend defiance. "What, you can play that game but I can't?"

I closed the door with him inside the house. "Later. Okay?"

He pulled on a serious expression. "You're right." He leaned forward. "But I'll remember you said that." He straightened and unleashed that stare of his. "I have to be honest. I can't *believe* I'm standing in your house right now. So what happened?"

I sighed. "It'll be easier if I show you. But you owe me a story, too." My phone call to him a little over an hour ago had been no more than "Please tell me you can come over?" and his surprising reply of, "I'll be there in an hour."

"Right." His face turned that cute tomato red. "That's what I need to tell you before we take a step. Because it might make me sound like a total asshole." He ran a hand through his still damp hair. "The only reason my parents didn't rip me a new one or ground me for the rest of my life is because of you."

I frowned, and he lifted his head.

Our eyes came together. *Magnets.*

"Lexi, I had to be honest with them about yesterday. Well" —he cleared his throat— "not *everything*."

I smiled as my face warmed to the color of his.

"But about why I took you up to Stinson Beach. What's going on with your parents?"

I nodded once. "I understand. And it doesn't make you an asshole."

"Really? Because my mom was looking at me like I was some sort've...superhero." He flinched. "It didn't feel like I deserved that after telling them your personal stuff." He groaned. "But my dad, the big-time FBI agent, kept pushing for more details. I felt like I was in the box at his office. Being interrogated?" He shivered. "Now I know what a *criminal* feels like."

A giggle escaped before I could stop it.

"It's not funny." He frowned. "I never planned on giving up what's going on with you."

I leaned toward him. "It's fine. I promise. And it's a good thing you told them the truth." I held out my hand, which he took, and our fingers joined. "Something pretty big happened earlier with me, my parents, and Aunt Daphne. Who *loves* you, by the way."

He smiled. "That's because people who *know* me think I'm pretty lovable. And cute."

I rolled my eyes. Even though everything he'd said was Very. True.

He followed me up the stairs. "Okay. Talk to me."

I led him right, toward my room. But he stopped in the doorway when he saw my three open suitcases filled with as much clothing as I could cram into them. And I still wasn't quite finished emptying my closet or dresser drawers. I'd also found some reusable bags and had filled them with items I couldn't live without. Hard-earned medals from dancing competitions. Figurines of beautiful, elegant ballerinas on pointe. Those had been gifts from my aunt. I'd even taken down my framed, black-and-white print of ballet dancers, in full costume, waiting in the wings. Another gift from my aunt, years ago.

I could have been one of those ballerinas. If not for my parents. But maybe, just maybe, I could do the next-best thing. And it hit me. Almost everything I cared most about in this room not only had to do with dancing, but had come from Aunt Daphne who was an incredible teacher.

Noah raised his eyebrows. "I know this one." He slid his eyes to me. "A guy and girl who are crazy about each other. Forbidden love. Her parents are cold and unreasonable, and want her to be with a respectable *Count*. But they, with the help of an adult, plan to be Together. Forever."

Grinning, I shook my head at the fact he'd just summarized most of *Romeo and Juliet.*

Defiance flashed through his dark eyes. "But you already ended things with the *Count*. And I'm not going anywhere. Your parents don't scare me."

And I loved him even more for saying all of that with such conviction.

I squared my shoulders. "No, you're not going anywhere. But I am. Today. That's why I needed you to come over—"

"Lexi, did they kick you out?" he asked, and with so much anger I drew back.

"No," I swiftly said. "I'm moving into my aunt's place. Today."

His face relaxed as his shoulders slumped. He then pulled me into his arms. "You could've just said that." He sighed. "So, it went that well with your parents." He squeezed me. "I was *kind've* kidding when I made the *Romeo and Juliet* reference."

I smiled into his chest. "We're *not* a guy and girl who are crazy about each other?" *He'd also dropped the word love.* "And my parents *aren't* cold and unreasonable?"

He laughed. "Okay. Fine. You caught me." We pulled away from each other and there came that soul-searching stare of his. "But I don't like forbidden with the word love when it comes to you and me." Hurt and confusion and a little anger settled into his eyes and face. "Your parents don't even know me. Or my family. At least the Capulets and Montagues had the excuse of hating each other for years." He huffed. "This is feeling more like me and my family are from the wrong side of the city. But we live in Pacific Heights, too."

I tightened my arms around his waist. "Noah, my parents are miserable, snotty—"

"*I hate Noah.*"

I froze, then blinked twice.

His eyes went right to the traitor, sitting in his cage. "That must be Coda."

I nodded, though this was the first time since Coda had come into my life I wished my parrot Couldn't. Speak.

"I guess I deserve you teaching him to say that."

"Noah, I promise—

"*Noah's so stupid.*"

I faced my bird. "Coda, be quiet!"

He squawked, then his feathers went *poof*.

Cringing, I turned toward Noah, giving me a blank stare. "I promise I'll get him to stop saying that stuff." I shot him my bright smile. "I can teach him to say *I love you, Noah.*"

He narrowed his eyes. "I've told you I can see right through that smile."

"But I wasn't being phony—"

He silenced me with a kiss that gave me yet another round of goosebumps, followed by the thick mist. And I lost myself in him. Again. But then we needed air. Again.

"I love you, too."

I giggled, mentally squeezed his words to my heart and soul, and hugged him.

"And thank God for your aunt," he added under his

breath. "Lexi, what do you need from me? Because I'll be *honest*. I love the idea of you not being here anymore."

I grudgingly stepped out of his arms. "Can you start carrying stuff downstairs? Because I'll be *honest*. I love the idea of not having to be here anymore." There was actually something else I needed and wanted to tell him. But I really needed to talk to Aunt Daphne first.

He gave me a quick kiss, then bent forward and grasped the straps of the reusable bags.

This also wasn't the time for more honesty. I—we—needed to focus on getting me and my traitor of a pet out of here and moved into my aunt's cozy condo. My new *home*.

* * *

I led Natalie down the hall toward my *new* room that was on the messy side, since I hadn't finished getting settled. I was down to just one unpacked suitcase, but had to put out all of my special dancing items. And Noah, before he reluctantly left, had helped me hang my black-and-white print of the ballerinas over my *new* bed.

When we walked into the room, Aunt Daphne turned from the closet where she'd been helping me hang my clothes and gave us a wide smile. Coda was currently in the living room until I could permanently move him in here.

Natalie paused, her eyes sweeping over everything, then she burst into laughter. "This is so awesome." She looked at me. "You're fucking amazing, and I love you."

Silence followed her strongly spoken words.

She flinched and peeked at my aunt, staring at her. "Sorry. It slipped out."

Aunt Daphne released a quick laugh. "It's fine. But mostly because I agree with you."

My face warmed at their words. And the fact they were

staring at me with so much pride and love. Something I didn't think I'd ever get tired of after my parents had lost that ability.

"I will leave you to it." Aunt Daphne headed for the doorway, but paused. "Do you know what you might want for dinner?" She laughed. "And breakfast? And lunch tomorrow? We'll have to go to the store." She shook her head. "I should have thought of that earlier."

I smiled. "Aunt Daphne, it's like you said. We'll figure it out."

She returned my smile, nodded, and left.

"You're also amazing," Natalie called out. "And I love you, too!"

Aunt Daphne's laugh drifted into the room from the hallway.

Natalie and I faced each other, and she threw her arms around me. We shared a long, tight hug. Then dissolved into ridiculous, girly laughter.

"Seriously," she murmured while pulling away. "What the *fuck*?" She stared at me with wide eyes. "You end up in Stinson Beach with Noah all of Saturday *and* night. Which explains why you guys didn't respond to anyone's messages," she accused. "Then when I finally do hear from you today, it's while you're moving in with your aunt." She grabbed my hand and nearly dragged me to the bed where we sat. "When I told Shane what little you told me earlier, he started choking on his drink of water." She laughed. "But he managed to say, 'Lexi Pfeiffer did *what?*' He also texted Noah."

I shrugged. "It's like you said last Saturday. I'd had enough." I then told her how yesterday had started, which led to falling off the grid with Noah in Stinson Beach. Until six this morning. And, *wow*. Had that really been almost twelve hours ago? I also told her about their unjustified, intense dislike for Noah. Also known as my official breaking point with them.

She growled. "That's total crap. Everyone loves Noah." She huffed. "But now all of *this* makes way more sense." Her eyes drifted over my room once again. "I meant what I said when I walked in here." She laughed. "I love this new, all-powerful Lexi Pfeiffer."

"Thanks. I do, too." I sighed. "But I'm not sure where this has left me with my parents. I haven't heard from either of them."

She frowned. "Do you really care? Do they even deserve you caring about that? Lexi, from what I know and have seen, they've only thought about themselves for a *long* time."

I nodded. "You're right." And she absolutely was.

"So don't even think about that or them right now. You need to relax. Soak up all the good vibes in your aunt's place." She hesitated, then said, "I never liked going to your house. Your parents' house." She made a sour face. "Too much darkness in the air."

Yes. The kind of darkness that can ruin a person's soul. Which is exactly what it had done to my parents.

"I'd rather talk about you and Noah instead of your crappy parents. Agreed?"

I smiled and nodded.

Without question.

She peered at me. "Where is he? I thought for sure he'd be here."

I twirled a lock of hair around my index finger. "His parents wanted him home tonight. It is Sunday, and we have school tomorrow." Another thing that seemed so unbelievable after everything that had happened in the last two days.

"And you were together most of yesterday and *all* last night." She gave me her wicked smile. "Tell me the truth. Did you two just fall asleep on the couch?"

My face became the temp of scalding as my eyes widened. I

leaned back. "Natalie, we haven't even been together a full week!"

She pointed at me. "You're the one going all rebel. Which is totally cool." She grinned. "Noah seems kind've perfect for that, too. The whole rebelling thing?"

Most. Definitely.

She burst into laughter. "What did you two do yesterday? Because your face is—"

"Okay. New topic," I said above her wicked laughter. I leaned toward her. "There's actually something I really want to talk to you and my aunt about. It's another reason I asked you to come over here."

Her humor vanished. "This sounds serious." She squinted at me. "What else does this new, all-powerful Lexi Pfeiffer have planned?"

I stood. "Let me go get my aunt."

New, all-powerful Lexi Pfeiffer.

I did love that description. And grinning like a *not-so* good girl, I headed out of my new room.

Chapter Twenty-Nine

I walked—more like bounced—in time with The Rolling Stones' "Start Me Up" blasting through my earbuds as I approached Noah's building. The lyrics made me grin, too.

Noah Luis Sanchez had known what *he* was doing when he told me listen to the song at the start of his rock music lessons. When I'd been technically unavailable and he'd been hiding behind his wall, now gone forever. And all it had taken to get his attention was having the courage to "Jump." Another incredible song he'd brought into my life.

I'd been doing a lot of "jumping" lately. After talking to my aunt and Natalie about my latest choice, which they'd beyond supported, I could barely remember my life before him and his Lesson One, Van Halen. I never wanted the lessons to end, either. Especially since it sounded like he'd barely touched on everything he knew about badass rock guitarists and their music.

Yes, Noah was a musician at his core. He made it look easy and definitely looked *hot* while playing. Still, I couldn't help but wonder if his true gift was music appreciation. Maybe not

Gershwin and other composers like him. At least, not yet. But his knowledge, enthusiasm, passion, and love for music had affected me. Forever.

He didn't seem to know what he wanted to do after high school, but all of those things would make him an outstanding music teacher. But would he take me seriously if I suggested it?

At that moment, he walked out and paused on the stoop long enough to shoot me his scrumptious, lopsided grin.

If he did take my music teaching suggestion seriously, girls would Fall. In. Love.

He sauntered down the steps and pointed at my earbuds.

I yanked them out, then reached into my sweater pocket for my phone.

"You were kind've bouncing there," he said when I reached him. "What were you listening to?"

I smiled. "Blasting 'Start Me Up'."

He nodded. "Great way to *start* the day."

"And you know, I think it's very interesting you told me to listen to that song. The lyrics?" I leaned forward. "And let's not forget about 'Hot For Teacher'."

His eyes widened in pretend innocence. "I have no idea what you're talking about."

I fought a lovesick grin.

He closed the tiny gap between us. "But speaking of The Rolling Stones, where's my kiss?" He placed his head beside mine. "I'm getting used to the way you '*Start Me Up*,' Miss Pfeiffer." He released his low, playful growl.

I didn't bother fighting my lovesick giggles.

He straightened. "Oh, you liked that, huh?"

"Pretty clever, Mr. Sanchez." I hooked my right index finger on the collar of his polo shirt, tugged him down, and greeted him just like yesterday. But the second time.

After our real hello ended, he pressed his forehead to

mine. "I think that'll get me through the day. But just in case"
—he lifted his head— "what are your thoughts on PDA at
school?"

I rolled my eyes. "Can you please stop being so cute? I
really need to talk to you. This is the only time we'll be alone
until after rehearsal. Oh, and I'm officially back today."

He slowly released me. "I kind've figured you would
be." He shook his head and cleared his throat. "Okay. I've
turned off the *so cute* to be serious. What's up?" He
frowned. "Did your parents do something after I left
yesterday?"

"No. I haven't even heard from them. And I don't want to
talk about them, either." Natalie had been beyond right yesterday. They didn't deserve it.

"Right. Done. So what's going on?"

I bounced in place for a few seconds, then blurted out,
"I've decided not to go to Berkeley next year. If I get in." I
smiled, scrunched my shoulders, and laughed. "I talked to my
aunt and Natalie about this yesterday, and they're totally
supportive."

He raised his eyebrows. "You decided this last night?"

I shrugged. "Not really. It's been in the back of my mind
since you asked me if I even wanted to go to Berkeley? You
know...*that* Saturday."

Surprisingly, guilt settled into his eyes and face, which
made my smile vanish.

"Why are you looking at me like that? It was a fair question, and I thought a lot about it."

"Did you?" He sighed. "Lexi, I think you need to slow
down."

I angled my head back. "What's that supposed to mean?"

He ran a hand through his hair. "*A lot* of stuff has
happened in your life since Saturday morning. Don't you
think you should wait to make a decision like that? I mean, at

least until you know you got in? It's only, what, another month or so?"

I stared at him.

Where was all *this* coming from? Yes, a lot of stuff had happened in my life since Saturday morning. But mostly amazing stuff. And none of that meant I wasn't capable of making more decisions when it came to my life. That was *finally* mine.

I crossed my arms. "I thought you'd be excited for me. You're the one who called me out on Berkeley, too. And what I really want to do. Which is dance."

He took a deep breath and slowly released the air. "So what does that mean?"

I smirked. "Are you sure you really want to know?"

He narrowed his eyes. "Yeah. I do. But I also want to make sure you're not throwing away *UC Berkeley* because of me. Or us."

Suddenly his reaction made perfect sense. His biggest fear about "jumping" had been all about me moving to Berkeley in the fall and getting lost in college life. Without him. But he'd ultimately decided to take a chance. And now he thought he might be holding me back in a completely different way.

"Lexi, I made my choice assuming you'd move across the bay in the fall." Our eyes locked. "I really hope me or us had nothing to do with this newest decision of yours."

I sighed. "Honestly?"

"Always."

I lifted my shoulders. "Of course it did."

He looked away and kicked a rock aside.

"But I *really* don't want to go to Berkeley. I *want* to teach dance. And not going to Berkeley doesn't mean I'm giving up on college altogether."

He brought his eyes back to mine.

"Noah, for the first time in my life I'm making my own

choices, and I *love* it." I laughed. "I don't know how all of this will work out, but I love that feeling, too. *Honestly,*" I added.

He cracked a smile. "Okay. That's fair. So you're going to work for your aunt?"

I nodded and shrugged. "More like work with her. Full time. Even take over some of her classes this summer. So she can take a vacation without having to close her studio." I grinned. "Between helping my aunt with some of her classes, working on the musical, and helping you on Saturdays, it recently hit me that I love to teach." I paused, then quietly said, "It's too late for me to pursue ballet *professionally.*" I huffed. "My parents made sure of that when they stopped the recitals and competitions, and summer-intensive programs. Before I started high school." *Because dancing was only supposed to be a "hobby."*

His eyes and mouth hardened. "Your parents really suck."

A giggle escaped.

"It's not funny." He reached out, clasped my hands, and pulled me into his arms. "You're an incredible dancer. I can't believe they did that to you."

I snuggled his chest. "They wanted me to be like them. And I *never* will be, Noah."

"I get it. Really." He leaned slightly away to give me that stare of his. "But it's UC Berkeley. Like you said, it's an excellent school." He frowned. "I'd never get into a school like that. But if you're positive—"

"You don't know that," I challenged.

He stared at me. "I don't get straight A's. And standardized tests and I do *not* get along."

I opened my mouth to protest, but he silenced me with a kiss.

"Not fair," I mumbled when we broke apart. "And you're too hard on yourself."

"I think we've covered that." He angled his head left. "Are you sure about all of this?"

I smiled at the fact he'd asked almost the exact same question as my aunt had yesterday morning. After my parents had stormed off. "I've never been more sure of anything in My. Life."

"Okay." His yummy mouth curved into his lopsided grin. "So I guess we should celebrate you *not* going to Berkeley this weekend? And wanting to be a full-time, *hot* dance teacher." He laughed. "Wow." He slipped his arm around my shoulder, and we started to stroll toward school. But then he stopped us and faced me. "Is there anything else I need to know before this day actually begins? Because you keep shocking the shit out of me."

I grinned. "Well, there are a couple more things. Questions, really."

He stretched his neck left, right, and said, "Bring. It. On."

"Where's my next lesson?"

He released a quick laugh.

"And have you ever thought about becoming a music teacher?"

He froze.

"I'm not the only one standing here who's a *great* teacher."

His face—of course—turned that fantastic tomato red. "Um...thanks. And no. I'd never thought about that."

I smiled. "Maybe you should?"

He cleared his throat and ran a hand through his hair. "I guess. I mean...yeah." He smiled. "But you're a pretty easy student."

I leaned forward. "Because of the way *you* talk about music. And how much you know." I slid my arms around his waist. "You'd probably like most of the classes you'd have to take, too."

He slowly nodded. "Maybe."

He stared blankly at a spot behind me.

It seemed he was really considering what I'd suggested. Which made me give him a genuine, bright smile and ask, "So, what's my next lesson, Mr. Sanchez?"

He blinked and slid his eyes toward me. "I'm afraid your teacher didn't come to class prepared today. But I have a few ideas, so I'll get back to you on that."

We started walking again.

"And when will I get to hear *you* play for real?" I asked. Yet again.

He hugged me to him. "Very soon."

Frustration at his continued vagueness caused me to release a tiny sigh. But it's not like Noah Luis Sanchez was going anywhere. Neither was I, for that matter. As relieving as that thought was, I'd eventually be having the UC Berkeley conversation with my *awesome* parents. Or would I? Considering their ongoing silent treatment, maybe my mom's "we're finished here" had meant something way more than that moment in time. Still, I couldn't believe they'd permanently turn their backs on me—their only child—because of choices I'd made for *me*.

Chapter Thirty

I joined the mad rush of P.A. students jogging down the stairs. But my final destination was the auditorium where the people I loved most in the world were at this moment. Ready to become their characters and continue working on the *big*, "I Got Rhythm" number, though we hadn't even introduced the dancing yet.

I cringed, remembering the chaos of almost *everyone* being on stage and trying to move without bumping into or stepping on someone. Their blocking definitely needed to be mastered before Aunt Daphne and I could—my eyes landed on *her*, standing near the staircase, and I halted. Several students ran into me, since I stopped so abruptly. A few of them even grumbled something about me being "totally rude."

My mother gave me a ghost of a smile, and I veered right to avoid more collisions.

"What are you doing here?" came out of me before the question registered in my brain.

I hadn't heard from her or my dad, and it was now Wednesday.

"To talk. And I figured this was the best way to catch you." She sighed. "As I'm sure you know, your aunt and I aren't currently on the best terms. Going to her condo wasn't an option."

I crossed my arms. "You could've called. And I have to be at rehearsal."

Her eyes hardened. "Of course you do. But this shouldn't take too long." She turned and joined the crazed, mass exodus from the building.

I paused, fighting the urge to run toward the auditorium. I'd expected to hear from her at some point, but not like this. Catching me off guard at school? Some part of her had probably been hoping to find me with Noah, too. But I'd texted him to head to the auditorium with Shane, Heather, and Liam and Maddie, because my last period had been released late. Thank *goodness*.

She had already disappeared from view by the time I forced my feet toward the doors.

I had no idea what she wanted to talk about. Command me to come home?

Not. Happening.

She was at the bottom of the outside staircase piled with students when I emerged.

What would actually be nice to hear from her was *I love you, Alexis. And we'll figure this out.* But those phrases seemed to belong only to Aunt Daphne. And Noah, in his own, oh-so cute, supportive way.

When I cleared the last step, she went right. I had to assume she was parked that way, and I fell into step beside her. The chill in the air matched everything about my mother right now.

A painful silence fell between us, and I peeked at her. Like Dad, years of misery had settled around her mouth, eyes, and forehead in the form of deep wrinkles. She—they—easily now looked ten years older than they were. I also couldn't remember the last time she'd worn her honey blonde hair loose. It was always pulled up into a tight bun or ponytail.

Years ago, when they'd loved each other and being parents, her hair had bounced around her shoulders in soft, pretty waves. Especially when she'd laughed, a sound I couldn't recall.

We reached where she'd parallel parked her car. Perfectly, too.

She stopped and faced me. "I'm here to say you've made your point, Alexis." She shook her head and shrugged. "You win. Because that's clearly what you want to hear."

I frowned, because she clearly still didn't understand. But was I really surprised by that?

"It's quite obvious this boy, Noah, means a lot to you," she calmly continued. "Your father and I want you to stop all this ridiculousness. You need to come home."

Of course.

"You won't be grounded and can see Noah as much as you want."

Something about this didn't even feel right, but I stayed silent.

She tried on a genuine smile, and Noah's "I can see right through that smile" drifted through my brain.

"You're eighteen and in love. My guess is for the first time, too. So be in love." She kept her cool, distant gaze on me. "But you do understand it won't last? After you move to Berkeley and become focused on college?"

So that was the real reason behind her sudden "acceptance" of Noah.

I smirked. And since she was being mostly honest for her, I felt no hesitation saying, "Then I guess it's a good thing I won't be going to Berkeley next year. Or ever."

Her eyes widened, and I raised my chin.

"Alexis, have you lost your mind?" She stepped closer to me. "You have been working toward UC Berkeley for almost four years." She stared at me. "And now because you're in love with some boy who's a year behind you—"

"His name is Noah!" I snapped. "And he has nothing to do with this." *Well, not entirely.* I leaned forward. "You and dad know what *I* wanted to do. And it never included UC Berkeley."

She nodded. "Yes. You wanted to be a dancer just like your aunt."

"There's nothing wrong with that. She has a great life and she's *happy.*"

Mom's eyes went back to hard and ice-cold. "If I had known putting you into dance twelve years ago would result in all this *nonsense,* I never would have done it."

I angled my head back. How could she say that about something I loved dearly? Something I was actually good at?

"Your father never wanted you to get involved with dance."

Big surprise there, considering he'd *never* liked Aunt Daphne, either.

She released a heavy sigh. "But I pushed it. I thought it would be good for you to be involved with an extracurricular activity. And that's all dance was ever supposed to be."

I crossed my arms. "Well, it became more than that. And I'm *good.*" My lower lip quivered, but I would not cry in front of her. "You and dad knew that, too, but you didn't care."

She held up her hands. "You're angry with us. So be angry." She lowered her hands. "But don't take your anger at us out on your future."

I stepped backward, beyond done with this. And her not listening to me. "I've made my choices. And until you showed up here, I was *happy.*" I took another step back. "I have to go."

She reached out and grasped my hand.

I drew back at her eyes and face radiating anger, panic... and some desperation?

"Alexis, I'm hanging on by a thread here!" she hissed. "Your father has basically put all of this on me. Talking sense into you and bringing you home."

Because it was way more important for him to get to his new life in Chicago, then deal with me. His now rebellious daughter.

She took a deep breath, freed my hand, and again tried a smile. "Now, feel free to text your aunt to let her know you're okay and that we're going to her place—"

"*No.* I told you on Sunday I'm done listening to you." At that moment, I felt my phone buzz inside my sweater pocket. It had to be Noah or my aunt wondering where I was right now. "I have somewhere important to be." I gave her my back.

"I was really hoping it wouldn't come to this," she said. "Your father and I agreed that if you continued behaving like this, and refused to come home, we'd make sure your aunt was sent the bill for your tuition the rest of the school year."

I froze, blinked twice, and slowly faced her.

Her expression had become an emotionless mask.

I knew, like everyone else, what P.A. cost. And though my aunt wasn't at all poor, that didn't mean she could afford P.A.'s mind-blowing tuition. Even three months of it.

My breath left me at the fact my *parents* had brought it to this. And all because I—their daughter—wanted to be happy. Make my own decisions about my life. I peered at her and asked, "What happened to you? To Dad?"

She frowned.

"I'm your daughter, and Aunt Daphne's your sister." I stared at her, my mouth hanging open. "How can you two be so cold? Do something like this to me? To her?"

Mom narrowed her eyes. "It's called the cost of rebellion, Alexis. Your father and I raised you better than this, and your nonsense won't be tolerated."

I pressed my lips together and nodded.

Yes. Punishment. Because I'd proven I'm not the perfect *good girl* they wanted me to be.

My phone buzzed again. I needed to get out of here. Away from her and the ugliness that had taken over her heart and soul. When had she become a person I really didn't want to know?

"Alexis, are you coming with me or not?"

I shook my head and took two giant steps backward. "Aunt Daphne and I will be fine." I glared at her. "We'll figure it out." *Hopefully.* I turned my back on her and speed-walked toward the doors. And it hit me—my mother staring at me with so much coldness might be my last memory of her for an *extremely* long time.

My phone buzzed yet again as I walked back into the building.

I darted past the office, the staircase, and went left. Where the people I loved most in the world, and who *loved* me, were at this moment.

The tears I'd successfully fought while outside with my mom now blurred my vision, and I paused in the empty hallway. It was so silent I could just hear the music and cast singing "I Got Rhythm," and a couple tears slid from my eyes.

What was I going to tell Aunt Daphne? She didn't deserve any of this. Actually, neither of us deserved this. More tears fell as full-blown panic shrouded me.

What if she couldn't afford three months of tuition? Would my parents really stop paying as a way to punish me for my *rebellion*? Three months. That's all I had left. It wasn't even a full three months. The seniors got out earlier than the rest of the school. Graduation was in mid-May.

I struggled to get air into my lungs as I wiped my wet cheeks.

"Lexi? I've been texting you. Noah texted you, too."

I raised my head at the sound of Aunt Daphne's approaching voice.

When she saw me, she halted and her eyes became round.

She practically sprinted toward me, then placed her hands on my face. "Sweetie, what happened? Where have you been?"

I managed to take a shaky breath and say, "With...my mom."

She angled her head back. "Your mom was here? When? I didn't see her."

"She...was waiting for me...by the staircase."

"She ambushed you at the *stairs*?" she said with so much outrage, my tears paused.

I sniffed and nodded. "We...have a big problem."

Aunt Daphne put her arms around me. "What did my *lovely* sister say to you?"

I opened my mouth, and the tears began again as I told her what happened.

Chapter Thirty-One

Aunt Daphne sat beside me on her warm, cozy couch and gave me an affectionate smile.

Being the most amazing aunt on this planet, she'd excused us from rehearsal to bring me *home*. And to start "undoing the damage your mom caused."

"I just got off the phone with my financial guru."

I sniffed twice and swiped my nose with the tissue.

Surprisingly, she laughed. "Apparently, your parents were under the impression—when they gave you that unforgivable ultimatum?—that I wouldn't be able to swing the last three months of your tuition. They, in their uptight, lawyer minds, must see me as a pauper."

I slowly sat up and asked, "And you can afford the tuition? Really?"

She reached out and grasped my left hand. "I made pretty good money when I was dancing professionally and invested as much as I could. It's how I was able to start the studio. Which is another investment." She squeezed my hand. "I'll definitely have to take money from some of those investments to cover the tuition, but it's going to be fine. *You're* going to be fine," she firmly added. "So stop crying." She smiled. "That adorable boyfriend of yours is supposed to be here soon and you, being a teen girl, probably don't want him to see you like this?"

I gave her a tiny grin. "Actually, he has seen me like this. Saturday morning? Before we took off for Stinson Beach."

She nodded. "After your dad broke the news about Chicago." She sighed. "I've honestly never liked him. There's always been a selfishness to him I couldn't stomach."

I picked at the pillow I hugged. "I don't remember him always being like that. Or her."

She leaned right, into the cushions. "Lexi, you were young and most children adore their parents when they're little. They were also happier people back then."

I peeked at her. "What happened to her? To them?" I'd asked my mom the same questions, but she'd ignored them. Nothing new there, either. "I don't understand how they could be so awful to me. Or us. And for what? Because I'm dating a boy they don't *want* to like, and because I don't want to go to UC Berkeley?" My tears returned as I shook my head.

"Sweetie, I can't answer where it all went so very wrong with them. I'm sure their jobs haven't helped," she added under her breath. "Your grandparents tried talking your mom out of focusing on family law, but she—surprise, surprise—wouldn't listen to them." She lifted her shoulders. "I think she thought it would be a noble area of law. Saving people from unhappy marriages? Saving kids from parents who didn't want them?"

I frowned. "I've never thought of their jobs that way. But it still sounds *depressing*."

"And that's what your grandparents tried to tell her. I can't believe your parents haven't burned out by now. Between what they deal with on a daily basis and the hours they work?" She huffed. "But I'm really surprised by your mom."

I rolled onto my left side. "Why is that?" Because she seemed perfectly happy pretending to be so perfectly happy with her life. Just like my dad.

She hesitated, then said, "I shouldn't be telling you this, but after what my *lovely* big sister did to you today, I'm going to break her confidence. You also deserve to know the truth."

I held my breath as I hugged the pillow tighter.

"Your mom was a dancer, and she was the reason I became one."

I froze, then blinked twice.

She flinched. "Well, the better wording would be *tried* to be a dancer."

My mouth inched open.

"But..." her voice trailed off, and I knew exactly where she was going with this.

"But she wasn't as good as you," I stated.

She barely shook her head. "Or you, for that matter." She laughed. "I think you, my beautiful, gifted niece, are better than I was at your age. And I'm not saying that because I'm your very proud aunt," she added. "Come to think of it, your mom's dancing back then reminds me of Noah's."

Now I flinched.

"He has rhythm," she swiftly stressed, "and works hard. But he wasn't born to dance."

I shrugged and nodded. Because those were certainly fair comments. If he were here, he probably would have agreed with her, too. But my mom? *Wow.* I couldn't even imagine her as a young woman, dressed in tights, a leotard, ballet skirt, and pointe shoes—I glanced at my aunt.

"Did she want to be a ballet dancer?"

"I think she was simply open to being *any* kind of dancer." She gave me a pained expression. "But it wasn't her gift."

Yes. But it was my gift. And Aunt Daphne's gift.

A thought so powerful landed in my brain it stole my breath. "Was she jealous of you?" My aunt did say on Sunday she and my mom had always had a "love-hate relationship." I'd seen it firsthand, too. My mom was also the one who'd started dancing first.

Her eyes wandered away from mine. "I don't know. Maybe?" She glanced at me. "Sweetie, we've never been really close, and I'll always be surprised she—they—allowed you and me to become so close. She was right when she said your dad never wanted you to get involved with dancing." She grinned. "Yet another reason he and I have *never* liked each other."

I cracked a smile, but said, "I'm wondering why she even let me get involved with dancing. I mean, Dad wasn't supportive and it was supposed to be an *extracurricular activity*."

She became silent for several seconds, then said, "Do you want to know what I think?"

"Yeah. Definitely."

"I think your mom expected that you would inherit *her* feet; not mine."

My mouth formed a Big. Fat. *Oh.*

"It's just my opinion," she continued. "But then you wanted more dancing classes and competitions and intensives, which turned into you wanting to pursue dancing professionally."

I closed my mouth so hard my teeth clicked. "And because *she* couldn't be a dancer—"

"I think it was more about them having way bigger things planned for you than dancing."

Yes. Very true. Pre-law, pre-med, something professional. That's what they'd wanted for me. Still, I couldn't help but wonder if my mom's motives for pulling me from all things dancing, as best she could, had come from a slightly darker, selfish place.

"Lexi, I'm not fond of your parents right now," she quietly said, "but I can't let myself think any other way when it comes to the topic of your dancing."

I pressed my lips together and nodded. And did I even really want to go there?

She sat up. "I hope knowing all of that might help you better understand your mom?"

I tried to smile. "Yeah. Thanks." But I wasn't sure I did understand her any better. Or why she and my dad had chosen misery to consume their lives.

What kind of people choose misery over genuine happiness?

A couple loud knocks on the door caused both of us to jump.

She frowned and stood. "That can't be Noah." She turned and headed for the front door.

No. It couldn't be. Just like his building, visitors had to be buzzed—

"It is Noah!" she called out around a quick laugh.

I heard his yummy voice and sat up. I quickly wiped away the last of my tears. And ran my fingers through my hair. I finished right as Aunt Daphne led him into the living room.

He stopped and gave me that soul-reading stare of his.

Every part of me zinged at the sight of him. As if I hadn't seen him for days instead of just hours. Lunchtime, to be exact.

"How'd you get into the building?" my aunt asked him.

He tore his penetrating eyes from mine and smiled at Aunt Daphne. "A very friendly neighbor of yours let me in as she was leaving. I think she said her name was June?"

I rolled my eyes. Because June happened to be over sixty

and had probably mentally swooned at the sight of him and his smile. The same one he was giving Aunt Daphne.

"Of course she let you in." She focused on me. "Sweetie, are we good?"

I nodded, though I was better than good now that he was here.

"Okay, then I'll leave you two alone."

"Actually, can we go to your room?" he asked me.

My aunt paused, and a heavy silence descended.

I giggled as his face turned that ridiculously cute tomato red.

"Yeah, that didn't sound right." He cleared his throat. "I mean, I have a surprise for you. But I was hoping to be alone with you when I—" He groaned. "That sounded worse."

Aunt Daphne laughed. "It's fine." She eyed me. "Keep the door mostly open?"

Her question caused my face to feel the same color as his, and I grumbled, "Yes."

Seconds later we were in my room, behind a mostly open door.

"*Hi, Lexi.*"

"Hi, Coda."

Noah dropped his backpack on the floor, pulled me close, and I melted into his arms.

Chapter Thirty-Two

I snuggled his chest, buried under a black hoodie, and took a long, deep breath.

He must have come straight from rehearsal, since he wore black basketball shorts. His hair looked as though he'd run his fingers through it about a dozen times. Probably out of Gershwin frustration. Or concern over me.

"How was rehearsal?" I asked as we squeezed each other. *And I never wanted to Let. Go.*

"It totally sucked because you weren't there. Again." He released an irritated sigh, then leaned back enough to catch my eyes. "My sister dropped me off. I had to stop at home to pick up your surprise. It's on my laptop. But as she drove me over here, I couldn't stop this one, selfish thought that'll probably make me sound like an asshole."

"Noah, stop calling yourself—"

"*Noah's so stupid.*"

I moaned. I'd moved Coda in here Monday and put him by the window. Like he was used to. But the spoiled traitor obviously didn't deserve what I'd done for him.

"Hey there, Coda," he replied without a trace of humor.

I released him. "I promise I've started working with him on *I love you, Noah*." Which I said loudly in Coda's direction.

He tapped his bell.

"Right." Noah shook his head. "Anyway, my selfish thought was that I'm looking forward to the time when your parents can go more than a few days without making you cry, because they've upset you so much." He stared at me. "And I'm not pissed at *you*. But I knew something was wrong when you didn't show up at rehearsal. You were supposed to be right behind us. Then you weren't responding to me or your aunt." His eyes and face softened. "She went looking for you because I couldn't. And when she came flying into the auditorium without you, and left after saying something to Mrs. Chaplin, I knew they had done something *else* to you." He paused, then said, "That's what's pissing me off."

I pressed my forehead to his chest. He already knew everything. There wasn't any reason not to tell him what my *lovely* mother had done. "My mom showed up at school and, basically, gave me an ultimatum. And it scared me, because it had to do with...P.A.'s tuition."

His muscles tightened before he said, "Are you saying she said come home or they'll stop paying your tuition?"

I lifted my head to find him staring at me with a combo of anger and disbelief. Which was exactly how Aunt Daphne had looked when I'd told her this *lovely* story.

"Yes. But my aunt is the most amazing aunt on this planet."

He narrowed his eyes. "Your parents really do *suck*. Who does that kind've shit to their kid? To their family?"

He tried to step back, but I tightened my arms around his waist.

"I love you so much right now, but they're not worth this. Aunt Daphne said she'll work everything out with the tuition." I laughed. "My parents should *not* have underestimated her."

He released a long, slow breath. "Okay. You're right. Especially about them," he added under his breath. Our eyes then locked. "You're sure you're okay?" Humor finally flashed across his face. "Because if you need to punch something" — he leaned right and grabbed a pillow off my bed— "I have a good grip." He held it up as if it were a shield. "Years of growing up with an older sister who has a mean streak." He grinned. "But payback was a real bitch."

I grabbed the pillow, tossed it aside, and hooked my finger on his sweatshirt's collar.

As soon as we came up for air, he said, "Lexi, seriously. Are you okay?"

I tried to smile. "I'm not a hundred percent." Especially when I remembered everything Aunt Daphne had told me about my mom. "But I will be. Because of *you*. And Aunt Daphne and all of our friends. And the fact I can dance whenever I want without being given a guilt trip."

Irritation returned to his face, and I brought him down for another kiss. And another.

"Okay," he said on breath. "So I guess you want to change the subject?"

"Finally," I teased. "Noah, I promise everything will be awesome." *And it would be, too.*

"*I hate Noah.*"

I cringed.

He eyed Coda. "I'll be honest. I *don't* see an awesome ending for your parrot."

I placed my hands on his face and forced him to look at me. "And you said something about a surprise. Twice."

"Yep. And I actually have two surprises for you." He bent down and picked up his backpack. "Well, more like three."

"*Three* surprises?" I laughed. "You've been busy." I

grabbed his hand, led him to the foot of the bed, and dropped to the floor. I then gave him my *not-so* good girl grin. "Are you brave enough to sit, Mr. Sanchez?" I patted the spot next to me.

He sat. "You don't scare me, Miss Pfeiffer," he said in his mesmerizing lowered voice, followed by a kiss. He then went into his backpack and pulled out a folded piece of white paper.

I quietly clapped. "That looks like Lesson Six. Is it the guy you said died too young?"

"No." His mouth inched into his lopsided grin. "I'm saving him for the perfect moment." He handed me the paper. "But I think you're ready for who I picked this time. And that's another really short list of my favorite songs he's done. Mostly his *early* stuff with a band called Cream."

I unfolded the paper. Like with The Rolling Stones lesson, he'd typed a list of songs, but included the band's name beside the song or just one name. "Eric Clapton? He's the guitarist?"

His eyes lit up. "Oh, yeah. He's considered the second-greatest guitarist of all time and—fun fact—was a huge influence on Eddie Van Halen." He smiled. "Another reason I chose him."

I returned his smile as I stared into his eyes, bright with excitement. Passion. Over music.

"You also said you wanted a history of rock-and-roll." He pointed at the paper. "Clapton was heavily influenced by the blues." He shrugged. "I figured if you liked his badass guitar playing, you'd be ready for the history of rock-and-roll. And the guitarist who died too young."

I hugged the paper to my chest. "I promise I'll start this lesson tonight." And his contagious excitement caused me to shiver from exhilaration. "And call you about it."

I could definitely listen to him talk about music the rest of my teen life. And way longer.

"You better." He again reached into his backpack and

withdrew his laptop. He took a quick breath and fully faced me. "I did something for you." He laughed, but it sounded a tad on the nervous side. "So here's the thing. I can't play my electric guitar unless I'm wearing my headphones. It's a strict rule my parents have, because we live in a condo?"

I frowned. "Oh. Right. That makes total sense." And could be why he'd always been so vague about when he would play for me.

A hint of defiance flashed through his eyes. "But I broke the fucking rule last night."

I burst into laughter. "How'd you manage that?"

"When I got home from rehearsal, *nobody* was there but Beelzebub and Lucifer." He raised his eyebrows. "I couldn't believe it. That almost never happens. And so I made this."

As he opened his laptop, I snuggled against him and placed my chin on his shoulder. I also had a strong suspicion of what'd he done for me.

I held my breath as he went into a video he'd made of himself, sitting cross-legged on the floor in the music spot in his room, and holding his beloved electric guitar. Seconds later, he started playing—my eyes widened and I leaned closer to the screen. To better see him as he played an awesome guitar solo. While looking oh-so *hot* in the process.

My mouth inched open while I concentrated on his busy, confident fingers. And though he wore an expression of total focus, I saw the corner of his mouth in a half smile.

Giddy laughter rippled out of me, and I slid my eyes in his direction. But he was staring somewhere off to his right. If he'd been standing, I knew he'd be kicking at nothing on the floor.

I continued watching him. Listening. Determined to make this a memory I'd *never* forget. He wound down his badass playing, and gradually stopped. The song was less than a minute. Then the video ended. Silence, outside of Coda playing with his bell, filled my room.

"Wow," I said on a breath, followed by a giggle. I faced him. "Is that *your* song?"

"Oh, *hell* no. It's called 'Eruption'." He eyed me. "Eddie Van Halen."

I smiled. "That was So. Cool. Can I have that video, so I can listen to my hot, guitar playing boyfriend anytime I want?"

He burst into laughter. "Yeah. Just don't post it anywhere, okay?"

I tugged him toward me and sealed his request with a long, delectable kiss.

"Thank you for doing that," I whispered as I caught my breath. "That was the best surprise. Ever." We kissed again. And one more time just because we could.

I went back to snuggling his side. "Play it again?"

"Actually, I have one more surprise for you. And this one" —he cleared his throat— "is a little harder for me."

I lifted my head, and our eyes connected.

"You just asked if what I played was my song, and it's not, but I do try to write songs. To challenge myself." His face flushed. "But writing is *not* my strength."

I hugged him as tight as I could.

He went into his backpack for a third time and withdrew a piece of notebook paper. "This is a song I've been working on." His face went from flushed to crimson. "It's handwritten. Besides my family, teachers, and former tutors, nobody else in my life sees or has seen my actual writing. But I want to share this with you."

Speechless, I slowly pulled the paper from his fingers.

"Try to ignore all the spelling mistakes?"

I nodded. "Yes. Of course." I held my breath as I unfolded

this piece of paper that was really so much more. It was like Noah Luis Sanchez had handed me a part of his soul.

I carefully read what he'd written, and I grinned. It was a super sweet love song. The spelling mistakes weren't that bad, either. He mixed up his E and I placements. Left E's off the ends of some words. And other mistakes here and there.

"Can you even read it?" he quietly asked.

I lowered the paper and smiled. "Yes." I leaned toward him. "The hot, guitar playing *bad* boy is writing a love song?"

He grinned. "That's what happens when a bad boy falls for his *hot* dance teacher."

I giggled. "I think it'll be beautiful when you're done." A thought occurred to me, and I asked, "Or maybe we can finish it together?"

He gave me that soul-melting stare of his. "I'd love that. And *you*."

Our mouths came together, and for as long as we could stand it.

"Now will you play the video again?" I asked the moment we separated.

He situated his computer on his lap, hit play, and we nestled together. Then his Totally. Badass. Guitar playing burst from the speaker.

Epilogue

"**I**'m choosing our warm up song today, Miss Pfeiffer."

I opened the studio's street door. "My next lesson?" I'd lost track of lesson numbers somewhere around George Harrison from The Beatles, Robby Krieger from The Doors, and The Edge from U2.

"Yep. And you'll love it."

Excitement shimmied through me at another badass rock music lesson. And he still had yet to start his actual history of rock-and-roll lessons. But I Couldn't. Wait.

The door hit something on the floor. I looked down and spotted a thick manila envelope. I nudged it out of the way with the toe of my Vans and walked inside with Noah right behind me.

He picked up the envelope, then slid his eyes to me. "It's for you. From UC Berkeley."

I stared at the envelope.

"You obviously got in."

"Yeah." I rolled my eyes. "How nice of my mom to slide it through the mail slot." I glanced at him. "It's the only way it could've ended up *here*."

He slowly nodded. "I think she's coming around. What do you think?"

Fighting a grin, I said, "Just toss it." I turned and headed into the studio.

"You don't want to open it? See in writing that you, Lexi Pfeiffer, got into UC Berkeley?"

I stopped at the closest metal chair and removed my backpack that contained a surprise for *him*. "Not even a little bit." I frowned. "In fact, I'd love to send it to her, or my dad if I cared about having his new address in *Chicago*, unopened. With a big, black X over the label." And was the complete opposite reaction *all* of our friends had experienced after getting into their first-choice schools. But they were on a different path than me. And Noah. With that thought, I lifted my chin and said, "No regrets. So toss it."

He threw it over his shoulder with enough force it landed under the windows with a *plop*!

I burst into laughter.

"Oh, you liked that, huh?"

I nodded. "It was perfect. And before we start our second-to-last tap dancing rehearsal, I have a surprise for you." I gave him my bright smile he no longer challenged. "It's a very belated birthday present."

He smiled. "Does it include you changing into your *hot* ballet clothes?"

I rolled my eyes, then went into my backpack for my sketchbook. Which I handed to him.

He stared at the book. "You're an artist, too?" He opened it and stopped on the first page that was a drawing I'd done of an elegant ballerina on pointe. "A fucking *good* artist." He lifted his eyes and his mouth fell open. "Why haven't you told me you can draw like this?"

I laughed. "All part of my surprise. But you have to keep going."

He shook his head while slowly flipping through the pages. Then he stopped again.

"Whoa." He looked up, his eyes and face full of awe. "When did you draw this?"

"I've been working on it for weeks and just finished it the other day." I bounced in place. "Do you like it?"

He laughed. "I love it." He went back to staring at *his* picture. "I can't believe you drew this." He grinned. "I really am hot."

Very true. But I said, "I'll take it back if you act like a silly—"

He grasped my left hand, pulled me toward him, and gave me a too-quick kiss.

"Thank you," he murmured. "I really love it. And *you*."

I smiled and nodded.

"So, Miss Pfeiffer," he said in his addictive, lowered voice, "ready for our second-to-last Gershwin rehearsal?" His smile slipped. "Believe it or not, I'm going to miss this."

My smile also dipped. "Me, too. *But* you have come a long way since January, Mr. Sanchez." And, *wow*. It was already April. *Crazy For You* would be running two weekends from today. Then it'd be May. Graduation month.

"Mostly because of you and Nicolas being dancing drill sergeants," he teased. "But speaking of him, you ready to do *our* dancing warm up?"

I shook my head.

Yes. Focus on the now, because Nicolas would be here soon.

Smiling, Noah set my sketchbook down on a chair, but kept it open on *his* picture.

I went into my backpack again and pulled out my bluetooth speaker. "You know," I threw at him as I walked right, "I'm not sure you can top my song choice from last week."

"And I *love* the fact you chose a badass ZZ Top song."

Also known as a guitarist, band, and song he'd led me to through a lesson.

"But this guy you're about to hear—" He whistled long and low when he stopped beside me. "He's usually referred to as the *best* guitar player of all time." He went into his phone. "He's also the guy who died way too young."

"Took you long enough," I teased him. "Who is it?"

He grinned. "Johnny. Allen. Hendrix."

I stared at him.

"That was his real name. But he went by Jimi Hendrix. He's legendary." He bent down to turn on my speaker. "You'll see what I mean in a few, short seconds." He scrolled through his phone's music library that contained so many amazing songs that went with amazing bands and guitarists, I didn't know how he kept it all straight. Except that music was him.

What sounded like high-pitched guitar playing came from the speaker as he stood.

He held out his hand. "'Shall We Dance'?" he asked, quoting a song from *Crazy For You*.

I grasped his fingers. And Totally. Badass. Guitar playing exploded from the speaker, followed by a guy singing.

"Wow," I said as he led me to the center of the studio. "I love it. But what's he singing?"

He pulled me into his arms and gave me his devil-worthy grin. "The song's called '*Foxy Lady*'." He released his low, playful growl.

Lovesick giggles rippled out of me as we started dancing as best we could to a rock song.

"But I like to think of it as *your* song," he added before spinning me once.

I concentrated on the lyrics. And my face became tomato red hot.

He laughed. "Out of all the rock songs I've thrown at you, this one makes you turn red?"

He spun me again, and we continued our dancing.

"I guess you have a point." Especially when I thought about the lyrics to "Hot For Teacher" and "Start Me Up." "What are we going to do when the lessons are all over?"

"That'll never happen."

I smiled. "Because there's so much badass rock music? And the blues lessons?"

"Those are two reasons." He hesitated, then said, "I've been thinking about your music teacher suggestion and" —he cleared his throat— "I really like it. So does my family."

I angled my head back to catch his eyes. And he gave me that piercing stare of his.

"I also thought it'd be cool to teach playing the guitar."

"More like totally cool."

"Does that mean you'll be my first student?"

I gave him my *not-so* good girl grin. "Oh, *hell* yeah."

He laughed. "So maybe we can start this summer?"

I hooked my arms behind his neck. "I'd love that. And *you.*"

We sealed our latest deal with a misty kiss as my new favorite rock song surrounded us.

~The End~

Acknowledgments

I'm a huge lover of rock music, and pretty knowledgeable about the guitarists and bands Noah leads Lexi to through his lessons. But I'll be honest. *Rolling Stone Magazine's* article "100 Greatest Guitarists," published a handful of years ago, really helped me narrow down who to focus on in Lexi and Noah's story. I referenced it quite a bit and will always be grateful for that article. It was super fun research, too!

Thanks again to The Killion Group for bringing the entire series to life through such amazing and cute covers, and for turning my characters' stories into actual books.

Last but not least, to my proofreader extraordinaire, who always catches the little stuff, THANK YOU. In the words of Noah, Best Mom In. The. World.

About the Author

Christine Miles is a full-time writer living in Albuquerque, New Mexico.

An avid reader and writer since elementary school, her passion for literature inspired her to pursue a BA in English and an MA in Creative Writing. She writes YA and Adult Contemporary Romances with sassy, independent heroines and swoony heroes who love them for their strength.

When not writing romances, she loves traveling, binge-watching shows on streaming apps, reading mysteries and thrillers, listening to music, and spending quality time with her family, friends, and dog.

You can find her on Facebook and Instagram. Sign up for her newsletter to get ARC's and updates at www.christine-milesauthor.com.

www.ingramcontent.com/pod-product-compliance
Lightning Source LLC
Chambersburg PA
CBHW061617190726
48288CB00007B/2361